# THE SAGE, THE SWORDSMAN AND THE SCHOLARS

TRIALS OF THE MIDDLE KINGDOM 1

Revised and Enhanced Edition

PIERRE DIMACULANGAN

Cover design and illustration by

Pierre Dimaculangan

Copyright © 2018 Pierre Dimaculangan

All rights reserved.

ISBN-13: 978-1-7292-1206-6

# INTRODUCTION

"The Sage, the Swordsman and the Scholars" is an-action adventure, martial arts, historical fantasy set in late medieval Ming Dynasty. It also employs figures and concepts from ancient worldviews unique to the Middle Kingdom, a civilization known today as "China". It therefore creates an alternate history and fantasy epic for modern readers while drawing inspiration from the popular Chinese genre of Wuxia (martial arts fantasy) for the mainstream audience.

The philosophical insights that have largely influenced The Sage, the Swordsman and the Scholars have been inspired by a unique interpretation of Tao or the "Way" (classical Chinese science, philosophy and metaphysics), ancient Chinese Heaven worship, and key teachings from Mozi (Master Mo) who, during his time, was as prominent a philosopher as Confucius or Mencius. The tides of history however , have brought Confucianism at the forefront of Eastern thought and Mozi's teaching, though largely forgotten, has been experiencing a small revival in academia.

# Name Pronunciation Guide

### PROTAGONISTS
Sun Xin – soon shin

Famin Jie – fah meen jyuh

Zuo Shilong – z'woh shee long

Meiling – may ling

### MARTIAL SCHOLARS
Lu Guanying – loo gwun ying

Tian Qiu – t'yen cho

Zhang Sunzan – jang soon zan

Shang Jian – shang j'yen

Zhen Shu – jen shoo

### IMPERIAL MILITARY/ GOVERNMENT OFFICERS
Zhu Youcheng "Hongzhi"(present emperor) – joo yo chung "hung jee"

Zhu Di "Yongle" (past emperor) – joo dee "yung-luh"

Xuanda emperor – shwun-duh

He Feishen – huh fayshen

He Jin – huh jin

Liu Quan – lyoo chwen

Han Bin – han bean

Zhou Liang – jo lyang

Wei Qiuyuan – way cho ywen

# A FATEFUL ACQUAINTANCE

HE HIKED PENSIVELY THROUGH THE marshy and sparsely wooded landscape of the province of Guangxi. His head hung low and though his body moved in a purposeful direction, his mind spun and wandered more than usual. He had just returned from the desert regions of the western edge of the Ming Empire after a long campaign hunting down a troublesome warlord who had long caused havoc and unrest in the region. However, the success of his mission no longer left him with the same feeling of satisfaction. Something was missing and the meaninglessness of his deeds was becoming more and more apparent. Sun Xin was entering the tenth year of his wanderings in the empire yet for all his accomplishments, he felt emptier than when he had first begun. He was hardly the man he was when he took the first step on his lonesome journeys throughout the Middle Kingdom.

Over the years he had made friends and enemies and forged fragile alliances with rivals if he had not already eliminated them. His greatest frustration however, stemmed from the questions that plagued his mind. *Does anything I do even matter? Are the pain and anguish worth the effort?.* Though his personal crusade had entered its first decade, a sense of vanity was beginning to consume his life's mission. In fact, it appeared that the more he tried, the worse it became. It was not enough. He just had to keep his blade sharp and his mind even sharper.

So many years had been invested into his sword, but how much longer would he have to continue these quests? Just three years from the age of thirty and already the endless journeys through unforgiving weather conditions and incessant fighting on every quest would in time leave little room for additional scars on his body. Reality was weighing more heavily on his mind than anywhere else. However, the utter hatred he carried for those he considered unworthy to be kept alive inspired him to continue the fight. Sun Xin was without a horse so he undertook his long and uneventful journey on foot. The lack of speed added to his frustration.

His thoughts and feelings continued to conflict as he cut his way through the marsh. He ignored the fact that he had just entered the misty dominion of the Crimson Moon Sect —one of the many bothersome rebel groups experiencing resurgence across the land. They were naught but deluded cutthroats who have deemed themselves worthy of a "righteous crusade".

Away from the noise of his troubled soul, it was the rustling of leaves, the melody of a stream, and the whispers of the wind that produced the sounds of the forest in the morning. Even the locks of his long black hair danced to the left and right of his face. A melancholy song slowly enters in harmony with the music of the forest. Sun Xin played his flute to the rhythm of that flowing stream to calm his spirit and clear a clouded mind. Into the heart of the forest he strode under the rays of sun light beaming between the trees.

The peace and the music were abruptly disturbed by the sudden, though expected appearance of the Crimson Moon Sect. Out from the undergrowth they leaped and stood before him motionless, hooded, and clad in black. The whole forest fell silent, leaving only the menacing sounds of their rasping breaths and the faint rattling of their chained sickles. The silence of the air was broken by the sudden whistle of a rushing arrow rapidly approaching from his rear. In one swift motion and a spin of the heel, Sun Xin drew his sword and slashed the arrow mid-flight. Together, the occultists attacked when his back had turned but they were quickly dispatched by the masterful strokes of his blade; a deep thrust into the chest of the first followed by a diagonal slash across the belly of the second were a blur to the assailants. More arrows darted toward him but he dove away from their trajectory. The bowman was obscured amongst heavy bamboo foliage so Xin made a mad dash to his position and cut the bamboo to reveal the shooter who then vanished in a plume of white smoke.

What was left of the bodies he had slain had seemingly vaporized into thin air. Empty. It was typical of the trickery practiced by the dark ones. He scoffed at their pathetic attempt to ambush him but such was the nature of his journeys across the countryside.

"They never learn," he muttered to himself.

He drew a sharp sigh, sheathed his sword, and tightened the chin strap of his broad-brimmed hat. He continued down a hidden trail deep into the thickness of the forest. The foliage canopy eventually led into an opening revealing a small river valley. In the distance, embracing a mountainside engulfed by mist and mountain fog stood a small homestead surrounded by colorful vegetable gardens. Gray smoke ascended from the rooftop eaves that gently curved up to the sky. A sign above the door post of the cabin read *Heaven watches over this home*. He had passed by the remote homestead before. It looked inviting and perhaps whoever called the shack 'home' would allow this weary traveler food and brief respite. It was in the moment when he approached the front steps of the cabin that Sun Xin suddenly staggered and struggled to keep his footing.

His vision narrowed and a terrible burn scorched the back of his neck. When he had felt for it, a crimson stain streaked across his palm. An arrow had indeed managed to leave its mark on him. He fell at the doorstep of the cabin and faded into unconsciousness…

He awakened with a start, though dazed, in a sweat, and inflicted with head pain. Half a dozen fine needles were embedded into the vital points and nerves of his neck and shoulder. He was greeted by a silvery-haired man noticeably older than he and wore on his face a peaceful and kind countenance. It was the hermit of the home.

"It was by no accident you have arrived to my humble home, Master Swordsman," he said while handing Xin a pitcher of water. "I hope those horrid bandits did not give you too much trouble. They have tried to enter my home before only to discover that this sign speaks the truth." He chuckled while pointing toward the sign outside.

"You mean to say that Heaven intervened?" Xin asked as soon as he guzzled a tankard of water.

"Indeed, it was also by the Will of Heaven that you have made it here," he replied with a satisfied grin. "You were in a slumber for three days since the poison needed to run its course. You, my friend, are quite fortunate. The poison you received was but a fraction of the intended dose."

"Did you really say 'Heaven'?" Xin muttered trying to shake off the disorientation. "You sound like my old master."

The hermit simply smiled.

Sun Xin was not sure how to react to the stranger who seemed to have saved his life but his instincts dictated that he was at least trustworthy… and harmless most of all. His wounded neck was patched in herbs but the burn remained. He should be grateful but was not so sure of how to express it, not to mention that this was the first time anyone had saved his life in such a way.

The hermit was of average stature, though rather taller than others of his ripe age and had a light beard encircling his mouth. He was neatly dressed and groomed for someone who lived in seclusion upon a mountain far away from any village or township.

"That is a very fine sword you carry, Wanderer," he commented as he cast his gaze upon Sun Xin's straight sword. "I have yet to see any other such as yours, so ornate and fine. It bears the elegance and skill of a master craftsman. I certainly hope that it has not been misused in any way. A gentleman's weapon should not be used for selfish gain," he said smiling as he plucked the needles from Xin's body.

It had been a very long time since Xin had met a man who conducted himself with such peace. He turned his gaze to where the sword leaned against the corner.

"It is both a gift and a burden and my answer to those who seek other times than peace. In this sword lies my purpose," Sun Xin answered. *It is curious that a hermit would show interest in a sword*, he thought.

"Ah yes, I see, I see," the hermit nodded.

Sun Xin stayed well after dark with the mysterious man whose name he did not even ask.

They talked over tea and hot stew until the moon peaked its arc across the night sky. Their conversation went to and fro discussing such things the ancient philosophers once pondered and taught.

"So tell me your story," said the hermit. "Tell from whence you came that you would stumble upon my home, barely alive while brandishing a crossbow and a fancy sword that, um, I assume has tasted much blood."

Sun Xin lowered his gaze and leaned against the bed frame. "The all me a 'Youxia' – a knight-errant. But I am naught but a lone swordsman. For years I had been drifting through the lands serving as an independent agent employed with the League– er…" he stopped mid-sentence, being careful about what he would reveal.

"I am under contract with an underground guild of intellectuals who have dedicated themselves to the swift eradication of corruption and crime in the Middle Kingdom. They seek to preserve the domestic peace but are independent from the tiresome politics of the imperial bureaucracy. They're not bound by the burdensome complications of law and war. Before landing here I was on my way to Guangzhou to meet with them."

"Ah, so they are what you would call 'glorified vigilantes'," the hermit commented.

"More like unofficial secret police," Xin corrected him. "Though their order is largely secretive, they operate in plain sight. It is important you realize that I am no mere bounty hunter easily sold to the highest bidder, nor am I an assassin puppet who couldn't care less about the corruption of government officials high and low. I fight for a cause of the highest calling, one that has value for countless generations to come."

Sun Xin was quite surprised with himself. He had never divulged such information so easily especially with a stranger.

"And yet you seem largely dissatisfied. I can see it in your eyes. A conflict burns within your soul," the hermit said.

"You would know of such things, hermit?" Xin asked redirecting his steely gaze to the face of his host.

"I have experienced much and received plenty. But I know nothing on my own other than that which has been revealed to me," he answered plainly. "The cause of goodness is always like swimming upstream against the raging currents of a mighty river. Those who swim in it are becoming fewer. Evil however, enjoys an easy route, and is practiced with little effort by countless followers. Pursuing the path of evil is like riding the downstream current of that river and it pulls you faster and farther with every passing moment," the hermit changed his tone to a whisper. "… until you've drifted so fast and so far you can no longer turn back."

"You're telling me this because…?" Sun Xin questioned with a raised eyebrow.

"Because I see your pursuit of right, or at least the enforcement of it, is genuine. But you tread a thin line as fine as the spider's silk. One wrong step and you'll be riding the river downstream and headed for a waterfall too!" chuckled the hermit. He nearly coughed from it.

"So you've got me all figured out, is that it? You don't have to worry about me, 'Uncle'," muttered Xin with a hint of sarcasm. "I'd rather die than be anything like the criminal or rebel scum I have learned to hate."

"That is exactly what I mean," the hermit answered.

"Like what?" Xin said, this time his tone more terse.

"The hate. It will make you paddle downstream."

Sun Xin did not answer. He grimaced at the reminder. It was a lesson his master had long instilled in him. But the very precepts of the sword art he wielded were left buried and forgotten in a deserted crevice of his hardened heart. It was a heart that now burned with a fiery rage that fueled his curse, a bloodlust and callousness to the sight of death. He considered himself to be a righteous man even though he had long discarded the sacred principles his master had bestowed upon him since childhood. He refused to accept it, but deep inside, Sun Xin knew the moral path he had chosen was one in which there would be no return.

The cost of his own humanity was the price he was ultimately willing to pay for the realization of his vision.

*Mercy? Forgiveness? These were weaknesses that yielded no results for the swift eradication of evil!* he kept telling himself. He believed his master was mistaken, even naive for adhering to such doctrine, and apparently so was this hermit.

The hermit reached for the tea pot. "Let's shift to a more light-hearted topic, shall we? You were asking about the sign posted outside my door."

The hermit spoke continuously of Heaven whom he called Shang Di, the "Lord of Heaven" whom the ancients once worshiped, honored, and obeyed.

"The Way is Heaven's gift – a revelation and the transcendent path of righteousness that humanity has been ordained to walk," he proclaimed. "Through the Way all things were created. It is only through the perfect Way that the imperfect world can be saved."

He made further mention of outlandish antiquated beliefs

concerning the invisible things like the so-called spirits inhabiting the world. He also spoke of the machinations of darkness and the personification of it that worked furiously to lead men far from the knowledge of the Way, presenting in its stead a false path. "All such things," he claimed, "would only become more evident in the days to come."

The hermit sage shared his convictions of such ancient things with a doctrine that Sun Xin found unusually old-fashioned, overly superstitious, and riddled with dogma. He would usually ignore the crazed ramblings of such old men but there was something about the hermit that Xin found intriguing. He was wise and collected as if he was completely sure about the truths of which he spoke.

"Such teachings have been forgotten or regarded as outdated belief neither practiced nor studied in its orthodoxy for more than two and a half thousand years," said the hermit.

Still, it was intriguing and unusually frustrating for Xin to have to absorb. The hermit preached of Heaven's will and the indispensability of impartial love for all people. Love, he said, was the cure for all the evil and injustice of man. It is, as he said, the supreme ethic that embodied the nature of the "Way"…

"*Whatever it was he meant by it*", thought Xin.

On the other hand, Xin stubbornly stood firm in his convictions in the enforcement of law and in the administering of justice by force.

The hermit intrigued him. He was such a curious character because he shared a wisdom that had been largely forgotten and strangely difficult to refute. In many ways, he reminded Xin of his old master for they were similar in their convictions and philosophies.

"You speak like a man from the age of sages, but I do not see any disciples?" Sun Xin inquired.

The hermit redirected his gaze to the floor. "I traveled from province to province telling others of my revelation but there was no room in the hearts of the people. Those who would listen fear ridicule or even estrangement from their homes."

"And what is your message?" Xin asked with a raised eyebrow.

Before the hermit could answer, the cabin rattled and shook. An obnoxious hammering and crashing suddenly plagued the house. Savage whoops and shrieks pierced through the nooks and crannies of the home and could be heard echoing across the valley beyond. It was intimidation in one of its more aggressive forms. The Crimson Moon Sect had returned. They seemed to have followed Xin into the hermit's home and wanted his blood in revenge for their fallen comrades or for perhaps the priceless bounty that had been placed on his head. He quickly reached for his sword but was stopped by the hermit.

"Stay your blade, Swordsman! They cannot enter here," he snapped.

Xin started to protest. "They will break down your door and–"

"No, they most certainly will not." The hermit said, this time in a low voice, almost a whisper.

Xin was most uncomfortable with the situation. He scrambled to his sword and gripped it tightly. His vision focused and his heartbeat quickened. The incessant banging on the walls and the door grew louder and he almost drew his blade before the hermit stood firmly in front of him with both his hands resting on his cane and he declared:

"I rebuke you, foul agents of the enemy! Be gone; you have no place here! This home belongs to Heaven! You have been warned!" A mighty gust likened to a monsoon wind rushed through the interior of the cabin causing the candle lights to dim to a near simmer. The air grew cold and the night fell eerily silent. As quickly as it began, the terrors of the night had ceased and the echoes faded into the valley. The cultists had fled deep into the black forest from whence they came. Sun Xin stood motionless and stunned, unable to comprehend what he had just witnessed. What sort of trickery was this? He sought an explanation but was not sure what to ask first.

"What happened? What did you just do?" He questioned as he stood clutching his sheathed sword. The hermit sighed but with a smile said:

"Well, you did ask me what my message was, and what you have just witnessed is but a small testament to that," said the hermit. "Knowing Heaven is the great endeavor. Walking in the Way negates the necessity of sheer force. A sword may have its uses in the hands of the righteous, but it is not a staff which one should lean upon."

Sun Xin was not fond of preachy philosophy. He merely smirked at the hermit's answer. But nonetheless, he slept that night pondering the mysterious words of the hermit and nursing the toxic wound inflicted by the poisonous arrow.

The events of that night continued to bewilder him. Xin did not consider himself to be a superstitious man and he considered such spiritual teaching, for the most part, a hindrance to the progress of society. It most often served as an avenue for violent fanaticism. However, he felt something strangely different with the hermit even though he could not fully understand the meaning of his words. Was he some sort of sorcerer? He could not be, Xin thought. The hermit was nothing like the fabled wizards or mages in ancient times. How was it that he was able to stop the attack so quickly and effortlessly? His thoughts kept him awake for another two hours before he finally found sleep.

When morning had arrived, the sun cast rays of gold into the valley and the sun beamed brightly through the open window. His sword leaned against the hearth, and the lion's face engraved upon its golden hilt glistened against the morning light. He slung the sword across the back of his hip while flexing away the stiffness in his joints. He had grown eager to return to Guangzhou and already had spent too much time lying around in the hermit's home. The old man was outside sitting silently by the stream possibly praying or meditating.

Xin joined him outside for breakfast. After a bath in the stream, he was presented with his robes – newly washed and neatly folded next to his dusted boots. After donning his mail vest and dark blue robes, he secured his hard leather bracers into his forearms and secured the tightening straps around them. The crossbow he slung behind his back. The sword he refastened to his hip. Finally, his trusty rattan hat now rested upon his crown strapped firmly around his jaw and chin.

"I must take my leave. My allies in Guangzhou are expecting my arrival very soon. Thank you, most of all for nursing me back to health. I will also not forget your kindness, your words, or what I have witnessed last night. My name is Sun Xin," he said with a slight bow and fist wrapped in hand – a salute and gesture of gratitude.

"I am Famin Jie. It was a pleasure to have accommodated your stay. Safe journeys my friend. May your path lead you to the pursuit of righteousness," he said with a bow as he exchanged the salute. The hermit set him on his way packed with provisions. Famin Jie was the hermit's name. He would be sure to remember it.

He left the small valley with the words of Famin Jie still impressed into his mind and with the events of the previous night replaying through his memory. He found his way back to the old trails and roads, passing by farms and isolated communities. A small country temple not far from the beaten path was abandoned long ago but provided shelter from a storm. There, Xin sat patiently on the floor, eyes closed with arms and legs crossed amidst the ghastly statues of a pantheon of deities for all whom the temple stood. They seemed to hauntingly stare at him as the rains poured and the wind howled. To Xin, such idolatry was vanity and mere illusion. Quite ironic that he found shelter in such a place. He scoffed at the idols adorning the walls of the derelict temple while he waited for the storm to subside and the thunder to fade into the mountains. It was curious, even to him, that he did not the harbor the same feelings for the teachings of Famin Jie. They were food for philosophical thought rather than objects of ridicule. He did not understand it, really. It did at least give him something to think about until the rains passed.

He continued his journey further south walking briskly through rice fields and lakes ornamented with lotus and water lilies. A procession of Ming imperial troops making its way toward the provincial garrison marched down a main road. It was headed by mounted commanders in imposing armor and winged helmets topped with bright red tassels. They were accompanied by haughty high-ranking government officials wearing brocade uniforms of bright colors. Their approach was heralded by the uniform rhythm of their pounding boots and the clatter of their weapons and armor. He walked to the side of the road and the soldiers passed him with a glare of suspicion that screamed "We're watching you, vagrant. Tread carefully." He had a healthy respect for most the imperial army and had no desire to engage them at any time. They had often proved to be as strong and skilled as they were intimidating. Sun Xin smirked as he recalled some of his past experiences.

Other travelers became more frequent as he neared Guangzhou. Many of them simply gave Xin a nervous grin and leaned to the opposite side of the road as they passed him by. Villages and towns became more frequent as well. The people would always take a brief moment from their daily activities to observe the strangers making their way through their town. Sun Xin had grown accustomed to their staring. People have grown overly cautious of travelers carrying weapons. It was always in the smaller and more remote settlements where blending with crowds was impossible for the lack thereof. At least the chickens roaming about the streets paid him no attention.

It was not long until the silhouette of the walled city appeared in the horizon. It overlooked the sea which faintly sparkled in the hazy distance. Many great ships from various seas of the known world were docked at the harbor of Guangzhou, a city nestled beside the sea. A dozen other vessels anchored not far from shore. Columns of smoke rose from the shapely colorful rooftops of countless establishments. Across the districts, the streets sprawled with thousands of citizens like ants of a vast colony, and thousands more came and went through the monumental city gates. A large pagoda overlooked the districts majestically, casting a shadow that shaded many street blocks. Guangzhou – The Ming Empire's gateway in the South has stood for nearly one thousand five hundred years and has become a crossroads for the maritime world.

It was late into the afternoon by the time Sun Xin approached the vast city gates. They were guarded by light detachments of spearmen from the local Ming imperial garrison. They were posted on both sides of the gate keeping watch for suspicious and wanted persons filtering through the bustling crowds. High up on the walls archers and crossbow units were stationed. Past the gates, the city truly opened up before Xin. The streets were lined with vendors selling food and condiments of all sorts. Shops providing exotic fabrics, textiles and various garments, spices and herbs from all over the known world lined the stores on another street, and beyond were restaurants, herbal medicinal shops, offices, and large pavilions. Thick and thin crowds hurried about their business, buying and selling, meeting and eating. Craftsmen from the province had set up shop in the streets to peddle their wares. Olive-skinned foreigners wearing long surcoats of ornate embroidery walked past Sun Xin but the light company of soldiers patrolling the streets paid them no attention.

"Even visitors from the desertous West have become common," he thought.

Most buildings went up two and three stories and they riddled the street canopies with lanterns, flags, and various banners. Along the main avenue, a trio of musicians played their flutes and stringed instruments together in harmony with costumed dancers. Across from them stood a congregation of acrobats, jugglers, and street performers hoping to win the crowds for some coin. Further down the dusty street, Xin paused to observe the local outdoor performance of an opera. Many children ran about and the smell of street food filled the air.

The city can truly be an overwhelming place – a sharp contrast to the province. It was festive, lively, and colorful, yet, suffocating, and exhausting. The districts divided the residential from the commercial, although they were, for the most part, thoroughly diffused. The heavy crowds were straining the sense of urgency he had developed since he left the hermit's homestead. He dashed towards a nearby wall and used a combination of momentum and friction to scale it to the rooftop with ease. With a quick and steady pace he cut through the streets by gracefully leaping from rooftop to rooftop while being careful to avoid slipping from loose tiles. He launched himself from a ledge and watched the ground as it rushed toward his feet, his long scarf trailing behind him like the tail of a kite. He dropped into a dim alley and hit the ground with a roll swiftly and silently far from the awareness of the people nearby. He brushed the dust off his shoulders and secured the satchel strapped to his back. He casually continued to his destination on level ground. At the top of a broad and shallow hill, a large multi-storied structure stood mightily inside a walled courtyard complex.

A stately academy for music, literature, statecraft, history, philosophy, and martial arts served as the face of the League of Martial Scholars' official headquarters and it stood loftily upon a hill at the edge of one of Guangzhou's greener districts. A wide stone staircase led to the large red doors that stood in between the stone statues of mythical beasts. A prestigious sign hung attractively at the top of the door post: School of the Way of Culture. Many students from various walks of life attended the school seeking to gain skills and knowledge far beyond business and agriculture and it served as an attractive alternative for those who desired something different, even nobler besides passing the maddening civil service examinations in which many aspiring scholars dedicate their lives. The Academy also offered its students a means to a life of higher purpose other than civil service. The school was known for graduates who have proceeded into success in various disciplines. Throughout the empire, it was the only school of its kind. However, it was only a means to an end – a façade to continue the never-ending vigilantism of the political cabal that was the League of Martial Scholars.

The academy which the Scholars headed was alive with culture.

There were many students at work, writing and studying, playing or composing music, and in another courtyard at the center of the academy grounds, one hundred students practiced combative art forms in unison training in the armed and unarmed fighting systems. After completion of their studies many of them move on to civil service examinations and become virtuous government officials. Others become writers, artists, architects, doctors, and musicians to name a few.

From among the students who attended the school, candidates of exceptional skills and unique backgrounds were carefully and secretly chosen to be initiated into the League's mysterious brotherhood of warriors. Many have been given a chance to enter League's inner circle as official Martial Academicians and were obligated to swear an oath of allegiance that indoctrinated them with a creed to uphold justice and defend peace through blade and brush. Wherever they may be or whatever path they choose in life, their oath would always stand.

Behind the main hall of assorted musical instruments, book shelves, and calligraphy brushes were several halls for study, dormitories, and quarters for martial and musical practice. The walls displayed a wide array of traditional weapons. Spears, sabers, various swords, and halberds decorated the rooms.

Sun Xin entered the school through the main gate which opened up into a spacious courtyard. At the center of the courtyard stood a heroic stone memorial of one of the Middle Kingdom's greatest warriors – Yue Fei who had valiantly led the armies of the Song

Dynasty against the marauding armies of the Liao and Nuzhen nations in the north some three hundred fifty years earlier. The image of Yue Fei served as a powerful symbol and daily reminder of the meaning of loyalty, patriotism, and superior martial skill. For the likes of Sun Xin and the Scholars who fought for the people's cause largely in secret, the story of Yue Fei served to remind them of the necessity of abstaining from the burdensome yokes of politics and the complications of government affairs. For Yue Fei, his timeless devotion and impeccable military record did not suffice to save him from being betrayed, imprisoned, and executed by the corrupt officials in the very government he swore to protect. The League of Scholars and those who associate with it therefore avoid corrupted politics and legalism in exchange for swift judgment founded upon a sacred written oath formulated in shadow many years ago.

Xin proceeded through the courtyard and entered the main office. There upon the second story of the pavilion he was immediately greeted by the Head Scholar of the League, Lu Guanying who also happened to be the school's headmaster. He was a most superior combatant and was especially well-versed in nearly all studies offered in the school. He was also very knowledgeable of the teachings of the great Master Kong whose philosophical teachings allowed the Middle Kingdom to achieve unprecedented developments in society and government or the last two thousand years.

There was also Tian Qiu the polymath, somewhat short and clean-shaven, but was a man of rare skills ranging from the philosophy of science to the application of mathematics. Where wisdom should have been however, there was but an abyss, an insatiable desire for knowledge – knowledge in which he took great lengths to achieve. He took great care to not make it so evident to his colleagues, though he could always be seen carrying with him a scroll or a set of books.

At the other end of the room was Shang Jian, a brilliant tactician and strategist unlike the Middle Kingdom had seen since the legendary Zhuge Liang of the Three Kingdoms era. He was a handsome man with effeminate features yet was exceptionally skilled in unarmed hand to hand combat as well as an erudite of the ancient Seven Military Classics. He had declined a coveted prestigious position in the capital in exchange for applying his abilities for a more profound, albeit secretive calling within the League.

With him stood Zhen Shu, the wealthy descendant of a long line of legendary master craftsmen and armorers. His family's forge was renowned all throughout the Middle Kingdom for superb craftsmanship in weapons and armor. He was olive-skinned and muscular from the many years of forging iron and steel. Only the finest warriors of the Ming Imperial Army were able to obtain his fine work and a chosen few were gifted his special weapons and armor. Some of his pieces were bestowed to Sun Xin for his valiant efforts in enforcing the creed of the League. The sword hanging from his hip, the mail covering his torso beneath his clothes, and the hardened leather vambraces wrapped around his forearms were his very handiwork. Such were a few of the key members of the League, diverse, but joined for a single noble purpose whilst taking into account the cultivation of the mind of the scholar.

"Ah, Sun Xin you have finally arrived," he said delightedly. Lu Guanying was a kind man with his years full of experience. He was strong-willed and in good health. A maroon cap covered the top-knot of his long silver-streaked hair. The rest of the members of the League stood to greet Xin's arrival. Sun Xin greeted them with a salute, his left hand covering his right fist. They returned the gesture. He unfastened his cap and loosened his scarf as he looked around to survey the old familiar place. His connection with them gave him a sense of belonging, not that he felt he needed such a thing, of course.

"How was your campaign in the deserts of the Far West? What of your training in solitude?" Lu Guanying asked Xin since he had spent weeks abroad.

"I have not found peace in the field; there are only common thieves and bandit gangs that the army refused to bother itself with. I have however succeeded in destroying a bandit safe-haven in the northwest and had the pleasure of hunting down a notorious serial killer during my return journey."

"Quite eventful, it seemed," Tian Qiu commented. "May I ask whom it was you slew?"

"The Crossbones Killer. Have you heard of his rampage in the northwestern provinces? Prints of his face are on every notice board of every city and town there," Xin answered. His arms were crossed and his posture was erect.

"Indeed," said Tian Qiu. "He was permitted to commit his

atrocities for far too long. The Subprefectural and District Magistrates in that region would rather fatten themselves on pastries and politics rather than offer a bounty an experienced tracker would accept."

"Or have enough sense to coordinate with the bureaus at the capital to prompt an imperial response," Shang Jian added.

"And it's for such things that our organization exists," continued Lu Guanying.

"Nevertheless, the Crossbones Killer is no more," Sun Xin remarked.

"How did you do it?" they asked.

Sun Xin redirected his gaze downward. "I had been tracking him for several days. He didn't make it difficult. He could not help himself from killing. Persons missing for weeks were turning up dead at every turn with each killing as gruesome as the last. The things he'd make them do to each other and themselves were nothing short of atrocious. He knew I was on his trail and thus led me to an abandoned outpost in the middle of nowhere."

"Knowing it was a trap you had naught left to do but spring it," said Zhen Shu.

"Naught left to do but spring that trap," Xin echoed. "That abandoned outpost was a den – a mass grave where many corpses were hanged in display. He thought such a sight would have caught me off guard; he then proceeded to harass me with hit and run tactics. After I had become familiar with his attack pattern I cut him down. Before I landed the killing blow he smiled at me and said 'b'fore long, your entire world will turn upside-down.' I thought nothing more of it drove tip of my sword through his throat."

"Surely the ramblings of a deranged psychopath," Lu Guanying remarked. "I am truly impressed with this feat. Tis a great burden that has been lifted from society, but a crying shame for the victims we cannot resurrect."

Xin switched topics. "On a more geographically political front, now our troubles with Lin Xuan the Warmonger are over. I tracked him down at an inn near the desert and deceived him into thinking I was one of his henchmen. He and his trusted commanders will no longer be our concern. Word of his death spread rapidly across the region. The Menggu tribe of that region has disbanded their alliance with his men and the people are celebrating his elimination. The nearest army garrison mopped up the remnants of the forces there. The army now occupies his territory and is still clueless as to the cause of his death. Not even the governor of the province was aware of my presence there," he said as he leaned back against the wall with his arms crossed. He paused for a moment.

"Upon completing my objective I found a map outlining the other nests where many of his followers reside in wait. Your Academicians can raid them to eradicate their presence from that province once and for all." Sun Xin said plainly as he pointed at the map.

"Well done, Xin," Guanying said nodding with satisfaction. The rest of the members of League murmured with excitement and approval of the mission's success. They have been tracking Lin Xuan for many years and it was Xin who had finally removed him once and for all relieving the Ming Empire from a painful thorn in the flesh.

The government however, will never truly figure out who killed him and that is perhaps for the better.

"That was quite a feat but we must keep one eye open. The worst may be in the loss of the balance of power upon the death of the desert warlord. The region under his influence has surely been agitated. Get your fill to eat and rest a while," Lu Guanying said as he tossed Xin a fat sack heavy with coin.

Though Xin was not a member of the League, he had long earned his place among them. He was even requested to officially lead the Academicians but better judgment or perhaps even pride prevented him from assimilating into their brotherhood. Still, Lu Guanying felt quite fortunate to have had such a skilled fighter and assassin to carry out the combative causes of the Martial Scholars. They have once said that if the enemy does not sway with words and civilized diplomacy, the sword was but the last tool implemented to enforce justice. Such was the creed of the League of Martial Scholars. Sun Xin's first encounter with them went back some years ago, when the Academicians led by Shang Jian had been hunting the same target he had been tracking for many weeks. When Xin struck first blood on the target, the Scholars' attention refocused on him. A professional relationship with the League and their brotherhood of Academicians had begun from that point forward.

Xin paused for a moment to recall his trek through the woods. "I was making my way through the outer edge of the dominion of the Crimson Moon Sect. During my scuffle with three of their scouts I was wounded by a poisonous arrow. Living alone in the mountain, there was a hermit like the sages of times past, who had nursed me back to health. When the evening had come, the occultists attacked the house and attempted to harass us with their usual terror tactics. The sage however, claimed that he was under the protection of Heaven and so with one statement alone, the occultists fled into the night as if they had felt a power against which they knew they could not contend. I have never seen such power or authority projected from man before." Xin and the Scholars stood in silence unsure of what to make of the story.

Headmaster Guanying broke the silence. "There are stories of a more fantastical nature circulating throughout the Middle Kingdom since time immemorial. Many have merely neglected such news as myth or superstition but not even I can deny that dark activities have grown frequent of late. I do not find your encounter with the occult nor the resurgence of crime or even rumors of wars too surprising. We must stay vigilant and dutiful to the people within the borders of the empire. But tread carefully, Xin. These days charlatans abound and run to and fro," he advised to Xin. "Even so, this hermit or sage has made himself a friend of the League."

"I sense that something dark is on the horizon for the Ming Empire," Tian Qiu expressed rather unexpectedly. "All of us, even among the Academicians could sense its approach though they remained largely silent about it."

"Explain yourself," said Xin in a rather commanding tone.

"Our information network spread throughout the districts and prefectures across the empire has fed the League with vital information that I find is of great concern. Middle Kingdom's state of affairs grows dire. Our informants indicate increased hostile activity from many criminal groups and underground rebel organizations. Such news was troubling though no one could produce an explanation as to why. You've already personally experienced this truth with the Crimson Moon Sect."

Shang Jian the strategist stepped in. "The rebel groups and secret societies have grown bold of late. Even the imperial government has grown anxious. We've heard that the bureaucrats of the palace in the capital are scrambling for solutions. However, we ourselves are unsure of what their spy agencies in the Eastern and Western Depots already know. Their lackeys in the Imperial Secret Police are largely untrustworthy and corrupt – most being mere pawns of the powerful eunuchs heading the Depots."

"The war ministers and officials can do little to initiate military action," added Zhen Shu. "Most are occupied in defending the northern and western borders from hostile nomad horse tribes, enemies of the Middle Kingdom since ancient times. Furthermore, the rest of the troops have been allocated along the southeastern coasts to defend from marauding pirates from the island nation of Riben across the Yellow Sea. The cities' prefects were ill-equipped to combat the rebel and bandit raids on the outlying provinces and cities. Military responses were less than satisfactory."

Headmaster Guanying rubbed his chin in contemplation. "The

League does not officially meddle in the military affairs of the empire and leaves such matters to the emperor and his court. Still, there might be a time when our involvement in war would become inevitable. There are however, troubling reports from the neighboring provinces regarding the arrival of foreigners never before encountered in any of the seas. They've congregated in Guangzhou and are treating with high ranking officials who've bothered to come all the way from Beijing. The eyes of the League have been set upon them for some time now. I believe we are right to do so…"

Though their day to day routines have provided them with a feeling of security, recent unfolding events have changed that feeling to anticipation and anxiety.

Sun Xin did not consider himself to be a part of the cabal, but took pride as a lone agent with an alliance with those who shared his philosophical views of justice, punishment, and national security. The Academy had been a sort of home for a number of years now and was currently the only place where he could find respite and training for his body and mind.

How he ended up with the League was a long story and he would never forget how Lu Guanying had bailed him out of a great demise while offering him a place amongst their ranks not so long ago. Sun Xin owed the headmaster much and he did his best to repay that debt by fulfilling his missions in the name of their cause and creed. Across the large courtyard, Xin entered a study and rested. To his wonder, the wound on his neck had almost completely healed.

Now he felt as he had another new debt to the sage living on that small mountain. Famin Jie's words and actions on the night he had spent in his home was one he would never forget. Sun Xin remained bewildered and awed at what he had experienced there. He had seen and heard many things, but he never thought he would meet a man whose words held so much power that even the darkest minions fled upon hearing them. In the back of his mind, Xin hoped that one day he would meet the hermit sage again.

# MYSTERIOUS FOREIGNERS IN GUANGZHOU

THERE WAS QUITE A COMMOTION throughout the city as word spread like wildfire concerning the recent arrival of mysterious foreigners from an unknown land. They have harbored in Guangzhou and have already begun establishing relations with the city and the officials who have arrived from Beijing. The League of Martial Scholars, being naturally well-informed, had many allies in the city's high and low places serving as keen eyes and ears. Consequently, news surrounding the activities of the mysterious foreigners came to them fairly quickly. "They sought to establish long-term trade relations, dealing with medicines, special spices, and knowledge," Xin recalled in the League's report.

Sun Xin made his way through narrow alley ways and corridors deep into the heart of the city to investigate this commotion. The local government headquarters stood in the distance and a crowd was gathering around the complex as a procession of oddly dressed figures made their way through the street. Armed guards kept the crowd at bay as curious onlookers craned their necks to observe the arrival of a foreign embassy. Dozens of them, very tall, wore elaborate garments adorned with ornate accessories and carried with them unfamiliar flags and banners. Xin again took to the rooftops for a fresher perspective of the scene. The procession was accompanied by tall soldiers clad in heavy plate armor of dark metals and silver. Their heads were covered by a helmet of horns and their faces obscured by angular plates of metal. At the fore of the procession was a hooded and cloaked swordsman clad in light armor, abbreviated in form from those worn by the accompanying guards. Underneath the armor he wore robes of red and on his hip hung a long, slightly curved blade with no scabbard.

The procession was taken as a surprise to Xin and the observers since foreign delegations of this size were hardly ever allowed to leave the harbor premises. The faces of the foreign delegates, however, were in plain view and they walked haughtily under the shade of broad parasols to preserve their pale complexion. To his shock they did not resemble the faces of men. Very pale, they were, with eyebrows high and arching, eyes red as fire, and their ears pointed and curved along their temples. Xin continued to observe them until they entered the government office while the city's prefects remained posted alongside the government guards. The hooded swordsman turned and unexpectedly directed his gaze towards the rooftop where Xin was perched. He smiled and nodded before returning to join the delegation that proceeded indoors.

Xin took a breath and left the scene in haste. The arrival of the Foreigners was of great significance and unbeknownst to the people of the Ming; their easy access to their land would have unforeseeable consequences.

In the academy's main office and behind locked doors, the Scholars convened concerning the recent events taking place within their own city. "I take it you have seen the parade of Foreigners in the streets leading to the office of the magistrate? I have already heard they are nothing like us," remarked Lu Guanying.

"I have seen them. They walk like men and behave like men… but they are not. The people are fearful of them. They carry the stench of treachery," replied Xin with his arms crossed and head lowered, hat covering his face.

"After ousting a century-long occupation under Menggu warrior horsemen, the Middle Kingdom receives a new threat from the sea. What is it they want?" Tian Qiu questioned while rubbing his chin.

Headmaster Guanying continued. "According to my contacts in the prefecture, the foreigners claim to only wish to trade and establish intimate diplomatic relations. In fact they have already won the favor of the governor and magistrate of the province despite the imperial policies concerning the tribute system imposed on foreigners. I have also just received word from our contacts in the capital. Surprisingly our illustrious emperor somehow felt compelled to allow the foreigners to trade on equal terms."

Whispers and murmurs echoed in the hall of the Scholars. Many of them considered this imperial decision to be controversial. Such a decision was unthinkable. Has the emperor gone mad? This drastic change in policy was unprecedented in the history of the Middle Kingdom. All other nations arrived as inferior powers to pay tribute to the Emperor as a gift in exchange for trading rights and diplomatic relations. What allowed these barbarians to have the right to negotiate on equal terms was a mystery even to the listening eyes and ears of the Scholars.

Sun Xin grunted. He was unamused at the prospect of foreigners meddling in the already-complicated situation in the Middle Kingdom. The horsemen continued to raid the North and Wo pirates of Riben plagued the coasts. "If these barbarians become hostile, the empire may not have the immediate resources required for an adequate defense of the empire," he stated. "I do not trust the snow-skinned foreigners. They carry themselves with an aura of superiority that I find unbecoming."

"The citizens, however, can only wait upon the decisions of the authorities. This unexpected leverage the foreigners seemed to so quickly possess over the government was curious indeed. Just how the capital and the emperor will continue to react to their arrival remains to be seen." Lu Guanying massaged his forehead. "The best we can do is observe these recent changes and be wary of their intentions. Our counterparts at Hanlin Academy close in the capital may be able to provide further insight about the activities of the foreigners in the country. We cannot risk what nearly happened when mere horse nomads sat on the Dragon Throne." A courier urgently entered the council chamber. His clothes were dusty from a long journey on horseback and he smelled of the noon day sun. With both hands, he presented a sealed document to Lu Guanying. He unsealed the document and began to decipher the encrypted message monogrammed with a symbol that could have only come from Chancellor Wu Chan of the Hanlin Academy – an imperial institution that provided the emperor with secretarial tasks as well as the most intelligent staff to take government duties whenever the need arose.

Upon reading the letter, Headmaster Guanying paused and sighed. "Well this just answered some of our questions. Our pale guests have made appearances in other cities along the coast. Not all too different from what we are seeing." He said. "This changes many things. It is vital we know their intentions before it is too late for us to take preventive action."

Tian Qiu the polymath was more curious than concerned than the rest of the Scholars. He was fascinated with the arrival of these foreigners and was enticed by the wealth of knowledge they could offer in the many disciplines he practiced. "Why do we cloud them with such suspicion? Is there not so much we can benefit from them? They apparently have the means to arrive on our shores from a distant and unknown land. If they are sophisticated enough to have accomplished such a feat then maybe they may not be so indifferent to our ways," said Tian Qiu with uncharacteristic optimism.

"Whatever cultural sophistication they may possess could only serve as a greater capacity to wage war against us… greater in comparison to the enemies we already know." Sun Xin replied.

Lu Guanying nodded and took a deep breath. "We can only wait…and trust that our government would exercise more vigilance and discretion concerning the foreigners' intentions than what they have demonstrated thus far."

Tian Qiu rubbed his bare chin in thought, still curious about the foreign visitors.

Shang Jian, a renowned strategist and tactician naturally maintained close ties to key officers within the military. "I have close connections with key commanders stationed in the garrisons along the coastline. Should the foreigners so much as imply hostile behavior, I am confident that imperial forces will be ready to administer judgment on land or on the sea." Shang Jian was ever at the ready to employ military force whenever necessary to defend the interests of the Empire.

Late into the afternoon, Sun Xin stood from an elevated balcony on the city's tallest structures. He extended his spy glass and peered through the lens. A handful of the foreigners' angular and curvaceous ships laid anchored offshore, sails raised and folded, cannon-like weapons protruding from port and starboard. A curved canopy arched over the deck of the ships acting as a sort of protective barrier. Was it perhaps a shield against the harsh sun of the open seas? The foreigners were pale after all. The ships were large and imposing, especially for being mere vessels of voyage, and were similar in size to some of the largest warships in the Ming Imperial Navy. Some of the foreigners could still be seen moving about the decks in rhythm hauling cargo and supplies of sorts. They moved purposefully and did very little conversing. Even the way they moved seemed almost unhuman and devoid of any sort of expression. Lu Guanying was right. The only thing they can do was be patient and alert. Perched on the highest tier of the city's pagoda, Sun Xin surveyed the ships until the sun had set. The air grew cold. The autumn season was upon them.

# IN THE SOUTHERN PROVINCES

TO THE YELLOW SEA in the East lay an old island nation ruled by a militaristic administration called the Ashikaga. Its inhabitants called it "Nihon" otherwise known in the Middle Kingdom as Riben. The country was simmering with civil unrest and had grown ripe for full-scale civil war. An elite warrior class natively called "sa-mu-rai" governed the provinces. Their swords were legendary, curved, and extremely sharp, wielded by a martial finesse honed through many years of continual combat. As the sovereignty of the ruling Ashikaga military administration in the archipelago began to weaken, the warlords of the various states raised armies to fight for the seat of power. Out of the brewing chaos of their civil war, many defeated members of the dishonored warrior class turned to banditry and piracy to survive. Onto the coasts of the Middle Kingdom they wreaked havoc for many years. Hundreds upon hundreds of elite pirates joined those who have defected from the Ming to patrol the seas and ransack towns and villages along the eastern coastline. Half-hearted military campaigns to combat the pirates were insufficient and the local leadership of the imperial infantry grew incompetent. As the confidence of the pirates grew, their invasions pushed further inland and they were left largely unchallenged. The activities of the pirates certainly did not go unnoticed by the Scholars who grew restless as the raids continued. As mediocre intervention of the local governments was not making sufficient progress, the League was compelled to take action from the sidelines. They reconvened to discuss the appropriate method to eradicate the pirates.

The most recent occurrence took place in the neighboring province of Fuzhou where a township was reported to have been completely taken over. Sun Xin volunteered to investigate.

"The imperial garrison within the town's province will provide the brunt of the fighting force to repel the pirate invaders. Sun Xin, you're to assemble with a battalion of soldiers and coordinate with General He Jin, a friend of the League and a close contact of mine. As we speak he is preparing for a preemptive strike within the enemy's defenses in order to create an opportunity for a full frontal assault," said Shang Jian. He provided Sun Xin with a badge to present to the General upon arrival. "Show them this when you reach the garrison. The general will know why you have arrived and who sent you," he instructed.

Xin accepted the badge and proceeded to leave the city. "Now I have a reason to take the fastest mount in the school grounds," he said to them.

Outside the reaches of the city, Xin pushed his horse to a full gallop across the hills and fields, passing by rice planters singing in unison, and farming communities on the edge of the province. Seeing such peace and security made it difficult to believe that warrior pirates were marauding and pillaging places such as these further in the North.

When night came Sun Xin camped under the stars beneath the hills where his flickering fire would not be spotted by any bands of outlaws or raiders roaming the wilderness. Out from his supply in the saddlebags, he neatly unpacked a meal and a small iron pot which he heated over the fire. With precision he conducted himself with discipline in the aim of perfection in any task he undertook.

He found no use in vices, vanities, or in any meaningless activity and useless speech. That is who he was and what he has chosen to be – a man of action as taught by his estranged master. Sun Xin found his master's ways as too passive and wasted his skills doing nothing but selling furniture and woodwork. Such a life was not fitting for a warrior. Xin grimaced at the memory of their last encounter. As he scooped the steamed rice into his bowl and dried salted fish on his plate, he wondered what his master was doing, perhaps taking a sip of hot tea just as he was at that very moment.

\*\*\*\*

On the top balcony of the Scholar's academy, Tian Qiu surveyed the trading posts near the docks where foreigners from neighboring nations arrived to receive a small portion of the Middle Kingdom's wealth. With the delicate adjustment of a few knobs, he optimized the focus of his mounted spyglass, to observe the activities of the pale foreigners. A large portion of the docks, however, was busiest of the rest. It was also there that the enigmatic foreigners stored their own treasures under the shadow of their behemoth ships. Tian Qiu took note of the activity taking place at the very moment. Government officials inspected the cargo brought by all foreigners. There were various fabrics, pottery, herbs and spices, precious metals and stones, trinkets, and ornate tools gathered from the ports of many nations along the seas. They were made ready to be delivered and distributed throughout the powerful and wealthy.

Guangzhou was one of the few cities in the empire where foreigners were given the "privilege" of trade after proper tribute was paid to the emperor himself. The pale visitors' trade items did not far differ from the rest although they brought with them many curious articles. Tian Qiu could not help but be captivated with the foreigners. They were after all, truly foreign. It is perhaps this very same curiosity that compelled the government to privilege them with more trading rights and diplomacy than all the rest. Countless questions riddled Tian's mind. From which distant, uncharted land did they sail? To what king do they swear allegiance? Nothing in the known records mentioned such a race of "people" or a civilization that resembled the foreigners in the slightest. Despite these countless questions, Qiu was careful to tame his curiosities and keep his distance, at least for the moment.

The foreigners were pale indeed, like corpses, as if their skin had been infused with snow. They were also tall and very well dressed. They favored hooded cloaks and fitted clothing and carried on their hips swords of various kinds. Despite their ghastly appearance, they were, by all outward appearances, very civilized. Their soldiers carried metallic elongated weapons with a visible barrel, obviously purposed for ranged combat. The delegates wore fine garments with ornate stitching and embroidery and carried themselves in the illusion of humility.

The Pale Foreigners had been given a patch of land to the West of the docks. They had hastily built a large outpost with several structures for living quarters and storage. Tian Qiu beheld their robust architecture, most of which was marked by towering spires and admirable domes. Plumes of steam and smoke ascended from the structures.

"Astonishing how quickly they can build even by Ming standards," he muttered to himself. There was much he wanted to know. The availability of new knowledge enticed Tian Qiu and all that these pale foreigners had to offer materially and mentally had a powerful allure. Just what was Tian willing to give to obtain such things? Nevertheless, he reported his observations to the other Scholars who were quite surprised and taken aback at what the Foreigners were permitted to do on their own soil. The judgment of the city's authorities and even the capital itself was becoming questionable in the eyes the Martial Scholars.

Lu Guanying purposed an investigation to uncover the government's unprecedented tolerance of the Foreigners' actions. His cohort and fellow Martial Scholar Zhang Sunzan was knowledgeable in law, diplomacy, and politics. His network was deep and cast a wide net over the empire. He therefore volunteered to make his own contributions to the investigation.

"The Foreigners have been frequenting the magistrate's office and have been seen paying visits to his home. The city's aristocracy has gained quite an interest in them. I fear their comfort is unhealthy," he said with a frown. "There are high-grade officials who share our political alignments. They would be willing to provide us with insights to what has become of our nation's foreign policy and perhaps provide us with clues to the Foreigners' true intent."

Lu Guanying nodded while Shang Jian rubbed his bearded chin. Zhang Sunzan continued saying, "I will also speak to my long-time friend. He is well informed of the city's activities and… underground dealings." With this, Zhang Sunzan released a pair of messenger doves from his study's window as he made preparations with his investigation. So was the gathering of the Scholars.

****

Sun Xin rode posthaste into the province of Fujian past green meadows, towering rock formations and trees, and bountiful farmland. He pushed his steed to a full gallop until he arrived at the garrison where he was to meet General Jin currently in command of the troops stationed there. He was halted at the gate where he showed the golden plaque Shang Jian had provided. The general was summoned and he greeted Sun Xin with a pleased smile.

"Ah, you must be Sun Xin the renowned swordsman. I've heard quite a great tale about you. Your deeds and mysterious persona have been quite the popular topic among common folk and elites alike."

"Well, I hope I can live up to your expectations, General," Sun Xin replied as he saluted him. The garrison was buzzing with activity as soldiers made their way to and fro the compound training and working, trying to look their best in front of the visiting General.

General Jin was a tall, robust man, with his uniform covering a strong and hardened frame. Confident and collected, he walked in lengthy strides with his left hand resting comfortably on his sword. His gate bore testament to prolonged experience in the art of war.

General Jin continued. "My orders come directly from the capital. The emperor is growing weary of these barbarous pirates. But I have just recently arrived myself. These men in particular have become undisciplined, complacent and lazy – a failure of the previous garrison commander. It is my job to get these men disciplined and ready for combat."

"Where are these pirates holding now?" asked Xin as they walked through the compound.

"We estimate over a thousand of them are currently occupying a township called Putian located ten and a half li northeast. Can you believe it? They have the nerve to hole themselves up within a stone's throw away from this garrison and other cities. Arrogant fools, they are."

"A mere one thousand barbarians and yet the 'mighty' Ming army is unable to repel them? I do not understand," scoffed Xin.

General Jin frowned. "These pirates are no mere barbarians, comrade. They are warrior class defected from Ashikaga Shogunate. It is only recently these pirates have united under one banner. They now answer to the notorious pirate lord Mizushima. I will give him credit; I have heard he displays significant skill on the battlefield even when greatly outnumbered. But those were said by the incompetent field commanders this nation has been producing in recent times," he said shaking his head.

"I was not aware of the growing incompetency our forces in the region," said Xin. "What would you have me do for your campaign, General?" They stopped in front of the living quarters where Xin was to stay. The general looked at him square in the eye.

"At dawn we will mount an offensive to destroy them so thoroughly that all the other pirates would not dare enter our shores. In the heat of battle you are to seek out Mizushima… and kill him. His death will greatly weaken our enemy's resolve and they will be defeated. They will be either drunk or extremely hung-over. Overconfident of their position."

Xin lowered his head. "A simple assassination, I see. Consider it done." As a freelance blade, Sun Xin was not accustomed to taking orders like a soldier. He volunteered his skills for what he believed was just and noble. He joined the Scholars on the condition they had the same goals and ambitions for the ideal society. Nevertheless, he agreed to cooperate with the general. It was part of his broader mission, and after all, the pirates were in need of eradication and he was willing to do whatever it took to see that it would be done.

"You will know Mizushima when you see him. He is known for wearing heavy red armor and a war mask during battle," General Jin said. "Be warned, Swordsman, despite how the Scholars have commended you for your skills, I guarantee that Mizushima is more than anything else you have faced before." He pulled on the hem of his uniform to reveal an old scar spanning the length of his chest. Xin's eyes narrowed. "Do not underestimate his capabilities," warned Jin.

"Tomorrow, justice will be done upon him," Xin replied coldly and confidently.

The garrison was alive with fast paced activity. Squads of soldiers performed push-ups, pull ups and other callisthenic exercises. Another company shouted with each strike as they performed spear and sword forms in unison. The rest sparred with each other – fists and feet flying and limbs interlocking with grappling maneuvers.

Sun Xin followed the general into his office within the garrison's largest building. Inside one of General Jin's captains stood in full scale and lamellar armor while examining a map that featured a miniature model of the town in the center.

"Captain Liu Quan, meet our newly arrived comrade Sun Xin. He is a special agent sent here by my comrades in Guangzhou. He will be of great assistance to us in our campaign against the pirate scum," said General Jin.

"Welcome to this lonely garrison, Master Swordsman," the Captain greeted him as he offered a fist-in-hand salute. Xin returned the gesture.

"Pleased to be of assistance," he replied.

Captain Liu redirected his gaze at the map. "They will not be expecting our sudden offensive tomorrow. Our scouts reported their current occupation of the town. They've been drinking and partying to a stupor for days, confident our government will take no action."

General Jin chuckled. "Then the fools are in no condition for combat. They will be easy pickings for us tomorrow. Additionally, I've had to ask some special favors but we have one dozen cannons for tomorrow's Pirate Massacre," the General smirked. He positioned the troop and cannon models on the map to the South of the town. "The capital has given us permission to flatten the town if need be. Tomorrow our heavy guns will bombard from the South. While the bombs fall, the pirates will attempt to flee to their boats and ships on the shore just outside of town only to find them already destroyed. The pirates are not accustomed to cannon warfare so they will panic."

Captain Quan continued: "They will attempt to flee to the north and to the west. Our archers and gunners will devastate their numbers in the east and my heavy cavalry will charge out of the trees to cut them down on the north side. The survivors will retreat back into the town to make their stand. There the infantry will meet the pirates head on."

The general turned his attention to Xin. "You will be charging into the town with the spear and saber companies. Like I have already said; there you will find the pirate lord and kill him in heat of battle." Sun Xin agreed to the General's strategy.

"What of the townsfolk?" Xin asked.

"Any civilian casualties will be minimal, if not present. They have either fled or were unfortunate enough to fall at the hands of the pirates," the captain replied.

Later that day, Xin sat atop a guard tower observing the garrison troops training in hand to hand combat, weapons technique, and battle formations. The bellowing of the General's elite commandos could be heard all over the compound, disciplining the troops and restoring their combat readiness. On the roof of that guard tower, Xin meditated to prepare his mind and spirit for what was to come. Most of the guards looked up at Xin with suspicion and distrust. The rest of the soldiers were unsure of what to think.

****

The time had come. Many years of a lonesome life on the mountain was at an end for Famin Jie the hermit. The clouds of despair were approaching the Middle Kingdom and the age of the Ming was being threatened. By this Famin Jie grew ever more troubled, so he headed north in search of answers. With a hefty wicker backpack and a small cane, he made his way north reciting the hymns he composed himself:

"Though the paths before me be black as night, I fear not. Though darkness stalk my footsteps, I fear not. The blades of evil that seek my flesh nor the greed of men and the schemes of demons, I will not fear, for the Light goes before me and the darkness retreats before its brightness for it cannot overcome it."

As he continued through the lonely trails of the forest, the vegetation and foliage canopy grew denser and thicker until he no longer recognized the road he traveled often many years before. A heavy fog rolled down the side of the cliffs blanketing the forest with a sort of heaviness that clouded the air. He struggled against it.

He then beheld an ancient forest witch emerging from the fog and she presented herself before him a form that was young, healthy, and radiant. She walked a circle around Jie with light-footed strides. She laughed and it resonated through the fog and it plagued the air. She was powerful and ancient. Famin Jie felt it. She carried with her a fallen spirit which had gifted her great power and long life. It was the case for all those who wielded such powers. Supernatural afflictions were not inhibited by the limits of human physicality. Famin Jie knew that the witch's realm extended throughout the forested area of the southern and central provinces and for many years had become a horrific legend among travelers and adventurers. Though many have scoffed at stories as mere superstition, he knew better than to take such matters lightly.

She had come that she may oppress him and he knew this well. "Say what you must and be done with it, thou who art fallen and damned," Famin Jie remarked. Her laughter shrieked even louder, piercing the sage's ears.

"You have a bold tongue for one so small… and irrelevant. Yes, we know you, prophet. We know whence you came and what you seek to accomplish. Do you think that one who has lived such a pitiful life can achieve what you have set out to do?" She whispered with a devious smile.

"It may be so, but I know of One who knows of thee and of the final defeat that thou and all of thine kind will face. Try to impede me if you must. I walk in accordance with the Will of Heaven and nothing you say or do will have me alter my path. Neither my days nor my destiny are my own for they are at the disposal of Shang Di," Jie retorted.

The witch scowled and glared at him but then quickly composed herself. "Your life is well acquainted with grief, loss, and poverty. We are powerful, prophet. Lay down your burden; spare yourself the tiresome journey of your fruitless life, and surrender to us. A great wave fast approaches the Middle Kingdom. We can restore your loss a hundred fold, grant you the knowledge of the whole world, and all of the Middle Kingdom shall know your name. You will become greater than the Ancients if you but raise your hands and surrender your breath to us."

"Away with you, foul spirit, and make haste back to the void from whence you have emerged! Your fate has been written and has been decreed. The riches you promise are worthless in the face of eternity," Famin Jie shouted pointing at the vile witch.

She shrieked and cursed. "You have chosen poorly, prophet. You know not of the mighty dark forces of which you oppose. Your path will be nothing but pain, death, and destruction. We will not rest until your very life force has fallen into the abyss! Darkness has already enveloped this land and soon the forces of our newly-arrived lords will overwhelm you and your kind."

"The sovereignty of Heaven determines all things that come and go. There is no plan that can succeed against Shang Di. Now leave me in peace, fallen creature, lest you be tormented by the light that is truth," Jie decreed.

With that said the witch and the spirit that dwelt within her retreated into the forest. She could not lay a finger on Famin Jie for he was covered by that which was far greater than she. The fog receded and calm was restored to the forest. After his encounter with the ancient witch had come to pass, Famin Jie made camp and prepared a fire where the smoke ascended together with his prayers in meditation…

\*\*\*\*

The investigation concerning the Pale Foreigners continued for days in Guangzhou's districts as Martial Scholar Zhang Sunzan made appointments with his informants – the many eyes and ears of the city. They were acting spies within the businesses, the local law enforcement and government, and were friendly to the League of Scholars.

A discovery was made that the Pale Foreigners have been bribing the provincial and city governments in order to gain unprecedented trading and territorial privileges in the country. Details were rather uncertain but it became clear to Zhang Sunzan that the corruption ran deep all the way to the imperial court involving the lowest officials within the city's government to the powerful eunuchs in the emperor's palace.

"Their growing influence has already caused the Middle Kingdom's own tributaries to be driven out as the Foreigners monopolized trade and commerce along the coasts and among other nations in the Southern Seas," Zhang's contacts said.

On the second floor balcony of a popular teahouse, Zhang Sunzan and his most trusted informant – a very reliable source nicknamed Fox discussed matters concerning the Ming government's relations with the Pale Foreigners.

"Lately our own government has been plagued by corruption and it has only worsened with the arrival of these Pale Foreigners. Those eunuch snakes in the imperial palace are cunning, Zhang. They have been proven to conduct secretive business with the Foreigners away from the watchful eyes of the more virtuous bureaucrats and our well-meaning emperor," said Fox as he took a sip of tea.

"This only confirms our prior suspicions about them. Our worst fears are coming to fruition," Zhang sighed. "What about the imperial spy agencies? What role do the Eastern and Western Depots have in all of this? And what of their officers the Jinyiwei secret police? Surely it is impossible that all of these recent developments unfolded without their approval, if not direct participation."

"One can only guess the ins and outs of what occurs in the Depots or the Jinyiwei. There is compelling evidence to suggest that not even the emperor himself completely knows what is transpiring right under his nose. I've little doubt of this. The emperor may be young, but he is uncompromising and unwavering in his principles," Fox said, pressing his fists against the table for emphasis. "As for the Depots, there are rumors that even among the agencies there is division. Some may have even gone into hiding and set up shop elsewhere. I cannot confirm anything. But I too suspect that most of them have a stake in all of these recent events, with the eunuchs being the very drivers of this conspiracy. If anything, I think the League can do deeper digging than I or the others can. I suggest you reach out to your contacts in Hanlin Academy."

"Something tells me they want more… more than just the profits gained from monopolizing the trade and commerce of the seas," Zhang Sunzan said as if in contemplation.

"I concur. I fear they will proceed to conquer all the trade routes by land in the West and take the kingdoms directly in its path. If this pattern of events continues, we could possibly find ourselves outflanked on land and sea. Even now they have the nerve to build their foul structures on our own land!" Fox said in disgust.

"It is because our government allowed it. We must know their true intentions," Zhang said.

"I must ask of a rather heavy favor from you, Fox. I'll be sure to reward you handsomely."

"No need for a handsome reward. I have a duty to protect my home just like you," Fox replied. Zhang nodded.

"As soon as you are able, make haste for the capital and seek out my old friends holding office in the Censorial Office. They are Wei Qiuyuan and Zhou Liang. They can surely provide more details on what is really happening in the court. If anything, it would be they who could shed some light on all that is unfolding. I have reservations about making contact with Hanlin for a full investigation. It is wise to be patient. Take this badge with you and present it upon your arrival to their headquarters. It will ensure you can speak to them directly and not be harmed. You will find my late parents' estate on the southeast corner of Beijing adjacent to the street lined with medicine clinics. You will know it by the yellow pillars supporting the corner eaves. My housekeeper resides there. Tell him you have arrived to send your findings to me using our family hawk. Launch her on the balcony facing south. She will know to come to the first station in the next city. My network will ensure that the message will continue from station to station." Fox agreed. "Go by sea and travel light. Here is some coinage for your traveling expenses and a dagger lest should you encounter hostility on your long journey," said Zhang as he handed him the items. "Please take care, friend." With a final sip of tea, the two exchanged farewells and bid each other good fortune.

****

Zhang Sunzan summoned the council of the Scholars the following morning eager to share the developments with his colleagues.

"Brothers, in recent days, I have been at work gathering information concerning the Pale Ones and it may appear we were correct to suspect them for it is consistent with what we have been hearing from other sources."

"What is the extent of the threat they pose to the people, Zhang?" inquired Lu Guanying.

"For now, any threat they could pose to our civilization is at the least economic and political. Their presence extends far beyond the Middle Kingdom and they have already begun to dominate commerce between the Ming Empire's tributaries in the southern seas." The council shifted uneasily in their seats. The wooden chairs creaked as Shang Jian and Lu Guanying leaned closer towards Zhang in interest. "They do not appear to be an honorable lot, brothers. They have been known to use cunning, intimidation, and have been seen resorting to bribery. It's a terrible shame," said Zhang shaking his head as he tucked his arms tucked into his sleeves.

Lu Guanying sighed and paused for a moment in thought. "This is such a sharp turn of events for all of us. Are we able to identify the officials involved with conducting relations with the Pale Foreigners?" he asked.

"I am yet to have any neither specifics nor am I able to disclose names, but I can tell you the majority of the conspiracy and secretive business taking place within the capital are being initiated by the emperor's eunuchs. Their influence on government affairs has become very powerful of late I'm afraid, and our virtuous emperor, never leaving the palace, is with little doubt being misled concerning the events unfolding within his own court. I have a friend setting sail for Beijing as we speak. He will be making contact with trusted allies holding offices in the Censorial Office though it may be some time before we will receive news. He is sailing upwind after all. The Censorate's inside perspective of the situation will be invaluable to us," continued Zhang.

"What of the Censorate? Is it not the Censorial Office's duty to prevent and punish this corruption?" Shang Jian questioned, outraged. "Surely there are righteous officials opposed to all this! The Emperor cannot be kept in the dark forever." Zhang agreed with Jian's questioning.

"That is one of the many things we must uncover but I'm afraid that this 'disease' runs deep within the palace administration and within the governments across the cities and towns along the Eastern Coast. I strongly suspect that those involved are too powerful to be challenged by the virtuous. It is also important to note that the Jinyiwei imperial guards do not only answer to the Emperor as they once did. They are now the pawns of the conniving eunuchs."

"What on earth could the Pale Ones possibly offer that would compel the government to sell their nation's sovereignty so easily?" The question bewildered the Scholars. Lu Guanying rose slowly from his seat and said,

"As soon as we have received news from Zhang's allies in the

Censorate, I believe it is appropriate that we meet with the Hanlin Scholars at Beijing. There is a great possibility we must step outside of the shadows for the sake of the empire. We are now the nation's only equalizer against the eunuchs and these foreign powers."

"Bah, forget the investigations! Were it up to me, I would have already mobilized our forces and kicked them out by the edge of our swords. Their very presence is enough justification alone," Shang Jian said. His face had turned red.

# DEALING WITH PIRATES

IT WAS BUT A FEW hours before sunrise in the neighboring province of Fujian, northeast of Guangzhou. A battalion of 1,120 imperial soldiers led by General He Jin made preparations for their advance toward Putian Township now occupied by the pirates from Riben. They comprised mostly of the fallen, masterless, or dishonored warrior aristocracy of the Ashikaga military regime whose rule dominated an island nation for over one hundred fifty years. The ground beneath the mighty garrison shook as hundreds of archers, hand gunners, and spearmen assembled into formation while the general's personal detachment of mounted commandos rode out of the garrison gates. Their scaled and lamellar armor reverberated with the pounding hooves of their war horses. The red tassels on the tops of their helmets flew in unison with the flags and banners they carried into the battlefield. The faces of dragons, lions, tigers, and mythological creatures decorated their shoulder pieces and breast plates. Coupled with their personalized lances, war masks, shields, and spears, they were truly an awesome sight and an intimidating force for the rest of the troops. Above all, they were terrifying for any enemy that should face the receiving end of their charge.

General He Jin rode out with them wearing armor befitting his prestigious rank. It protected his whole body and appeared adamantine despite its ornate design of hues of gold and bronze-like textures. The faces of two dragons rested on his shoulder armor and the golden wings of a phoenix spread out from the left and right sides of his helmet. He wore the armor with great pride and rode with his head held high in great anticipation of the impending battle.

The general and his elite commandos sat high over the rest of the troops. Sun Xin secured his sword diagonally on the rear of his hip and slung a long range crossbow across his back. A quiver full of barbed bolts was fastened to the strap on his waist which he placed conveniently towards the front for ease of draw. Among all the men in the field, he wore no armor save for the specially crafted vambraces and the steel mail vest that hugged his torso beneath his clothes. With the matching hat, his dark blue attire was almost entirely suited for practicality and comfort during long distance travel. He stereotypically fit the look of a knight-errant, but Xin's skills and knowledge went beyond the men who were given such labels. He knew it well.

He mounted his steed and rode ahead of the troops towards the general and the captain who had initiated the march. No words were spoken and the only sounds in the air were boots and hooves pounding the ground in unison to the rattling of armor and gear.

"I will survey the terrain ahead to eliminate any enemy scouts lest they spot the dust rising from the hooves of our horses," said Sun Xin to the General.

He rode his horse posthaste through the dirt road pulling away from the troops. The wind rushed against his face and his long hair danced to the wind. He enjoyed traveling on horseback. It was not only fast and efficient; it gave him a feeling of freedom he could not enjoy elsewhere. The lush green landscape and semi-tropical vegetation flew passed in a blur for several li as he neared Putian Township – a town within reach of the provincial capital and several other settlements. The fact that the pirates had chosen such a place to plunder and occupy was a testament to their growing arrogance and overconfidence in the belief they would remain unchallenged. A signpost on the side of the road indicated he was approaching the town's limits. He slowed the horse to a canter and made his cautious approach into enemy territory.

Around the bend past an assortment of trees that formed a canopy over the road, the foul stench of death consumed the air and the sight that Sun Xin beheld horrified him. Even the horse neighed and reared at the sight.

Hundreds of bloodied and mutilated remains of what used to be the town's citizens were hanged on display along the stretch of road. The remains young and the elderly were not excluded from the horror. Ravens plucked eyes from their sockets. Flies swarmed the corpses and nested in them.

This was to Xin, one of the most important definitions of evil – a complete disregard for the sanctity of the life of innocents. The sight of it was infuriating and his clenched fist shook as the anger coursed through his body. He pushed the horse beyond the side of the road and parked him in between the trees a stone's throw away from the road. Xin centered his energy to his core to control the rage that would potentially cloud his judgment and compromise the task at hand.

Up into the trees he surveyed the area surrounding the southern face of Putian. Using the renowned Light Body techniques he attained during his brief training with the Wudang mountain priests, Xin free-ran along the large treetop branches, traversing them like the ledges and angular rooftops of the city. He precision-jumped onto an elevated rock formation and executed a lache maneuver on an extended tree branch before vaulting over a large tree trunk.

He needed to clear and secure path for the arriving troops and prevent any patrolling pirates from raising alarms. Away from the skeleton-strewn roads, he found the pirates lazily patrolling the township outskirts in a spread and loosely circular motion. With the miniature spyglass gifted to him by the Scholars, he observed the pirates from a distance. They were not alert and conducted their patrol like a burdensome chore. They were a curious sight. Their scalps were clean shaven at the top with a pony tail bun folded neatly against the back of their heads. Some wore leather or straw hats.

Their garments were loose yet appeared dignified and they wore a cold and hardened expression on their faces.

They were not the kind of savages that Sun Xin expected to see but after what he had witnessed along the path, nothing could change his mind about taking their barbarous lives. His anger continued to course through his veins and the familiar presence of the so-called 'Curse' was beginning to be rekindled because of his rage. Xin did not fight it. It gave him incredible ability. The cost was of little importance to him. He needed to neutralize them one by one with secrecy and silence. He carefully observed the movement patterns of the pirates and began to mentally isolate his targets one by one, playing and replaying his movements and executions throughout. He had the element of surprise. He would be striking from the trees. Enemies rarely ever think of looking up.

Perched on a large branch within the crown of an overgrown tree, Sun Xin chose his first target – a straggler furthest behind the patrol. He primed a barbed grappling hook and waited for the pirate to pass beneath him. He spun it round and round like a sling and flung the barbed hook deep into pirate's back. The iron sank into his flesh and dug itself deeper the more he moved. He shouted in extreme agony and fought furiously to unhook himself.

Xin dashed along the length of the branch and leaped off the end. Using the pirate as a counterweight, he dropped to the ground, leaving the pirate dangling helplessly in the air. Xin proceeded to tie the rope around a nearby tree trunk and took cover in the thick bushes. The pirate was shouting and cursing in a foreign tongue. His face was writhing with extreme pain, cursing and swearing as he struggled to pull his weight off the rope to alleviate the pressure caused by the hook gruesomely imbedded into his back.

The other pirates rushed to the sound of the commotion, bewildered at what had just happened. They drew their long, curved swords and gripped them firmly with both hands. One of them cut the rope with a single slash causing the dangling pirate to collapse to the ground. He laid there motionless. They began shouting in every direction. Xin could not understand what they were saying but he knew he was being challenged to fight in the open. *These pirates did not deserve the privilege of open combat*, he thought. Xin remained hidden and repositioned himself to take on his next target that was furthest from the rest. He quietly emerged from the bushes and grappled the pirate into a choke hold and cupped his hand over his mouth before he could squeal. Within seconds and a deep crack of the neck, the pirate lay motionless. Xin again repositioned himself strategically. Not two moments had passed until the body was discovered and the remaining pirates huddled even closer together, noticeably terrified and panicked. Nothing was more disarming for a warrior than an enemy he could not see. Now, Xin had them where he wanted – closely packed and well within reach of a short blade.

Xin removed two paper-wrapped pellets from his belt pack and tossed them into their midst, creating a bright flash and a large plume of suffocating, dense white smoke. Disoriented and in a panic, the coughing pirates cupped their mouths and swung wildly in the smoke.

They were immediately cut down by the lethally accurate strikes of Xin's dagger. Like a shadow he darted to the left and right of the group. One after another, they fell to each blow. The last had finally realized he was all alone. He shook as his head swiveled in every direction looking for his opponent. Sun Xin emerged from the underbrush and stood motionless before the pirate. With a shrieking war cry, the pirate charged at Xin with sword raised in the air. Xin side-stepped away from the blow and rammed the dagger into the back of the pirate's neck.

After the smoke had completely dissipated, he was the sole figure standing in the woods. His dark eyes glared at their lifeless bodies – cold and without remorse. They deserved a thousand deaths. But that, Xin felt, would not have even been enough to pay for the lives of the townspeople they murdered.

He wiped the blood from his dagger and locked it into its scabbard with a satisfying click. This was the side of himself his master had always warned. It emerged out of hatred and thirst for vengeance; some have called it the Swordsman's Curse – an addiction to bloodshed born out of a swordsman's fury. Xin denied that it would consume him and destroy him one day but he was beginning to feel oddly comfortable with the feeling, like a thirst that had been quenched. When it overtook him, his speed, accuracy and skill were unmatched.

He proceeded to greet the general and the arriving troops. After retrieving the horse, he regrouped with the nearby troops to meet General He Jin. The look in his eye was different, like there was no soul behind them.

"All possible threats to our surprise attack have been eliminated, general. The element of surprise remains with us," Xin said in a low cold tone that the even an accomplished soldier like General He Jin found somewhat unnerving.

"Well done, swordmaster. Now let us put an end to this pirate nuisance once and for all." When they approached the road lined with the corpses of the town's former inhabitants, the troops became agitated and horses whinnied. Some of the soldiers vomited at the stench.

"What sort of madness could have possibly come over these barbarians??" cried Captain Liu Quan.

"Not madness. Just evil," Xin answered.

As they neared the township, the artillery, infantry, and cavalry units took their elevated positions around the town's outskirts. Lying low in the distance amongst tall grass and trees, they awaited the general's signal. Xin stood among them, ready for the assault. Up on a hill under cover of foliage and vegetation, the general assembled seven cannons ready to fire. Plumes of smoke rose from inside the town and several pirates stood watch pacing around the gate entrances. Seven loud thunderous booms resounded from the hill as fiery cannon balls crashed into the town. Dirt, mud, clay, and brick flew into the air and shouts and cries followed suit. The pirates within the town panicked and ran in confusion to the sudden unexpected attack.

Chaos ensued as they scurried in various directions with their swords drawn though unable to find an enemy. The enemy blew a siren; their signature conch shell droned like a large horn signaled them to regroup. So far, it was going as planned for Xin and the general's troops. The pirates made a mad dash towards their ships docked at the harbor only to find them already sunken or engulfed in flames. The other ships were anchored far off shore out of reach. They proceeded to exit through the gates but were abruptly met by the general's cavalry that charged right through their ranks and trampling or cutting down all pirates in their path. The rest were met by archers and gunners who completely cut off their retreat. Arrows and ball bullets peppered the pirate company shredding armor and flesh. The volley devastated their ranks.

Back inside the town they prepared to make a stand —swords unsheathed, bows drawn, and spears at the ready. Those wearing armor or who were on horseback formed the front of their ranks ready to defend themselves from the Ming's unexpected attack. The Ming infantry charged into town for an all-out assault while Sun Xin trailed close behind. General Jin's cannons continued to bombard the town.

Deep into the streets, the imperial army collided head on with the pirates, and the sounds of clashing blades and spears were drowned out by war cries and shouts. The Ming infantry crossed blades and spears with the pirates – many of whom still wore the silk-strewn iron armor of their days as aristocratic warrior class. Some from the Ming cavalry charged through and collided with the mounted pirates. Many fell on each side. Sun Xin observed Captain

Liu Quan from a distance. The officer charged forward, leaped up onto a fence post and launched himself at a pirate, spear in perfect position. Afterward, he engaged several more, skillfully cutting down and impaling all who dared to challenge his onslaught.

Even the general joined in on the chaos. He barked orders from the sidelines while engaging a few pirates on his own. He cut them down without trouble.

The pirate lord Mizushima was Sun Xin's main objective. He evaded the brunt of the conflict in the streets by seeking elevation on the rooftops. A mounted pirate clad in red armor charged through the army's ranks cutting down the men with his long polearm —a curved broad blade mounted on the end of a shaft. Xin had found his target. He readied the crossbow and loaded a bolt. He crouched, took careful aim at the moving target and pulled the trigger. The bolt scored a direct hit on the pirate lord but only managed to dent the reinforced ridge on the back of the iron armor. After recovering from the blow, he turned to see Sun Xin perched on the rooftop.

Multiple arrows whistled past Xin's face while others shattered the roof tiles beneath his feet. As he evaded the second volley, he reloaded the crossbow and fired at the lead bowman perched several rooftops away. With incredible accuracy, the bolt pierced right through his forehead and pierced the other behind him, scoring a double kill. Xin leaped to the ground and softened the impact with a roll then made a mad dash toward Mizushima who was fighting in the chaos of several hundred men.

A stray cannon ball blew onto his position and knocked him off balance. His vision blurred and his ears rang but he looked up to keep his eyes on the target. One of the general's mounted commandos wielding a lance charged through the foray in an attempt to dismount Mizushima. They exchanged blows with their polearms; the cracking sound of wood and steel slamming into each other pierced through the chaotic noise of the battle. Both men then locked weapons and began exchanging fist blows. They eventually grappled each other off their mounts and onto the ground. They locked in full hand to hand combat. Mizushima bisected the commando's spear. The commando then grabbed the pirate lord's glaive, and tossed him into the ground with a hip throw. He drew his longsword and swung down to kill the pirate lord himself. Mizushima blocked the attack, causing the shaft of his polearm to shatter. He rolled backward onto his feet as he drew his curved sword and they crossed blades. The commando, despite his valiant effort fell to the pirate lord's sword technique. A stab into the exposed area of his armpit along with slash across the throat finished him off.

Sun Xin refocused his vision and shook off the disorientation as he drew his own sword. He charged full speed and flew into Mizushima with a powerful drop kick, knocking him hard into the muddied ground. The pirate lord stood and recovered his saber-like sword.

He spoke to Sun Xin with a heavy accent. He glared at Xin as if recognizing him. "You... I do not know what you think you are trying to do here but know your efforts are all in vain. You have no idea of the forces you will face. This is bigger than any of you, all of you!"

Sun Xin spat and twirled his sword into his combative stance with two fingers pointed at his enemy. "I know that right now, you are my enemy and that it will be you who will fall to my blade!" He charged at Mizushima with a series of consecutive sword thrusts and swipes but every attack Xin delivered was unable to break Mizushima's defenses. Well executed blocks and parries rendered Xin's usual techniques useless. The pirate lord's two-handed swordsmanship was not only exceptional, but heavily experienced and all too foreign. He proved to be one of Xin's tougher opponents. He found it hard to believe the pirate was holding his ground against his proven style. It seemed unnatural and even impossible.

They continued trading blows and combination attacks seemingly at a stalemate as the battle between the pirates and the Ming forces continued to rage in the background. Mizushima caught Xin's sword hand, twisted his wrist and grappled him to the ground. Xin retaliated with a sweeping leg kick that brought the pirate crashing onto his back. Xin rolled backwards onto his feet when all of a sudden the towering stone structure next to him began to collapse from the bombardment. Both men dove out of the collapsing structure's path as the general's cannons continued to fire upon the battlefield. Rubble and debris piled high on the street separating the two combatants.

In the waters towards the East, a handful of the pirates' box-shaped ships fired upon Xin and the Ming imperial forces. They were armed with a bizarre long ranged weapon never before seen by the men. The ships were from Riben no doubt, but the flashes originating from the ships were a pale blue and were much too far to be within firing range of even the best cannons. There was no time to consider such curiosities. Xin needed to eliminate his target. He crawled to the top of the rubble only to see that Mizushima had already mounted his horse.

"Take our duel as a learning experience, swordsman. You have my respect but not my favor. Next time, we will not part until your blood drips from the tip of my blade!" he said with a devious smile.

He and the surviving pirates then retreated towards the sea where the ships had docked while they continued to fire explosive projectiles onto the Ming forces. The Ming soldiers retreated and proceeded to escape the bombardment. Many were injured and dozens were dead, strewn throughout the streets and underneath debris. The neighs and whinnies of horses and the shouts of the troops were drowned out in Xin's mind as his body surged with utter frustration at his inability to accomplish the mission.

Fresh pirate reinforcements flooded out of the boats to cover Mizushima's escape. Dozens of them with longbows fired a volley of arrows that arced high over the town and rained down on the rooftops and streets. Soldiers took cover and raised their shields. Xin merely swiped and slashed them away as he made his exit. He rendezvoused with General He Jin who tried to salvage the remaining cannons whilst evading enemy fire coming from the distance. So began the long march back to the garrison where many of the injured limped or were carried back in stretchers and carriages. A few horses had no riders and carried only saddles where some of the cavalry forces used to mount.

Whether the battle was won or lost is a matter of opinion. Mizushima and his men were overwhelmed, forced to retreat and were only able to do so under the cover fire of their newly arrived comrades. To Sun Xin however, it was utter defeat. That was the first time he had ever failed at an assassination or faced anyone that had been able to defend against his swordsmanship so effectively.

The return trip to the garrison was spent in silence save for a few random orders shouted by commanding officers, and the moans and groans of the injured. Upon returning to the garrison, the injured were tended. In the General's office, Sun Xin and the key officers convened to discuss the battle that had taken place. No had expected the arrival of enemy reinforcements. Not only did this reveal an unexpected increase in their numbers but a new discovery of their combative capabilities. No one was aware of weapons that fired explosive projectiles that spewed from blue flames.

"It may seem that the empire's problem with pirates is slowly turning into a full-scale war and these turn of events, I admit, are very surprising," said General He Jin as he rubbed his forehead. "I have never seen such weapons capability in all my years in service. This changes many things for us in our fight against the pirate plague," His armor was soiled – stained with blood, mud, and dirt.

"The Ming Empire possesses the most advanced military weapons in the known world. There is no way pirates have the means or resources to design and manufacture such sophisticated artillery.

Even their homeland does not possess a culture of inventiveness and innovation," Captain Liu Quan growled. He was noticeably frustrated and confused with the outcome of the battle; he slammed his fist onto the map-covered table.

"That is because they were supplied with those weapons," Sun Xin interjected from the corner of the room. He stood on one leg, his arms crossed, and his back leaning against the wall. "And I believe I know from whom they were acquired." The others in the room turned their attention to Xin and stood quietly in anticipation of what he would continue to say. "Not too long ago, strange ships docked in the ports of Guangzhou and carried with them foreigners no one else has ever seen. None of the merchants from the South or near West have ever seen such 'men' nor of such ships in any of their travels until recently. These… pale-skinned foreigners carried with them many precious commodities for which the elites of Guangzhou have developed quite a taste and with careful diplomacy they have been able to acquire unprecedented privileges with the Ming government. Such privileges would be considered controversial under normal circumstances." Gasps and murmurs filled the room.

"Do you have any evidence that the weapons we saw in action today did indeed come from those Foreigners, Xin?" inquired the Captain.

"No, but that is the only reasonable explanation I have for the moment. It would appear that our visitors do not distinguish us from our enemies and are foolishly supplying them with weapons. That is going to be a problem," Xin continued. General He Jin nodded in agreement to his conclusions.

"Something tells me that this was no mere accident. Maybe the supplying of such arms to our enemies was deliberate. If this is indeed the case then the Capital must be warned that the Foreigners have been conducting business with the enemy." The general sighed shaking his head with his face in one palm. "There is something more serious, more sinister brewing in the shadows."

"It may already be too late to warn the government," remarked Xin. "The Foreigners may have already found their way into the pockets of many of our esteemed government officials. They have been in continuous communication since they have arrived. Something is definitely happening in secret."

The following morning, General He Jin and Sun Xin stood outside the garrison gates discussing the next possible course of action in their campaigns against the pirates and not to mention the arrival of the Pale Foreigners who could potentially be a new threat unlike the Middle Kingdom has ever encountered.

"My inability to carry out my mission yesterday cost us the victory. I must go away for some time to reflect on my failure. This means I must seek out my old master in order to find closure," stated Xin in a steely tone. The General patted him on the shoulder.

"Do not take the defeat too bitterly, comrade. We succeeded in ousting them from the shores. Mizushima has been known to elude the best of us as well as defeat the best in us. I will go to Guangzhou and report to the Scholars what we have discovered here. Perhaps they would know what to do."

Xin nodded. "Offer them my regards… and my apologies for my absence. I have… some unfinished business to attend to." They exchanged farewells and went their separate ways. Xin proceeded northwest and the General with a light detachment of his personal commandos headed south to Guangzhou to meet with the League.

It had been ten long years since Xin fled his master's instruction in defiance and arrogance. He regretted the state in which he departed from his master's home in the mountains of the Huguang region but he still clung tightly to the reasoning that justified his departure. He wondered anxiously if his master would welcome him after all these embittered years. He had a long road ahead which meant that he has a long time to spend thinking how he would greet his master upon his arrival. He knew that his training was incomplete and he craved to finish it in order to defeat Mizushima. However, the question remained: Would his master instruct him
again? Would he even look at him?

# THE WARRIOR MONK FROM SHAOLIN

THE ROAD HAD BECOME LESS lonely for Famin Jie. Farmers across the province had begun their harvest and many carried their new crops to several markets throughout the villages and towns. Ox-drawn carts full of fresh produce were just in time for the festival and caused quite a stir in Jie's belly. He craved a bowl of vegetable noodle soup. Aching feet and a growling stomach made him all the more eager to reach his stopover.

The town really opened up further down the road which led to the heart of a valley. The entrance to the town was marked by a large gate that arched over the road and on its face the sign said *Town of Fuza*. The festivities had already begun as the townsfolk hustled and bustled to and fro preparing for festivities. Colorful paper lanterns dangled overhead crisscrossing the streets, banners and posters were fixed to the walls, and succulent smell of street food saturated the air. Children ran about holding toys and snacks in their hands and only stopped to give the stranger entering their town a quick and curious glance before continuing to frolic through the streets and alleys. An assembly of musicians prepared their seats and instruments near the shops and houses where Famin Jie was headed.

"Ah, there it is," he whispered to himself smiling when he spotted the old noodle house he used to frequent in his younger days. It had not changed much after all these years. He unfastened his pack and took a seat near the entrance where he could get a full view of the street in all of its liveliness. Such was the innocence of the townsfolk inhabiting this place, free from the cares of politics and far away from the empire's enemies. Life was simple here but it also saddened his heart that they knew not of the Way.

As he enjoyed a bowl of hearty noodles, a man in the corner across the street eyed Jie. His clothes were old and worn and he paced nervously back and forth, restless and anxious. The man's restlessness did not go unnoticed by Famin Jie who paid him no attention but continued to enjoy his meal without worry. After he had finished his meal, Famin Jie returned to the street in search of an inn to spend the night. The inn, being on the other side of town, was quite a distance away so he rounded a corner that led into a lonely street full of many dark spaces. As he proceeded down the narrow street a shadow emerged from his rear. As he turned to see who approached, Famin Jie was violently tackled into the ground. It was the nervous man he had seen from the noodle house. He wrestled with Jie on the hard dirt ground and snatched the coin purse that hung from his belt. The man sprang to his feet with the coin purse in his hand and sprinted into the darkness only to be tripped and pinned back into the ground by a bald-headed young man wielding a wooden staff.

He was bald and wore the faded yellow and orange garments of a warrior monk from the Shaolin Temple. "You will not resist if you know what is good for you, thief!" declared the monk. The thief shivered and whimpered and nearly wanted to cry. It became apparent to Jie however , that the thief posed no threat and acted out of desperation. His appearance and expression testified to it.

"That is quite alright, there young lad. Take it easy, he is not going anywhere," said Jie calmly as he approached the thief. He brushed the dust from his shoulders. The monk snatched away the coin purse and tossed it to Jie. "I am sorry you had to resort to the coin purse of an aging man, sir. If you had just asked me for some coin, I would have gladly offered you a generous sum," Jie said gently smiling to the man whose hands were held up in surrender.

His lips quivered and his eyes watered. "Please, please do not hurt me. I am sorry for what I have done," he pleaded.

"Ha! How typical it is for one to become 'sorry' once he has been captured. I saw everything. You are a coward for preying on old men," the bald monk snapped. He pressed the base of his staff deeper into the thief's throat.

Famin Jie motioned for the monk to stay calm and to remove

the staff and provide some space.

"Come now, let us speak to one another like civilized gentlemen," said Jie kindly. He reached out his hand and helped the would-be thief to his feet. The bald monk observed them seemingly unsure of what think. He did not expect Famin Jie to have been so calm and forgiving about the situation. "Do not even dare to think about running. I will–" Jie stopped him mid-sentence gesturing for him to relax. "But he is a thief! His kind have become rampant in these parts, and they must be punished!" the monk declared as he tightly gripped his staff with both hands white knuckled.

Famin Jie gently put his hand on the man's shoulder and asked "What ails you, my neighbor?" The man lowered his head with tears falling from his face, feeling ashamed of what he had done. It became clear to Famin Jie that he was but a desperate man resorting to desperate measures. "It is my daughter, sir. She is gravely ill and I have nothing left for food and medicine. Bad fortune has fallen upon my household and my crops have failed this year. The harvest is dry." He began to sob.

"Do not fret, dear neighbor, for Heaven surely knows of your troubles. I do not believe our meeting was a mere accident," Famin Jie assured him compassionately. "You may find it well that I have a bit of experience with medicinal recipes. Come; take me to your home, neighbor. Monk, you come too. The crossing of our three paths was no accident."

The monk continued to suspect the man and continued to keep his eyes upon him. Together, the three of them made their way to a humble home on a hill not too far from the town outskirts. There Famin Jie laid eyes upon the farmer's daughter. Her breath was labored and her body was thin and frail. The sight of her broke his heart as he knelt by her side and felt her hands and pulse. He unfastened his pack and unpackaged a few herbs he had brought with him.

"I had a feeling these would come in handy sometime on my journey," Jie said smiling. He prepared the proper combination of plants and herbs, crushed them, and boiled them into a clay pot. After they had finished boiling, he administered the medicine to the young girl who could barely take a sip of the bittersweet broth. He unraveled a pack of fine needles which he cleansed under a candle's flame and pressed them into the girl's vital points to restore the balance of her flow of internal energy. "Now, we will just wait for the treatments to run its course while she rests," he said with a deep breath. The farmer and his wife sat anxiously beside their child just watching her breathe.

The bald young monk sat erect in the corner of the small house with his legs crossed and staff placed across his lap. His expression was blank as if unsure of what to feel about farmer's plight. He too felt compassion for the girl and a small part of him was glad he had not 'punished' the farmer for thievery.

"I have not had the chance to thank you for intervening when you did. I am not as fast as I used to be so I did not think I could have caught our farmer friend, here," Famin Jie said. "But if not for you, we might not have been able to help this family," he said as he took a seat beside the bald young man.

He rubbed his shaved temple and rested his head in the palm of his hand. "Yes, I am pleased that we have made it here to help them. But a large part of me earlier wanted to punish him for committing a crime. I did not know his story." The monk curiously observed the girl's parents sitting around her. He had not experienced the love and care of a mother and father and wondered what it would have been like to have been raised by his own. "Yes, I know your sentiments, but strict justice and protocol by themselves bear very little fruit, do you not agree? They fall short because they do not change the heart of a man," Jie replied. "Love – it is the greatest ethic," he said smiling at him. The monk looked at Famin Jie with a raised eyebrow apparently confused and unsure of what to make of his words.

"When a criminal is punished for his actions, he would be sure to think twice about repeating his crimes because he would fear the consequences. This form of justice saves innocent lives, sir"

"Punishments have their place for those who commit crimes and rightly so, but when a man's heart is truly changed in love, he will not only stop doing what is wrong, but he will become benevolent and begin doing what is good and beneficial to the people. If we had simply punished the man in the street, his daughter might have not lived."

Famin Jie prepared a meal for his company later that evening and upon their request he spent the night at the farmer's home. He awoke that next morning to the sounds of laughter and rejoicing. To his delight, the farmer's daughter was standing up and out of bed.

Her fever had gone and her skin no longer pale. She was swarmed with embraces and kisses from her parents. The farmer and his wife were in deep gratitude. Feeling ashamed for what he had done in the previous night, the farmer fell to his knees and begged for forgiveness from Famin Jie.

"Oh, compassionate sir, forgive me for what I had done. I was but a desperate man who resorted to wrong means. If there is anything I can do or give as a symbol of our gratitude, please just speak and it will be done." He kowtowed to Famin Jie who quickly brought him to his feet. "Now, now I am merely an instrument of the Orchestrator. It was Heaven that had caused our paths to cross. Give your thanks and praise to Heaven." Together on that day, they went into town and celebrated the recovery of the farmer's daughter and the season's festivities. As they observed the festival in town, Famin Jie questioned the bald young man who had been accompanying them.

"Judging by your unique attire and clean-shaven head, you are from an elite order of monks in the forests of Shaoshi Mountain, are you not?"

"I was a monk, but I was banished from the temple. Since then I have wandered the country side seeking work wherever I may find it and helping people wherever they needed. I have deviated from the teachings of my beliefs long ago, whether intentionally or unintentionally, I cannot even remember. Keeping my head shaved helps me remember who I am and where I come from. As for my banishment, I do not like to talk about it, sorry to say." Famin Jie nodded respectfully and continued to observe the holiday at the town well into the evening.

The sect of warrior monks from the forests of Shaoshi Mountain was a mysterious gathering, legendary for their physical abilities and renowned for their skills in close combat. They were also quite paradoxical, spending their days training in the martial arts while simultaneously adhering to the teachings and daily practices of an ancient mystical teaching that taught peace and abandonment of all desires. They rarely ever leave their one thousand year old monastery in Henan province which was in fact but one of several others.

The emperors tolerated their existence on the condition that they would be ready to fight for the nation if they were called. Despite their contrasting philosophical and spiritual beliefs, Famin Jie believed that even they could prove to be very instrumental for the cause of righteousness in the dark days to come.

"Since you have no definite destination, friend, perhaps you could join me on my journey into Huangshan. I am to meet an old friend in the mountains there and I would most certainly appreciate good company on the long, uneventful journey," said Famin Jie.

"I believe a new journey would be good for me. My name is Zuo Shilong. I would be glad to accompany you." It would be the first time he would have a friend since his banishment from the temple.

The next morning, Famin Jie spoke to the farmer and his family concerning the mysterious Way and the importance of living in it. "The blessings of Heaven are poured out to those who live in righteousness," told Famin Jie to them. "This is living the Way: Love, honor , and obey Heaven, love all people as you love your own self, help them sincerely with benevolence, be generous with what you have, always forgive those who wrong you and repay them with goodness. Live as such and you will find tremendous grace in your life. Never before have I seen a follower of the Way starve and go begging for food." With these words, Famin Jie bid the farmer and his family farewell and continued his journey north with the warrior monk Zuo Shilong trailing right behind him.

Their journey together, although not completely uneventful was made bearable with good conversation. The monk found the sage's company quite interesting and fruitful. Accompanying him restored a sense of purpose that he had lost since his banishment from the monastery. It was also the first time he had met a philosopher. Zuo Shilong found him most intriguing.

Far down the old and lonely roads many li away from the town of Fuza, they unknowingly entered the territory of a local gang of outlaws who called themselves the *Furious Tigers*. Their markings have been etched into trees along the side of the beaten path.

This fact did not remain unnoticed by the traveling duo as they were soon confronted by the bandits near sundown. The ones on horseback circled around them while those on foot blocked their path with spears and shields. Their leader, who was mounted on horseback, opened dialogue with mockery. He was a very large and powerful man with a booming voice to match his muscular frame.

"What do we have here?" he laughed mockingly. "An old man and a monk are trespassing through our territory without permission or tribute payment. This offense is punishable by death. What do you have to say in your defense?" he shouted. He was indeed a very tall and large man, muscular and burly, and sported a rough, unruly black beard that covered his cheeks, jaw and neck. He was clad in antiquated hard leather armor and sported bear and fox pelts around his waist. "We apologize if we have caused you any offense. We were just passing through and did not know we were treading on restricted ground," Jie replied humbly.

"Ignorance of our laws is not valid defense, fool! That you did not know on whose soil you tread is no one's fault but your own. Take them away!" barked the bandit leader.

Zuo Shilong brought his staff at the ready but Famin Jie motioned for him to stand down. "Please, sire. Hear what I must say to you first. Something dark approaches from the horizon and threatens our land and it is bigger than you, or me, or all of us," said Jie. "I humbly beseech you to forgive our offense and not impede our progress." The leader and his bandits looked at him in silence then broke into laughter.

"I give you credit for creativity, old man," the bandit leader said catching his breath, teary-eyed from laughter. "Since you made me laugh, I am feeling merciful. Someone ought to pay a pretty penny for your release. Tie them up and haul them back to camp until we can figure out what we want to do with them.," he barked to his men. Before his fellow bandits could obey the order and Famin Jie could make a response, Zuo Shilong charged through the assailants in a blur of motion, his staff gracefully twirling and spinning in the air and slamming into the bandits. The elegant circular motions of the staff testified to the monk's mastery of it as he brutally took them down one by one with every strike. His speed overwhelmed the gang and could not keep up with his movements to respond accordingly.

Famin Jie pleaded for him to stop but the monk had already rendered the bandits unconscious. The bandit leader was knocked off his horse but he quickly rose to his feet and grasped a large pole weapon. It was a heavy glaive called a Guan Dao crescent blade – a large and heavy steel broadsword attached to an extended shaft the length of a spear. Its size was well-suited for the bandit leader who stood a full head and a half taller than the monk, with veins throbbing out of his large biceps.

"I don't believe you realize just what you have done. Do you not see!? I am Buff Baby, the woodland wrecker!" he bellowed. He brought his Guan Dao glaive to bear.

He positioned his weapon and charged at the monk at full speed. Buff Baby skillfully swung and spun his glaive at Zuo Shilong at various angles effortlessly tearing through tree trunks and slicing bamboo stalks all the while the monk gracefully ducking and dodging each blow. As the glaive swung low at Shilong's ankles, he leaped and quickly spun around to bring his staff slamming into Buff Baby's face. He fell to the ground with a heavy thud while his Guan Dao sank into a tree stump and stuck. The powerful blow left Buff Baby unconscious, snoring on the ground, face down in an awkward fetal position. Zuo Shilong prepared to deliver the final blow to Buff Baby when Jie stopped him in his tracks.

"Do you really think that taking his life will stop any more of them from coming?" The monk halted mid-stride and just looked at him puzzled at the sudden question. "For every bandit you dispatch, ten more will take his place. He will cause no more harm to us and there would be no honor in taking his life. Come now," continued Jie. "A long journey lies ahead and we should not walk it with bloodied hands." Buff Baby lay on the ground writhing and moaning in pain while Famin Jie left at his side a packet of herbs to help manage the pain of their injuries. They were going to need it once they awakened. Leaving the bandits to tend to their own injuries, the sage and the warrior monk made their way out of the Furious Tigers' territory further north.

"I have a feeling as to why you were banished from the monastery, my friend," commented Famin Jie. Shilong turned to look at him with one eyebrow raised.

"So you think you have it figured out?" he asked.

"No, but I have observed that you are impulsive and prone to violence. An emotion courses through you and you act on it without thinking. Those tendencies can be harmful, especially for you."

The monk sighed and replied: "It is people like him that need to be eradicated. They are free to commit mischief as they pleased because those who are good leave them unchallenged. If I had not acted, we may not even be alive right now. I did what I had to do for our survival. They do what they do because they think no one will stand up to them." Famin Jie calmly replied to him saying,

"Buff Baby had no intention of killing us. Had he so desired he would have just done so without confrontation. If I had spoken to him more, he would have listened. He is living out of pain, Shilong. Not out of a senseless desire for mischief or evil." Zuo Shilong frowned.

"How can you be so sure of such things, teacher?" asked the monk. Jie paused to look at him and said "Because I was like him once – angry and rebellious. The results of violence against those who are wrong us are temporary and not far reaching. Despite its seeming necessity for the moment, its effects do not last very long. Do not be so quick to raise your staff to take the lives of those who act against you. Unless your life is under immediate threat, restrain your hand from reaching for your weapon," continued Jie. Shilong shook his head as he found it difficult to share Jie's view.

"I do not see your passivity as producing any benefit for the law or the people. Criminals like him truly need to die," he said coldly as he slung his staff across his back.

"Do you think their deaths will stop crime from ever happening, or criminality from forming in the heart of a man? No, the Great Way alone is the answer to all these things." Jie told him.

"How can this Way protect me from those who wish me harm?" asked Zuo Shilong. Famin Jie paused to look at him with a fatherly gaze.

"It cultivates meekness and humility."

Having lived most of his life at the temple, the very truth of the "Way" was quite puzzling for Zuo Shilong. There were very little teachings about it in the monastery. The only exposure he had to the teaching of anything resembling the "Way" came from his limited knowledge of the priests living in the foggy mountain peaks of Wudang who sought harmonious and peaceful coexistence with nature. However, they devoted much of their time in temples in front of statues of a pantheon of deities. They spoke little of the sort of message Famin Jie was sharing to him. He pondered on the words of the philosopher as they continued their steady march towards the Huangshan mountain range.

# RESEARCH AND INVESTIGATION

AT THE HEART OF GUANGZHOU, in the crowded streets of the commercial district, General He Jin and a light company of men rode their horses toward the Scholars' headquarters. They were to inform them of the recent events that took place at the Battle for Putian Township and the new developments concerning the pirates who defected from Riben. The city's harbor lay in the distance and He Jin paused briefly to observe the activities taking place at the wharfs. He extended a spyglass and watched the Pale Foreigners walking about as if they already owned the entire harbor. Under the shadow of the tall and imposing structure they had so quickly erected, the Foreigners conducted business with the city's local officials. Together they regulated the activities of the harbor and oversaw the comings and goings of various ships from around the known world. The elite Jinyiwei secret police guarded harbor entrances and patrolled the harbor compound. How unusual that a special task force that supposedly only answered to the Emperor was involved in such affairs.

"It appears that palace eunuchs have been scheming of late," he muttered to himself. He continued onto the Scholars' headquarters and was immediately greeted by Shang Jian the Strategist and by the rest of them. At the council chamber General He Jin informed them of all that had happened: the arrival of Sun Xin at the garrison, the battle of Putian, and the arrival of the pirate ships that fired upon them from great a distance using a mysterious new weapon. The news troubled the Scholars and they agreed that the only logical explanation was the involvement of the Pale Foreigners.

"One more thing, comrades," said the general. "Your swordsman Xin has ventured north. Has some unfinished business there, says he needs to talk to his master or something. He sends his regards and apologizes for his absence. He was… rather affected by the events of the battle."

"Sun Xin is a free spirit. He makes an appearance at precisely the moment he intends," Lu Guanying answered.

"The Foreigners have become more intrusive in their dealings with the people and they walk arrogantly amongst us with an aura of superiority and confidence. The corrupt ones in government have allowed this matter to get too far and our emperor sits on the Dragon Throne watching it all happen?" said Shang Jian.

Headmaster Lu Guanying stood and proclaimed, "There are still those righteous who desire to keep the empire free. We must speak with the emperor in order to take action against this blatant corruption. It is becoming top priority to eradicate the meddling foreigners." The General and the Scholars agreed. Zhang Sunzan awaited news from Fox concerning the state of affairs in the capital. "Word from Beijing will reach us soon. Any time now, my contact shall be sending vital information from my close allies in the Censorial Office in Beijing. His report will be most invaluable to us, and then we will know our next course of action." The Ming Empire was ripe for great change. Liberation was on the horizon.

☐

## Fox's Investigation

Exactly seven days since he had left Guangzhou, Fox disembarked from the cargo ship that docked at the capital's outlying district of Tangzhou where the Grand Canal reached its northernmost point. He continued on foot through the dusty, busy streets until he arrived at the main city gate imbedded into the monumental stone wall that surrounded the main districts of Beijing. He lowered his cap over his eyes and proceeded through the gate with a group of pedestrians being sure to stay away from the sight of the guards. The entire morning was spent navigating through the city's main avenue as Fox moved towards the center of the capital where the emperor's palace stood.

It was called the Forbidden City for only the emperor, his family, and his servants within the court were allowed to enter. It was the largest palace in the whole world – a city within a city. From a bird's view, it shone brightly with majestic walls, columns, and structures of vermilion red and glistened with rooftops of golden hues. Gaining entrance to the palace was not Fox's intention however.

Finding Zhou Liang or Wei Qiuyuan within the government's Censorate was his priority. He rented a room at the top floor of an inn which stood upon a hill not far from the Forbidden City. From the room of the inn he saw the Foreigners' small establishments just beyond the wall. They looked hastily erected but appeared sturdy. Guards wearing unusual foreign armor guarded the small compound. In the course of the next couple of days, he would be sure to learn something from them. He would leave one eye open for the Foreigners. The latter half of the day was spent in the premises of the Censorate compound watching for the censors that he was instructed to seek. The agency was quite infamous, as some of its members throughout history have been known to be corrupt and on occasion take bribes. If that were possible, then today of all days it was most likely to be with the arrival of the Pale Foreigners.

Fox made an effort to look natural and to blend with the environment to not be caught loitering around a "sensitive" government office. He waited for quite some time as he watched people move to and fro, all of whom were completely unaware of the possible crisis their nation is about to face. They were as it appeared, completely clueless about the corruption happening within their government. It was towards the close of the day that interesting activity really started to occur in the office of the Censorate. Fox watched from the sidelines across the street as five Jinyiwei Secret Police armed with broadswords and bows came knocking on the main entrance of the Censorate grounds. They barged their way through as soon as the gates were opened, and within moments, exited the premises with a man whose wrists and feet had been chained. "I will give you one more chance, Zhou Liang. Where is your colleague Wei Qiuyuan?" demanded one of the Jinyiwei agents.

"Even if I did know, I would rather suffer Ling Chi before I would betray my country. May shame and dishonor be upon you and all your comrades and may it follow you to hell," spat Zhou Liang.

The agent smacked him across the face with a backhand.

"Take him to the dungeons beneath headquarters. If death by a thousand cuts is what he would prefer, give it to him," the agent snarled.

Two of the agents dragged him away down the street as the remaining three proceeded to the opposite direction, possibly to the home of Wei Qiuyuan.

As they walked out of sight, Fox spotted a figure standing in a dim corner across the street. He was dressed in commoner's clothes and an old farmer's hat. He too waited for the guards to exit before he made his way down the adjacent street. Fox tailed him from a distance for several blocks. The man rounded a corner into a dark alley and disappeared. Fox looked around confused as to where he could have vanished. The sound of a dagger being unsheathed broke the silence and before he could turn around, a sharp point pressed against his neck. The man shoved him against the wall and he wrenched his arm high against his back.

"Calm yourself, comrade! I am an ally!" said Fox apparently very startled.

"How amusing; lackeys of paper pushers will try anything these days," said the man.

"I was sent by Zhang Sunzan. Reach under my chest pocket. I have a badge of the Scholars to prove it." Indeed the silver plaque of the League of Martial Scholars was secured beneath his garment and Wei Qiuyuan lowered his blade.

"My apologies, man. I can never be too careful," he said.

"I cannot blame you," said Fox. "It is important that I speak to you. The Scholars have been receiving little word from the capital and they must know of our government's state and the activities of the meddling Foreigners."

"We cannot speak here now. Just along the northern wall of the city at the eastern end of the commercial district, you will find an old wine shop still in business. At sunrise you are to go there and tell the shop owner 'I have urgent business from the South'. He will take you my personal guards who will escort you to see me. There is business I must first attend to."

When dawn had arrived, Fox had used the cover of darkness and evaded several Jinyiwei and city prefect patrols to reach the northern end of Beijing. The stress from several hours of waiting and a few more to reach this part of the city was beginning to take its toll on his strength. He restlessly entered the only wine shop in the district.

"I have urgent business from the South," he told the old shopkeeper who was busy with preparing the shop. He glanced at him plainly. "Follow me," he murmured. He was led to a storage room at the rear of the shop where armored men stood erect along a plain wall. "He has business with the official," said the shopkeeper. Two guards unrolled the large rug that hugged the floor and revealed a trap door . Fox went in climbed down with the guards and was directed through some old tunnels until they reached a damp, candlelit makeshift study. "Glad to see you have made it safely," said Wei Qiuyuan as the guards returned to their posts.

"I know why it is the Scholars have sent for you. They are right to worry."

"Yes, they have good reason to suspect the agenda of these mysterious Pale Foreigners and their influence upon the government of late. They believe corruption has grown rampant since their arrival. I believe this myself. My name is Fox. It is a pleasure to formally meet with you."

"I'm Wei Qiuyuan. The pleasure is mutual. They are not wrong, I'm afraid," said Qiuyuan as he massaged his head. He sighed and frowned. "However, I'm quite relieved to see you here. It means that the League is actively investigating this serious matter. I had hoped they would reach out to me. Our nation truly is at a crisis. Many high-ranking officials in the court have practically given themselves over to the Foreigners who call themselves the Terukk. In the past two weeks, I have been conducting intensive investigations concerning the Terukk dealings with the court. I myself have not been personally approached with any sort of proposition but I am nonetheless sure that dark dealings are being performed in high places. From the sidelines I have witnessed the Censorate's very own chief censor along with several eunuchs and scholar officials close meeting with them in secret… though I cannot be certain as to who is buying into their propositions. For the moment, I cannot name names. Too many are afraid to speak out and the line that divides allies from opponents has been severely blurred. I think you have witnessed my colleague Zhou Liang taken by the Jinyiwei last night? Such is the fate of those who would openly oppose this growing conspiracy. I warned him but he was too stubborn." Wei Qiuyuan felt great regret for his capture. Fox was not sure how to react and his mind raced with the realization of how deep the conspiracy was. He could hardly believe it.

"Has the emperor deliberately allowed this to occur within his own court?" Fox questioned.

"Our enemies have been very successful in keeping the emperor out of their way. And for good reason. Were he to discover the truth of the situation he would have sent his Capital Imperial Guards to arrest them all and have them executed." Sadness took over his face. "I have heard that his health is not well. In truth, he has disapproved of the Terukk from the very start and since then he has become strangely ill and has been bed-ridden for some time. Since then, the Terukk have been free to enact their agenda. I fear the new 'medicine' they are administering to him regularly is what is causing his affliction," said Wei with a sigh.

"So the young emperor himself has fallen victim to the deception of the bastards within his own court," Fox thought aloud. "And they're killing him slowly too."

"Speaking of medicines, there is more. The Foreigners have introduced a new substance, a drug of sorts that has become an addiction among those corrupted. I believe that this most of all is what's giving the Pale Foreigners so much leverage in our politics. I do not have a sample with me, but I have seen them passing it around. A small bamboo flask they drink. It morphs their minds. I have managed to smuggle a sample to my allies within the Hanlin Academy."

"Good Heavens…" Fox slammed his fist into the table. "It's beginning to make sense now, everything we've heard and learned of thus far. What of the imperial army? How compromised is it?" Fox asked.

"As far as I know, it has yet to be corrupted. I guess it's a blessing in disguise that the commanders and officers harbor a natural disdain for the civil bureaucrats along with the ministers who supervise them. As a matter of fact, I'm not so sure they're fully aware of what is transpiring in shadow though I don't doubt they suspect that indeed somethings are changing. The last thing we need is for the army to turn against the Middle Kingdom itself. They number in the millions!" Wei Qiuyuan leaned back into his chair and popped his knuckles. Fox struggled to wrap his mind around the reality of what was happening. The Censorate official's tone softened yet the coldness remained.

"What of the spy agencies? Now we know without a doubt they are active participants in this conspiracy. Their slaves within the secret police just arrested your colleague. The Eastern and Western Depots know all that transpire within the entire imperial bureaucracy, though I suspect there is division as the rumors say?" He said with some uncertainty. Fox was growing more rattled by the minute. He could no longer hide his anxiety.

"Yes, there is most certainly division. They think just because I'm a paper-pusher I cannot see for myself what is truly happening. How else would I be in the Chief Surveillance Office?" he chuckled. His smirk however morphed into a frown.

"The division among the Depots and the Jinyiwei secret police is more severe than what we can observe from the outside."

He presented Fox with a number of documents from a paper stack on the wooden desk.

"I've managed to intercept some formal letters exchanged between the agencies. Based on this communication alone, one can surmise that many within the Jinyiwei have surprisingly defected and have gone into hiding for fear of extermination. This information is of great import. They number in the tens of thousands, Fox. That's an entire army for a foreign kingdom. I need not mention that one officer alone is more than capable of eliminating a gang of bandits in single combat. But that is not the point. Most of them have submitted to the corruption running rampant in the Depots. Luckily, their internal division is causing much unrest. They're hardly able to function or conduct their duties effectively at this point. Still, many virtuous officials have already been arrested or executed. It won't be long until opposition is crushed completely."

"Blast it!" Fox shouted. "I've never felt so enraged and helpless at the same time! The tools within our own government are selling the empire to barbarian foreigners!"

"I cannot save the empire alone and I do not know whom to trust. The League must come to Beijing to help liberate us from this vast conspiracy and help the emperor reclaim the empire. With their resources, connections, and know-how, they can uncover exactly who is involved and formulate a plan to save the emperor and win back the court for him." He sat back and took a long deep breath.

"I would have reached out to the Martial Scholars myself but, the risks are just too great. If there is anyone with the connections, skills, and influence to equalize the schemes of the bastards within the bureaucracy, it is the League. The Martial Scholars can discover the ultimate goal of these foreigners."

"Then I must immediately send word of what I have learned here. The Martial Scholars must make contact with their counterparts in Hanlin Academy and unmask this conspiracy. We just might be able to rouse and embolden the virtuous in the palace to make a stand for the emperor and save the Ming Empire before it's too late," sighed Fox.

Before Fox could continue, the sound of commotion from the tunnels disturbed their conversation and shouts echoed down the corridors. "They have found us! You must have been followed. Come quickly!" Wei barked. He and Fox scrambled to gather his research. They proceeded further down the tunnel towards an exit.

"Halt! Stop where you are or we will shoot!" commanded one of the Jinyiwei officers.

"Keep going! Do not stop for anything!" shouted Wei. The tunnel led into several caverns lit with candles and torches where many of the capital's forgotten and unwanted have taken up a filthy residence. An arrow raced down the cavern and pierced through Wei's leg and he shouted in agony. He stumbled and fell into the dirt. "Go! Do not wait for me! You must tell the Scholars what you have discovered here for the sake of the Ming Empire!" shouted Wei.

"We will find you and get you out with Zhou Liang! I swear! For the Ming Empire!" shouted Fox. The Jinyiwei were fast approaching and Fox ran into the darkness of the cavern far out of sight. Wei Qiuyuan was dragged away for interrogation and a most probable execution. Fox ran and ran until his lungs felt as if they were to burst inside his chest. The officers were no longer pursuing him but the urgency of this mission weighed heavily upon his heart and he was desperate to send news to Guangzhou.

He ran through the streets, dodging patrols around the corners. He zig-zagged through alleyways and took shortcuts through some courtyard residences. Other officers made their way through the streets in haste signaling others to scour hidden enclaves in the district. Fox took cover inside a dark passageway between two large shops. Behind a stack of wooden crates, he waited for them to pass.

"I'm getting too old for hide n seek," he grumbled. He clenched his chest. The sensation of tightening worsened. An elderly woman creaked open the back door of the adjacent shop and glanced blankly at Fox, and casually closed the door. She did not want to get involved in any way.

It was dawn by the time he found the estate of Zhang Sunzan. He barely paused to catch his breath. He presented the Scholars' plaque to the keeper of the house and was immediately led into a study where ink, brush, and paper were immediately provided. He hastily scribbled a message to the League of Scholars. He wrote of everything of the conspiracy within the bureaucracy, the emperor's induced illness, and what had happened to Zhou Liang and Wei Qiuyuan. He rolled the letter tightly along with notes from Wei Qiuyuan and slipped them snug into a small bamboo cylinder. Zhang Sunzan's raptor was perched in a large cage in the room and he strapped the case onto its back. He released the hawk just as Zhang Sunzan instructed and it flew high and fast. He stood there watching it quickly disappear into the sky. In exhaustion, Fox collapsed onto the chair and passed out on the desk.

\*\*\*\*

It was the end of the week and night had come. After the Martial Scholars had all retired into their rooms and studies, Tian Qiu the polymath quietly made his way deep down into the Hall of Knowledge and Records – a large library and study where copied documents and original manuscripts of the Middle Kingdom's histories, known sciences, collected philosophies, and treatises on many subjects could be found. The hall had a hundred shelves of tomes and scrolls, and displayed a collection of great inventions from the geniuses and polymaths of history whom Tian Qiu greatly admired. Knowledge and technology lost to the dynasty in which it was learned had finally found its home in the Academy. A great armillary sphere adorned one corner of the room. On the other corner stood Bi Sheng's Moveable Type printing press first invented some four hundred years ago. Next to it was a replica of Zhang Heng's earthquake detecting device lavishly called "Instrument for Measuring the Four Winds and Movements of the Earth". On the opposite end of the room was an erect structure that nearly touched the ceiling. It was a model of Su Song's Cosmic Engine – a hydraulically powered clock tower that not only told the time in hours, minutes, and seasons, but traced the passing of the stars through the use of an attached armillary sphere and celestial globe. Such a complex and advanced device had been long forgotten in the Middle Kingdom since it fell under the occupation of the Menggu.

The only surviving model now remained safely in the hall of the academy and is now only known to the Scholars.

There, in the darkness of the hall, Tian Qiu brought the flame of his candle into an oil circuit running along the walls and the torches arranged along the length of the hall were set alight. Countless books and scrolls of paper and bamboo strips stored in the large underground library contained over two and a half thousand years of collected knowledge. Much of it has been lost or forgotten in society but it had found a safe haven in the Martial Scholar's Academy. It surpassed even the library at Hanlin Academy in Beijing.

Everything from government records from bygone times to entire columns dedicated to the comings and goings of every dynasty was within his reach. The hall was his favorite place and he often spent much time there in study. Tian Qiu spent the next several hours scouring books and scrolls on geography and the nations and kingdoms surrounding the Middle Kingdom and beyond. He searched for any clues in the histories that mentioned anything about the Pale Foreigners. He found nothing helpful. Not even the rarest records from the most distant lands led to any clues. Tian made his way to the far end of the library complex in an area where he had yet explored. Wiping away cobwebs and sweeping off dust, he found a chest tucked away in a dark corner. Stacks of papers and an assortment of books forgotten for many decades revealed themselves in the candle light as well.

He gathered the chest including the papers and pamphlets that accompanied it and moved to a desk at the corner of the room to examine what he had found. With patience and skill, he picked the lock and was rewarded with a solid *click*. The chest opened for the first time in several decades. The fact it had been locked so tightly was very curious indeed. What Tian Qiu had found astonished him.

They were in fact the actual preserved records of the legendary naval expeditions of the Imperial Treasure Fleet of the Dragon Throne led by the great eunuch admiral Zheng He.

"A great series of journeys that began seventy years ago and had abruptly ended some three decades later," Tian Qiu thought aloud, his eyes wide, and jaw somewhat dropped.

Records of the expeditions were laid out clearly in the documents. Tian blew away the dust and skimmed through the papers reading rosters and inventories, names and roles of the crew, diplomatic missions to foreign kings, lists of tributaries and their tributes, blue prints of various ships, illustrations of foreign cities, and even naval engagements against hostile powers had all been recorded in great detail.

This massive maritime project was started and funded by Emperor 'Yongle' Zhu Di and was quickly forgotten as soon as it ended. The very records that Tian held in his hands were thought to have all been destroyed or hidden decades ago by the vice president of the Ministry of War , Liu Daxia.

It appeared however, that the scholars before him were wise enough to have obtained them somehow, perhaps with the aid of scribes and other minor officials.

"Impossible. These should have been destroyed many years ago!" Tian exclaimed excitedly to himself. The great fleet of the Ming Empire was the most formidable of the known world and was on the verge of controlling all the known seas. No other navy came close to its size and majesty. It was quite a shame that the expeditions were abruptly ceased at the untimely death of the Admiral Zheng.

Tian, however, sensed there was a greater reason as to why the voyages were brought to a crashing halt. Momentarily distracted from his research he took the materials to a nearby workstation and examined what he had found closely.

The significance and splendor of the great voyages have unfortunately faded into history and is altogether just a distant and controversial memory in the Imperial Court. He turned his attention to a smaller iron box stashed inside the chest. He diligently picked the lock until he heard the metallic *ping*. What he found was just as fascinating. Specific accounts of Zheng He's later adventures were extensively written by his chief chronicler and interpreter Ma Huan. The log books were stacked in the box. Ma Huan's personal thoughts, feelings, and experiences were quite insightful and entertaining for Tian to read, but it was a few select days that caught his full attention. He unpacked the stack and untied the cordage that bound them together. He grabbed a chair and opened the first pages of the log.

## The Records of the Treasure Fleet of the Dragon Throne
### 13th Year of Reign of Emperor Yongle,
### First Day of the Eight Month

*Our return trip home was not without some spectacle and we were in a place to worry since our ships were heavy-laden with many precious cargos and foreign envoys from the nations in the South West. What we have encountered in the recent days could not be explained nor have we seen anything of the sort. Nowhere in the seas we have traversed nor in the harbors of the barbarian lands where we set foot have we seen such a vessel. It was a ship of admirable proportions and it approached us from the South with great speed, and the soldiers and the crew attempted to hail it to no effect. Had it continued on its course, a collision with the fleet would have been inevitable. Cannons were on the ready to defend the fleet formation should it have approached too closely. The lone mystery ship was not so much a concern as it was a curiosity and it kept a distance of approximately one half li at the rear of the fleet's formation. It trailed us for two days and a half whilst maintaining a consistent distance from our defensive formation. We remained curious however, but the crew became rather uneasy and on edge with the foreign ship following us closely. There were no visible men on board the deck of the foreign ship and yet it efficiently managed the raising and lowering of its silvery sails with relative ease. Upon the advice of the military personnel on board, we fired warning shots in the direction of the foreign vessel after which it came to a full stop when our bombs crashed into the waters around it. The vessel floated freely in the water where it had stopped and our fleet increased the distance from it. After we had distanced ourselves one full li, it returned fire upon us with spouts of blue flame that landed bombs with great range and accuracy. The bombs arched into the sky and fell harmlessly in the water landing quite precisely port and starboard of one of the Treasure Ships which, I should add, always sails at the heart of the fleet's formation. The foreign vessel had sent us a clear message and we understood. In fair circumstances, I doubt the Admiral would ever desire to combat ships with such weapon capability.*

Tian Qiu became enthralled with his discovery.

"Wait, could it be? The first mention of an imperial encounter with the Pale Foreigners! Astounding!" he exclaimed.

Despite what the other Scholars thought, he too held his country's safety and security a top priority. He did swear the same oath upon joining the League, after all. He continued to sift through the historical records looking for more clues concerning the foreign ship they encountered while homeward bound. With further investigation, Tian Qiu began to learn the truth behind the fate of the Treasure Fleet. He continued to read through the accounts of Chronicler Ma Huan and the Treasure Fleet's records and perused the summary of notes attached to the official accounts:

*The passing of the Emperor Yongle many years after the first naval expedition marked a great hiatus in the voyages of the Treasure Fleet. The Yongle Emperor's son Zhu Gaozhi had ascended the throne as the Xuande Emperor and with the counsel of his most trusted officials ordered all ocean-going missions and the building of ocean-going ships to be banned permanently. The Ming Dynasty had turned into a nation of a closed-door policy and forsook the 'vanities' and the expensive projects of funding large expeditions across the oceans. Upon learning the news of a mysterious ship that had eluded the Ming fleet, a great flame of curiosity burst out of Emperor Zhu Gaozhi. In secret, he had purposed a new expedition for Admiral Zheng He to seek out the origins of the mysterious great ship that he had encountered on their journey home. Together they re-assembled the fleet to its largest size; three hundred vessels of varying proportions and purposes were built in the shipyards and they were armed with the latest naval weaponry the empire had to offer should anything go awry. Emperor Zhu Gaozhi ensured the palace officials that the expedition was strictly for the purpose of enforcing the peace between the rivaling tributary nations in the South West and to restore the relationship between the Ming Dynasty and the nations that paid the empire handsome tribute. He issued an edict saying the that lands beyond the Ming Empire have not been informed of his new reign and thus sends Zheng He to proclaim the news and inform the nations to obey Heaven's will and take care of the people in order to enjoy great fortunes and lasting peace. Therefore, the installation of many weapons upon the ships was most discreet to avoid any political complications within and beyond the court. Thus began the Treasure Fleet's seventh voyage. It began with stopovers at key harbors and ports in Maliujia and in Sumendala – the land of abundant gold. Here, Zheng He and his crew proclaimed the Emperor's edict and began their investigations, questioning any of the authorities who may have witnessed or learned news of the large and mysterious ships with silvery sails. The investigation bore very little results and any clues about the ships came in the form of rumors, sightings, and vague encounters made by merchants who frequented the southern seas. Unsatisfied with their findings in Maliujia and Sumendala, the*

Treasure Fleet sailed west towards Yindu – a vast land of many kingdoms and princedoms, gods, and spices. The journey to Yindu was not without its hostile encounters. A squadron of local pirates with their ships of triangular sails challenged Zheng He and the fleet and fired upon them. The Treasure Fleet managed to subdue the pirates and capture the captain of the flagship who was not in the least bit awestruck by the massive treasure fleet. Upon interrogation of the pirate lord as to why he attacked such an overwhelming force of ships, he only rambled what sounded like nonsense and continuously made claims of a great and mighty force from the Far South beyond the seas of Yindu. The pirate's surviving companions mocked the mighty Ming Treasure Fleet which they called "insignificant" and scoffed at Zheng He and his crew saying those of the Middle Kingdom who are under heaven "will be humbled" upon encountering the ones whom they claimed to be sent by Demigods". Unsure of what to make of the pirates' ramblings, the Admiral and the fleet continued on to another major harbor in Yindu where we restocked supplies, made repairs, and continued our investigations. According to the pirates, the mystery ships, it seemed, have been making visitations to Yindu during the Ming Fleet's absence. The governors of Yindu claimed to have described what they have seen as large warships with silvery-white sails anchored in the distance. Those on board landed on their coast and frightened the locals of the harbor. The officials described them as very pale, tall, and mysterious in their ways. They also appeared to be very wealthy and sophisticated and *presented a level of cultural development that not even the Ming possessed. They also spoke the language with an unpleasant and heavy accent and demanded tribute and allegiance to their name in exchange of jewels and precious stones never before seen in Yindu. They were thus obliged to comply and the pale visitors once again set sail unwaveringly south as soon as all diplomatic processions had concluded. Other shipping routes testified to the passing of the mighty foreign fleet heading southward at a pace that defied the prevailing wind directions Zheng He requested the princes and leaders of Yindu to reestablish their tributary relationship with the Ming Empire and vowed to be a powerful ally and defender . To his dismay they were compelled to refuse his request in fear of the consequences from their pale visitors whom they consistently called the Terukk. Zheng He was outraged at these unforeseen turn of events and vowed to continue his investigation in order to restore what he believed was the natural "international balance of power" where the Ming Empire reigned supreme over all the other nations who would pay tributes to the emperor. He and his crew of thirty thousand made preparations for their journey south to seek out the origin of the mystery ships and this new race of men called Terukk and once and for all "settle" their disputes. He wrote a letter to the Xuande Emperor telling of all the things they have learned thus far in their investigation and how he plans to proceed to south to the uncharted oceans. He then sent a small squadron of ships back to Beijing to deliver the message. The Treasure Fleet finally set sail to find the Terukk despite the insistent protests of the pirates currently being held in their cells below deck.*

What Tian Qiu found at the bottom of the records caused him to stay the night to continue his readings on these lost and forgotten accounts of Zheng He's voyages. The following records as written by Ma Huan chronicled the events taking place after leaving port from Yindu. The entries were as follows:

**First Entry Since Leaving Yindu Kingdoms**

*Our journey to the uncharted waters south of Yindu began with great anticipation and anxiety for the crew of this Treasure Fleet. We did not know what waited for us at the end of this voyage or whether what we were to find will be unpleasant or beneficial. The Admiral deemed the Terukk's demand for tribute to our subservient nations as an insult to the Dragon Throne and thus endeavors to "right this great wrong". The days become shorter, the nights grow longer, and the weather gets colder the more we continued on our voyage of discovery. It is strange to note however, that favorable, although, unexpected winds have been carrying our fleet in haste since we have left Yindu, as if some unseen "will" is conducting our journey. I cannot be certain.*

**Second Entry Since Leaving Yindu Kingdoms**

*We were fortunate enough to have been prepared for the frigid temperatures of this region. The seas in this place are forever locked in perpetual shadows and the waters flowed as an eternal sea of cold and ice. Many amongst the crew have begun to question the sanity of voyaging into such a realm or if we had entered into another world altogether. Many weeks of sailing have finally brought us to our destination though mere words would not suffice to describe what we have discovered here. As our ships continued to plow through the frozen sea, we entered a very dense fog with a thickness can be felt through our fingertips and in the lashes of our eyes. Upon emerging from the dreadful mist we beheld before us a monumental mountain of snow and ice of which an enormous cave had been carved into its face. On either side of the cave stood two towering figures of stone shaped like man and monster. Many of us could not decipher what the figures represented but many, including the Admiral, took their sight as an ill omen, very foreboding and mysteriously ancient. Nonetheless, Zheng He commanded the fleet to proceed into the mouth of the cave and into the shadows.*

### Third Entry Since Leaving Yindu Kingdoms

*For several hours now the fleet has been navigating through this colossal cave of stone and ice and the men could not help but marvel at its immensity, pondering upon the sheer scale of its construction. It was not complete darkness as we had anticipated for the cave glowed with a soft sapphire and cobalt blue emitting from the numerous stone formations that was laid throughout the walls of the cave. A steady wind is conveniently blowing through the cave, gently propelling the fleet at a sound pace. This cave seems to go on forever, barely meandering, and unwavering in size and shape. Many sections of the wall of the cave are carved with signs and enigmatic symbols that none, not even I, are able to decipher them. Ghastly images and statues have been mounted on either side of the cave as if standing guard, forever watchful of the pass, with their eyes of stone and metal seemingly following our ships as we passed by... although I observe that those following eyes were mere illusions, perhaps the making of my own mind. The air feels heavy and unnatural though I could not smell anything foul or out of the ordinary. The men have grown fearful and have resorted to burning incense and reciting prayers to various gods and spirits for deliverance and good fortune. The sheer weight of the cave is beginning to become overwhelming. Does this tunnel have an end?*

### Fourth Entry Since Leaving Yindu Kingdoms

*To our pleasant surprise the cave has finally released us from its clutches. Never before have I felt so relieved and delighted during a journey even in my younger days when I first began to travel. We are continuing the voyage as planned and the men are now breathing with more ease since they have been released by the overwhelming tunnel. A very large and imposing tower or structure of some sort guards the exit of the foreboding tunnel though it seems it has long been abandoned and left to ruin with its mighty black gates left wide open. The river of the tunnel has now expanded into another sea and on its edges are grasslands, hills, and snowy mountains. We are still sailing in loyalty to our general direction but our South-Pointer Needle no longer pointed in any specific direction but instead spun and twitched every which way. It is eerily mysterious. The sun does not shine here and the clouds thick and gray hang low over the horizon. We thought it best to sail close to the nearest shore so that we may observe the land beyond. I cannot even recognize any of the trees in the distance and the plants that grew in the grass are so foreign. Some even sparkled or shone orange and yellow like fireflies at night. Beasts I have never seen in any of the barbarian kingdoms we have visited roam this land in thunderous herds whilst wearing upon their heads swirling horns of ones or threes. I stood at their sight in absolute awe of their spectacle until a flying black creature akin to a phoenix swooped in and snatched away one of them and therefore disappeared into the clouds. The men were shocked and did not know what to make of it and stood there bows and guns pointed at the sky and their eyes wide open. The temperature here has become much more tolerable but the weather is not at all unlike the winters of the Northern Steppe where the horsemen live. I have just come to realize that this place has an eerie silence, one that has allowed me to listen to the creeks and groans of our ship. I have never heard them before.*

## Fifth Entry Since Leaving Yindu Kingdoms

*Our fleet has been sailing up against this river for some time. How we are able to proceed against the current is beyond my ability to comprehend. We had finally come upon a narrow bay where our ships managed to anchor not far from shore. Upon stepping foot onto the shore we were soon greeted by an entourage of soldiers clad in costumes and armor I have never before seen. A light company of soldiers amongst our crew immediately drew their weapons ready to protect the Admiral from these very strange looking men. The foreigners however, sat on their steeds calmly staring at us as if they already knew what we were. When the atmosphere had calmed, the Admiral and the officers respectfully introduced themselves though I could not tell if these natives understood. What was most astonishing however, were the features of their faces. Their cheek bones are high and strongly defined and their skin were as if it had been bleached with snow itself. They've ears pointing sharply away from their eyes, eyes which were red as molten steel. I have seen the eyes of men and they have always been black, brown, and even blue or green... but never red. I am beginning to question the humanity of these people. They ride upon large beasts as foreign as those we witnessed running in herds, and were heavier and more muscular than our horses, but just as imposing as the natives of this strange land. Even now as the men are setting up camp along the shore, the pale natives are watching us waiting to present us to their king, chief, or to whomever they have placed their loyalties. I am not comfortable in the presence of* the natives. Zheng He however, wishes to proceed with his diplomatic mission. We make preparations to depart as I write. I fear this will not end well. I depart with the admiral and a company of soldiers. My heart is trembling. This place is under the dominion of something dark and I feel oppressed here. The rest of the men sense it too.

## Sixth Entry Since Leaving Yindu Kingdoms

Half a day on horseback has allowed us some time to continue to survey the vast landscape in this kingdom. I suspect that it is but one of many on the fringes of a vast continent. The terrain has changed very little and the plains and cold grasslands have sparse tree lines with wooded areas covering the slopes of the distant mountains. Our communication with the welcoming party has been limited to hand gestures and bodily motions. I have yet to see them smile nor have I noticed any hint of pleasure in their demeanors which causes me to wonder if our arrival has left them somewhat displeased. Being around them has been quite unnerving to say the least. Telling time has also proven to be a challenge as there is no sun to gauge the hour nor is there any real sense of night and day. Here the pale sky does nothing more than change its contrast in the slightest. The only real wonder I can experience in this place comes from observing the strange new wildlife that roam the wilderness and the vast variety of enchanted plants spread all throughout the ground.

## Seventh Entry Since Leaving Yindu Kingdoms

*At long last we have made our way into what appears to be a castle or fortress of sorts. It is nestled in the heart of a deep frozen valley surrounded by steep towering mountains of rock and ice. It was a majestic sight our eyes could barely behold. We are now seated in one of their halls waiting to make contact with one who holds authority over the natives. Our journey to this castle has allowed us to bear witness to their dwellings —which feels much more like a garrison than anything else. They are a martial people. Their warriors patrol the streets around the fortress in small groups and all have given us cold hard glances as we passed them by —emotionless and stiff. There appears to be no room for festivities in their culture. Surely it is a military outpost. For this settlement harbors no restaurants, homes, and places of learning; we find instead storehouses, training grounds for troops, and living quarters for both martial and civilian people. Their structures are quite magnificent to say the least for they are quite fond of towers and spires made of very large and monumental stones upon which they engrave their art. Indeed this is some form of government outpost, not a town. As we wait to meet their commanding officer, I have had much time to admire their halls of dark stones and metals of black purple outlined with linear designs of gold. Zheng He and the soldiers in our company are exceedingly anxious and unsure of what to expect. A conflict of any sort is the last thing they wish on foreign soil.*

## Tenth Entry Since Leaving Yindu Kingdoms

*This will be my final entry until we return to Nanjing. Admiral Zheng He lays in his quarters severely injured from our failed diplomatic mission to the unknown civilization at the bottom of the world. These 'Terukk' are absolutely not to be trusted. They have charmed us with the fruits of their civilization, their wealth, and knowledge as if in an attempt to make us tributaries of them. Such a proposition is unthinkable and therefore we refused. I am fortunate to have been among those who survived. It was through sheer luck that we managed to escape their outpost. The soldiers in our company took great risks and paid a high price for our escape when the day grew eerily dark. Even the admiral was not unscathed. His condition worsens by the hour.*

*We pushed the horses for as far and long as possible barely able to reach camp by the bay. We scrambled to break camp and lost many precious hours trying to make it aboard our vessels. We have lost many ships and many brave warriors not to mention the loss of the eighth and ninth entry of this expedition. I am not even certain if the Admiral will survive our trip back to the Middle Kingdom. In short, our refusal to accept the Terukk lord's offer was taken as an insult in the same manner a slave would refuse his master's goodwill. We were ordered to leave the land at once to tell the emperor of what has transpired here but as we prepared to depart, their forces attacked us with bombards raining down upon the fleet. We returned fire with all that we had as we rowed and sailed directly to the dark cave while the enemy ships pursued us.*

*Our cannons and rockets kept them at bay while the mysterious and unlikely wind like the one we had felt upon leaving Yindu once again carried our ships through the darkness. This to me is unexplainable but I am forever thankful for the favor. We slowed them as best we could, spilling barrel upon barrel of oil from the stern and set it alight. Some of their ships were consumed by the fires. Others still pursued us. Cannons were aimed at the cave's ceiling, raining mountains of rock and ice in the path of our pursuers. This strategy costed us an escort ship. We could not rescue those who fell overboard.*

*As soon as we exited the long cave we exhausted all our bombs and rockets into its mouth and sealed it shut with so much stone and ice that only a dragon could roll them away. I doubt that it will hold them permanently but we will be able to land in Yindu in peace. I will never forget the face of the one who commanded that outpost. Exceedingly beautiful was she, but full of ill-will and malice. She desired for us to become the servants of her nation – telling us that her people heralded the creation of a new world. Should she and her forces arrive onto the shores of the Middle Kingdom, she shall experience the full wrath of our forces. Something must be done to prepare the people for this impending doom. Never before in the history of the known world have a people such as the Terukk possess such a capacity for arrogance and insolence. Of this I can be certain.*

# HOMECOMING

THE PROVINCE OF HUGUANG IS home to much history. It is a land of farms, tall vertical green mountains, the majestic river Yangtze –the life blood of the Middle Kingdom, and where Sun Xin's master had trained him in the combative arts, mainly the sword. It was also here where Sun Xin built his foundations and where he ultimately decided to find his own truth, just as he had told his master several years ago. He was headed for a wealthy village not far from the ancient city of Jingzhou. It was in this village where his master had carved for himself a life of simplicity crafting furniture and wooden goods. Xin was hesitant to meet him. He ran from his teachings in arrogance and disrespect so he had many doubts he would be overjoyed to see his prodigal "son" returning home, much less allow him to complete his training.

He sighed at the poor state in which he had left and regretted the utter disrespect he had displayed that day. He was naïve and immature. Nevertheless, he proceeded into the village on horseback and made his way slowly through the main road. The place was more beautiful than he remembered. The surroundings were lush and so peaceful and the homes were constructed with ornate beauty and classical architecture. Some of the townspeople turned to look at the handsome, dark, and mysterious visitor sitting erect on his steed as he headed towards the woodshop sitting on a hill above the village. He kept a straight face although he could not help but wince upon hearing them whispering as he passed by. They remembered him and what happened that day and he did not expect to be thought of highly in these parts.

His master was highly respected and esteemed here and Xin already felt as if he was unwelcomed. At the base of the hill, he parked the horse in a small stable and continued on foot up the slope where he could already hear the sawing, carving, and the hammering from the woodshop. The smell of fresh cut wood and processed lacquer revived many memories of life here, in this humble estate built in such a beautiful place. He took a deep breath and entered the woodshop where a few workers, some of whom he still recognized stopped to look to see what looked like a potential customer entering their shop. One of them, an elderly woman named Mang stopped what she was doing immediately and walked directly to Xin to examine his face. Her eyes began to water and she embraced Xin.

"You have returned!" she cried. "Our little Xin has come back home."

The rest of the workers crowded around him patting him on the shoulder with smiles and claps as he craned his neck in search for his master.

"Master Lo and the young lady went into Jingzhou with the wagon two days ago to sell our latest output this year. His business has blossomed over the years, dear Xin. We expect their return before nightfall," she said.

"I see. That is very good, granny Mang," he replied in kind.

"We are very glad to see you and I am happy you are safe in your adventures out there," she continued. "Oh, you've grown even more handsome. Have you had supper?"

"I am quite alright, granny Mang. Thank you. It is very good to see you too." Xin smiled slightly but it was apparent to Mang that he was apprehensive for his master's return.

"He was very devastated, you know. When you left that day it was as if his hopes and dreams had fallen apart. He stayed in his room completely quiet for three days with no food or drink," she commented. "We were quite worried about him."

"Do you think he will accept me again?"

"Oh, I'm sure he will be quite happy that you have returned although knowing him he will not show it. He is a good man and you were like the son he never had," she assured him. "He saved me too, you know, just like he saved you."

With one leg resting across the other, Sun Xin sat at the front porch of his master's home to await his return. He recalled the days he spent growing up here training, learning, and working at the shop and many times being the only playmate to his master's then very young daughter.

Huguang was quite a scenic province especially here, where he grew up. He wondered how did not appreciate such a thing when he was younger. Perhaps his experiences in the world beyond this village had opened his eyes to see more of the subtle pleasures in life. He sat there until the sun had begun to set behind the hills and the distant mountains of dense green. As the sunlight bathed the hillside with gold and yellow, the sounds of horse hooves and the rumbling of wagon wheels made its way up the hill. A covered wagon pulled by two horses stopped in front of the ancestral shrine. As the driver prepared to disembark, Xin approached him with his shoulders hunched, head lowered, and hat held loosely in his hands.

"It has been a long while, Master," said Xin meekly. Master Lo, as he was known, continued with his business as if hearing nothing, not even bothering to lay eyes on Xin.

"If you have come to purchase my wood work, you are too late. I have sold every piece at the city, but you already knew that so I am assuming you are here on other business," he said indifferently.

Master Lo had grown advanced in his years but he conducted himself with the same strength and discipline Xin had always known.

"Master, I have returned to humbly request that I finish the training I started in my youth… and to beg for your forgiveness," Xin said.

"Why do you call me 'Master'? I have not had a student in many years. I do not teach anyone any skills but that of the proper crafting of wood," he replied coldly.

Xin frowned though remained undeterred by his master's cold attitude. He fell on his knees and wrapped his fist tightly into his hand and pleaded.

"Master, if there be any ounce of regard in your heart for your lost student may it be that you find a place to forgive the insolence I have displayed before you many years ago," he beseeched.

Master Lo paused for a brief moment, looked up, and sighed. He then continued into his home without speaking another word. The wagon creaked and the sound of light footsteps emerged from it.

"Could it be? Is that you, Xin?" a soft and sweet feminine voice asked from behind.

Xin stood and turned to face her. A young and fair maiden emerged from the carriage, her eyes gleaming in the late afternoon sunlight and her soft flowing hair adorned a delicate and exquisite face whose radiance was only amplified by the golden sun. Xin was immediately taken by her. She emerged from the wagon, hair flowing down to her small waist. She grinned from ear to ear when her eyes met with Xin's.

"I cannot believe that it is really you! You have grown taller… but your face has not changed a bit," she remarked. She giggled cheerfully as she wiped a tear from the corner of her eye. She embraced him. An embrace. Xin could not remember the last time he had received one. It was very warm and comforting but it gave him goosebumps.

"You… er… have grown much as well, Meiling. Where the years have made me courser and darker you have blossomed like a chrysanthemum in the valley fields," Xin said bowing his head slightly.

He found it awkwardly difficult to lay eyes upon her without becoming… overwhelmed by her loveliness. He was not accustomed this feeling and it made him lightheaded. She blushed and laughed gently. Even the sound of her laughter was enough to lift the gloomiest of spirits.

"I'm overjoyed to see you again, Xin. Never mind my father, he does miss you, he just refuses to admit it."

"I know. I regret hurting him and I regret hurting you. I was so possessed by my self-centered ambitions that I did not take into account others I cared about," Xin confessed, still mesmerized by her.

"'Ling! Come inside. Now!" shouted Lo from the distance.

"Don't fret, dear Xin. I will speak to my father. I am overjoyed you are here and I know that he is happy as well. He will realize it soon enough."

That night, Xin stayed inside his master's old tool shed where he sat lost in thought. His vambraces, sword, and crossbow were neatly placed alongside his hat and boots. He could not help but ponder upon the past and remember the good life he enjoyed in this very place. He threw it all away. Was he a fool or was he right to have followed his heart?

A knock on the shed's door shook him from his thoughts as

Meiling walked in with a tray of dinner and some mats and a blanket. She smelled of plums and peaches –a sweet, rare fragrance to Xin who, on the other hand smelled of dust and mud. He felt rather embarrassed about it now that he was around Meiling.

"Forgive my stench. I reek from a journey of a thousand wilderness li," said Xin embarrassedly.

She smiled and so did her eyes. She could not take them off of him.

"Do not worry; I do prefer the smell of the wilderness to the stale, dusty city air. Besides, you can get a bath and a fresh batch of clothes by morning in the village's bathhouse if you need refreshing."

He nodded with a faint smile. He was… shy. Shy around her. The feeling confused him for he had never felt bashful before.

"I will see to that. Thank you for the food. Will you stay to dine with me?"

"I'll keep you company. I'm not feeling too hungry anyway."

She took a seat next to him on the blanket and watched Sun Xin eat. He was famished but he did his best to hide it by taking his time to savor every bite. The steamed rice was fragrant and sweet and the fresh stir-fried vegetables were cooked to perfection, sprinkled with garlic and spices just as he remembered. He had forgotten how much he had missed the food of home. It was far more satisfying and delicious than the bland rice cakes, stuffed buns, and dried-smoked fish he always packed on the road. He would be fortunate to have had even fruit on his travels.

She was amused by watching him eat. He had not changed the

way he took a bite or chewed his mouthfuls. He would always have bits of food on the corner of his mouth. She giggled at the fond memories she recalled as he chewed his food from his cheek pouches. This caused Xin to pause embarrassedly and eat less hurriedly.

"Do you remember when we were children, Xin? My father would always have to remind you to slow down because you would get stomach aches from eating too fast. He did say you ate too much. Half our food expenses went into your mouth," she said giggling.

Xin then did something he had not done in a very long time. He laughed. "Yes, I do remember. By the time it was time for training, I would still be too full to get anything done."

There was a sustained awkward moment as Xin continued to consume his food.

"I was heartbroken when you decided to set out on your own. I wanted to see you for as long as I could so I climbed a tree and watched you walk further and further away from the village," Meiling recalled, her eyes wandering around the room. Xin did not know what to say although deep inside he still believed his leaving was not without its fruits.

Meiling redirected her gaze toward his. "Over the years I began hearing rumors of a mysterious wandering swordsman eradicating wanted criminals throughout the country and even the most prominent of crime lords were looking over their shoulders in fear of his sword finding their backs. I knew immediately that swordsman was you."

"Yes, me. Over one thousand under the table contracts from prefects, nobles, and governors yet the work never ends," he said shaking his head. His actions compelled the Underworld to place a bounty on his head. He decided not to tell Meiling that he had almost lost his life to hunters and mercenaries several times. "Many of them tried coming after me since I started my campaigns. I guess I was fortunate to always be one step ahead of them. I have forged powerful alliances over the years so I am never truly alone," Sun Xin said to her with confidence as he took another bite.

"Why have you come back?" Her head lowered and tilted, her eyes trying to look into his.

He paused. "Well, I have missed this place and I wanted to see Master and you." Meiling just stared inquisitively into his eyes knowing his answer was only the half-truth. "…and I also desire to complete my training," continued Xin as he lowered his gaze.

"I see, I see" Meiling muttered as she looked away. "I am glad you are living the adventure you have long sought since your youth… and I am sorry that a simple life here did not suffice for you." Before Xin could answer, she picked up his tray and exited the shed saying "Enjoy your night and have a good rest. The blanket is new."

"Thank you, Meiling. Good night…" he said, his voice trailing away.

The following morning, Sun Xin was awakened by the hammering sounds of the woodshop. Production had resumed for that day. He dressed himself and stepped out into the high morning sun and was irritated upon realizing that he had slept in. Master Lo was in his ancestral shrine near the shed and he stood solemnly with his hands behind his back.

"This shrine and these tablets bear the memory and the spirit of my family from many generations past. My father before me and my grandfather before him always told me of the family's grand legacy. The name 'Luo' or 'Lo' carries a great responsibility, for through it lies a history of many virtuous and heroic figures that employed our unique style of swordsmanship. It has been coveted by countless many and has been passed down and developed for a thousand years." Master Lo continued to gaze upon the ancestral tablets as sticks of slow burning incense carried their unique aroma into the wind. "When my wife passed away giving birth to precious Meiling I had decided to never marry again, but I knew that one day she would marry and I would have no sons to continue the family name. My elder brothers and their sons perished in the wars against the Menggu in the steppe." He turned to face Sun Xin who stood stiffly outside the shrine's entrance. "Do you remember that day when I found you, Xin?" he asked pensively.

"Yes, b-but barely," Xin stuttered, unsure of how to respond.

"Shall I tell it again? Your village was ransacked by mounted raiders who had destroyed the light military presence guarding that part of the province. I had a wagon full of fresh lumber and I happened to be passing by when they began to set the place on fire. I rushed in to see if there were any survivors but only the dead lay strewn in the streets. I slew enough of the remaining raiders to force the rest of their troop to retreat." He sighed, looked up, and closed his eyes as he vividly recalled the events of that day. "I was about to leave when I heard horrific screams coming from one of the houses. I ran to see if there were any bandits remaining but instead I find you. Your parents and your baby sister lay lifeless in the corner. Around you were three dead men… and in your hand you gripped a bloodied sword. There you were, hardly eight years old and you had managed to slay your attackers. You defended yourself with that sword even though you could not save your family."

Sun Xin fell on his knees with his head slouched and a tear running down his cheek. "I do remember. I was not strong enough to save them." Suppressed memories of that fateful day came flooding back forcefully into his mind and the same fury that surged through his being that day was still fresh.

"A little boy should not have to bear the burden of protecting his family in any dynasty whether it is peaceful or full of turmoil. The fact that you were able to slay those three evil men was a miracle in itself," said Master Lo as he stepped out of the shrine and stood directly in front of Xin. Then he whispered, "You had a bright fire in your heart that I recognized immediately. I took you as my own, my only pupil –my apprentice. I taught you how to tame that fury and how to channel it into martial skill. You were a prodigy, Xin. Never before have I ever seen anyone learn the ways of the sword or the words of the Classics so quickly, and I was very proud. For a while I thought I had finally found someone who could continue my family's legacy." Xin sat on his knees with his head still slouched, his long black hair tugging in the wind. He did not know what to say. He felt shame, regret, and guilt all at once —all of which he seemed to be experiencing for the first time in a long time. "Did you find the fulfillment you sought out there in the world, Xin?" Master Lo asked him seriously. "Did killing all those men fill the void inside your soul and bring you peace? Are you fulfilling your destiny? You certainly must be fulfilling something. I can smell the blood on you."

Xin was not even sure if he was supposed to answer the questions. He would not have known how to answer anyway. He was unsure himself.

"Tell me something, my former apprentice. Why have you come back?" Master Lo asked with a tone that was distant and cold.

"I came haughtily thinking I could finish my training. But now I realize that I really should have come asking for the forgiveness that I do not even deserve," replied Xin with a hint of guilt… and resentment.

"You walked out on me ten years ago and have never visited until now and yet you think you can come here expecting to complete your training? You think you can just come here thinking you're worthy to fully wield my family's revered sword art for your petty and childish wiles?? You are not a sword master; you are an insolent brat that thinks he can save the Middle Kingdom just because he's learned a few techniques of an undefeated sword style!" Master Lo shouted as his face burned red with anger and eyes that glared down at Sun Xin. He had every right to vent his fury on him. Xin was not worthy to be his apprentice and he knew it. It was his pride that caused him to walk away from this place and it was his pride that made him think he could just walk right back into his master's life whenever he pleased. "The sword arts of the Lo family are sacred and you just used it however you pleased. Your blade is as guilty as those of the men you slaughtered. Tell me, Xin. Have you ever once considered the men whose lives you took all these years? Have you ever wondered that perhaps some of them were merely acting out of desperation or were in a way forced to enter the life they did? Many of them had families, homes, and carried with them loyalties and convictions as strong as yours. Continue resting your life's principles and values on the Way of the Sword and in the end it might just be the very thing that takes your life," he preached.

"My sword has saved countless innocent lives and I can confidently say that I have very little regrets with what I have accomplished through your training over the years. With respect, I must tell you that one cannot put a price on the lives I have saved. You haven't seen what I have – what the Underworld practices, what the crime syndicates plot in shadow, or the corruption that occurs among the officials who collaborate with them. Were it not for me, thousands of innocents would have perished or have had their lives destroyed forever," he protested.

Master Lo scoffed. He walked into the house and returned with a sword in his hand and presented it to Sun Xin.

"Draw this sword. If you can cut the hem of my garments I will consider your actions justified and I will call you 'Master'. Surely your combat skill is equally matched by your personal philosophy!"

Xin hesitated and wondered if this was some sort of test. "Go on. Try to see if you are able to land a cut on even my cloth," Master Lo said seemingly tauntingly. Xin bowed, drew the sword, and assumed his stance while Master Lo stood before him completely at ease. His hands rested behind his back while his face sported a smug smirk. With the twitch of an eye Sun Xin lunged at him with a thrust of the sword that missed cleanly as Master Lo simply stepped to the side. Every succeeding attack was blocked, dodged, evaded, or thwarted with ease until he disarmed Xin and landed a solid open-handed strike to his chest.

It was no use. Master Lo could predict his every move. He knew him too well; and knew even better the techniques he employed.

Sun Xin doubled over and gasped for air, frustrated and angry. He dashed towards Master Lo and right before his fist could land on his face he slammed to the ground, in a daze, and barely awake. When he came to, his nausea was brought about by a headache that kept him from standing to his feet. Master Lo crouched to Sun Xin's level and pressed down on vital points on his head to relieve the pain. Master Lo sat on the grass across from Xin.

"You are arrogant, impulsive, overconfident, and angry; defeating a bunch unskilled of crooks wielding fancy weapons does not make you worthy to wield the techniques of the Guardian Lion Sword. Before one can take or save a life he must first learn the true value of it. You have yet to learn this principle. You can't just go around killing enemies just because you can. The administration of justice is a high calling and you are not yet qualified. One cannot walk with a sword and live virtuously and righteously when he himself is empty. The condition of the heart that is inside you at this moment is a comfortable home for the Swordsman's Curse. It grants its host unparalleled ferocity and martial ability at the cost of your own self-destruction. Think very carefully about the path you trod, student, and consider what meaning really means in your life. If the sword is the foundation of your life's purpose, it will be the death of you." Master Lo left Xin with these very words as he entered his woodshop and continued on with his day as usual.

From a window in her room Meiling looked at Xin concernedly, worried for his very soul. It was hard even for her to think he was the same boy she used to play with in the grass and fields. Xin did not want to admit it but a small part of him knew that his master was correct. His pride had blinded him to his own ignorance about the way of the sword and the art of living. How can one who has yet to find the meaning of life be able to take it so quickly upon one's own judgment? Xin could not even clearly define the moral law that stood for the basis of his actions. Xin remained outside Master Lo's house staring at the old sword while reflecting on himself and the life that he had led for the past several years and wondering if he had done all the right things. Has anger and hatred been leading his life this whole time? He could not tell. He had been this way for as long as he could remember. The images of his murdered parents and sister forced their way back into his mind. Over the years he had forgotten the very reason why he began his campaigns. He had completely lost sight of the purpose of his mission. Now he remembered from where it was his inner rage was birthed – reminded of the reason why he set out on his own. Then the rains came and poured down on the valley while Xin climbed to a steep, tall hill and meditated under a pavilion that overlooked miles and miles of the landscape below and beyond. The faces of every single one of his targets —hundreds of man hunters, sect members, crime lords, mercenaries, gangsters, corrupt officials, and other bladesmen were flashing back into his sight. He still believed they deserved the death he had granted each and every one of them.

\*\*\*\*

First thing in the very next morning, Martial Scholar Tian Qiu presented his discoveries to the rest of the core group in the League and together they read through and analyzed the preserved documents of the Ming chronicler Ma Huan. The Scholars were speechless at this revelation of history and became even more troubled now they have confirmed the foreigners that have landed on their shores were the very same ones that Zheng He had personally encountered.

"The information provided in these presented sources will prove to be invaluable in combating these Pale Foreigners," said Lu Guanying. "I commend you for this discovery. We also have the previous generation of Hanlin Scholars to thank for salvaging these documents."

"Thank you, Headmaster ," replied Tian Qiu. "I found it quite odd that an advanced civilization such as these Pale Ones would have no other prior documentation from the past. Logically I decided to search through our copies of historical records, thanks to the benevolence and cooperation of the old Hanlin Academy. Not surprisingly, the great Admiral Zheng He indeed has had a first-hand experience with these foreigners in their native land – a land which appears to be on an uncharted continent in the southern-most point of the sea, where all other seas converge."

Excited whispers made their way among the members of the council and Senior Academicians present in the council hall. There were mixed feelings of awe, disbelief, and even fear. Most of them were apprehensive about an impending conflict with the Pale Ones.

With such a valuable discovery and its circulation amongst trustworthy government officials, war it seemed would be inevitable. The League of Scholars began to consider reconnecting with the Chancellor of Hanlin Academy whose access to the emperor would prove to be useful for their movement into the government and potential courses of action against the corruption. They continued to examine the chronicles of Ma Huan and took several moments to comprehend the magnitude of their current situation. How could knowledge of such momentous events be hidden away from everyone? It seemed impossible and utterly foolish to withhold this great turning point in the history of the Middle Kingdom and the rest of the world. Hard questions were exchanged between the council though none could rationalize what they have learned.

"How could such a monumental, world-shaking event in history been so easily censored and forgotten from all memory? It seemed so impossible!" they said amongst themselves.

An Academician unexpectedly entered the council chambers and presented Zhang Sunzan with a rolled sheet of paper. He leaned his elbow against the armrest and read it with great care line by line. The others sat at the edge of their seats, looking to him in anticipation. Zhang Sunzan stood from his seat and presented to the Scholars' Council the message he had just received from his trusted contact Fox. The avian had just swooped in with the message from Beijing.

"A trusted colleague of mine has sent word from the capital," he said as he reviewed and scanned the document.

"He had successfully made contact with Wei Qiuyuan of the Censorial Office; according to them, it too has, unfortunately but expectedly, been corrupted by these meddling foreigners. Furthermore, Wei Qiuyuan has reported his observations regarding secret dealings between key officials and eunuchs and the Terukk. He has discovered extensive instances of bribery occurring in court. Bribery with addictive potions that can be consumed by mouth in small amounts. Some have even become… grossly addicted to it. In exploitation of this addiction, the Pale ones ask for land rights, ridiculous trading privileges, and unreasonably high leverage within the Ming political system. In summary, any virtuous within the bureaucracy who would dare 'squeal' have been imprisoned or are threatened with death or blackmail. In conjunction, the spy agencies along with the secret police have been compromised, with reports of widespread divisions, dissention, and desertion occurring in the bureaus. This renders them too dysfunctional for official government duty, according to Wei. The emperor is kept in the dark, largely unaware of what is transpiring in the empire, within his own inner court." Zhen Shu squinted at the scribble on the paper.

"Apparently, according to Fox, the emperor is ill. He and Wei believe it is most probably an induced illness to keep him from intervening in the rampant corruption." Zhen Shu sighed deeply and looked up from the paper. "Now it seems that our last direct and reliable line of contact with the court is our counterparts at Hanlin Academy."

Headmaster Lu Guanying shook his head in disbelief yet he could not say that he was surprised. Murmurs and whispers filled the council chamber. "It appears that the Foreigners' agenda is beginning to reveal itself. Clearly their foreign policy seeks to destabilize our civilization completely. For what ultimate purpose, this we must uncover."

Tian Qiu nodded in agreement. "It seems that the memory of the Treasure Fleet's visit decades ago is still fresh in their memories. Perhaps this is some form of retribution."

"Wei Qiuyuan is correct. I think it is time. Those of us here in the council are to meet with the scholars at Hanlin Academy to make our presence known before the emperor. Hanlin Academy's Chancellor Wu Chan will be able to make the proper arrangements for our maneuvers after our arrival. We must make haste to Beijing before the Pale Ones do any more damage, especially ones that may be irreparable. Revolution from within the capital is at hand," declared Guanying, "and I am afraid, blood will be spilled."

Some days later, the League made arrangements for a trip to Beijing via the coast leaving their academy to the care of Senior Academicians. Not far from the harbors of Guangzhou, a fine ship was being loaded with preparations for an extensive voyage to the North. There, General He Jin and the men of his company oversaw the preparations for the Scholars' very own warship the Phoenix Spirit. It was nowhere near the size of a massive treasure ship but it was of admirable proportions and was more than capable of sailing to the farthest reaches of the known world with ease and utmost efficiency. It was sleek and streamlined, built for speed and featured a wide deck that allowed for elevated combat platforms. Its sails of red silk would soar high —designed to tack into the wind with utmost efficiency.

Thanks to the efforts of General Jin, the ship was being outfitted with new cannons and the latest developments in military technology. The ship was almost too good to believe. It was a true marvel of naval engineering and it was an object of great pride among the Scholars. They approached the ship with a sense of a renewed awe for the vessel. The ship's handpicked crew moved about the ship and harbor making preparations to depart. They saluted the Scholars and the company of Academicians as they arrived.

"She looks even more beautiful than the last time I saw her," breathed Shang Jian as he gestured his greetings to the general. General He Jin reciprocated and nodded in agreement.

"It was built with sophisticated techniques largely forgotten among shipwrights of late. This Fuchuan class warship is a classic. Only the finest ships within today's Ming Navy could match the Phoenix Spirit's in the open seas or in a river, take your pick. I have made some arrangements to have your ship refurbished with the best weaponry thanks to the contribution of an old friend," said He Jin with a raised eyebrow. "He is quite a brilliant engineer…" he paused to look around and leaned towards the Scholars whispering "but just between you and me, he is a bit cracked and rather deaf. You would have to shout more often if you would like his attention. Explosions appear to be rather unfriendly to the ears."

The Scholars chuckled at his jest as a short man entered the scene. His hair and beard were wiry and rather unruly with the ends scorched to a near crisp. His face was dirty as if he had been working in a coal mine, lightly seared by black powder. He wore a foolish grin and walked with a stiff awkward gate as he approached Jin and the Scholars. "Gentlemen, I would like you to meet the benefactor and designer of your refurbished ship. Meet 'Fung', better known as Big Bang like, you know, an explosion… for obvious reasons," said General Jin. The Scholars greeted him gladly.

"A pleasure to meet you all!" exclaimed Big Bang enthusiastically. "Hope you like the new babies I put into your ship. Can't wait to see it blow something up! Sixteen heavy iron cannons waiting to spit!" he giggled with a foolish grin. Everyone else just smiled and looked at each other awkwardly.

"We need sixteen, huh? Most ships in the Ming Navy get a minimum standard of eight or ten!" commented Shang Jian. Big Bang and the rest of the ship's crew proceeded making final preparations for their departure as the sun had begun to dip beneath the horizon.

"I would like to thank you for all, comrades. Now, the League of Martial Scholars is one of the beacons of hope left in this country," lamented the General. "I must take my leave and return to the garrison in Fujian to take care of unfinished military business. I must ensure the troops are combat ready should things turn sour in the empire," he said with a frown and determined eyes.

"Take good care, friend. We will see you again real soon," said Zhen Shu.

"May you have a safe passage to the North, friends. Sail far from the coast and go under cover of the morning fog and send my regards to the emperor. May Heaven help him," advised He Jin. With that, he and his light company of commandos mounted up and proceeded to make their way out of the city.

"The cloud line in the east meanders through the sky like a dragon and the stars are unveiled that we are able to see them in the light of the setting sun. Nature is on our side. A heavy fog will conceal our departure early in the morning," said Tian Qiu, alluding to his knowledge of the Classics and the Book of Changes.

"Let's blaze a trail of fire to the capital!" Big Bang screamed maniacally.

# REVELATIONS

It was at the prosperous and charming town of Xidi at the foot of the majestic snowcapped mountains that an exiled monk and a wandering hermit sage decided to settle for the night. The light from the setting sun bathed the western face of the mountain cluster with yellow and orange, making the view from where the sage and the monk were standing quite spectacular and mystical.

"Tell me again, why we have come to the Huangshan range?" Zuo Shilong asked respectfully.

"I have come to meet an old friend… to commune in spirit so I may know Heaven's will," said Famin Jie softly. "We head for Celestial Peak, a few days march and climb. It would be well worth it. There are some things that I must attend to, questions that need to be put to rest."

"What is at the top of Celestial Peak?" asked Shilong wide-eyed and curious with childlike excitement. The two checked into an inn and sat down at one of the lobby tables to dine. Famin Jie looked at the monk and chuckled.

"There is an old friend living in a Sanctuary in seclusion and relative obscurity somewhere on that mountain. Nobody, not even I really know his story but he possesses knowledge and wisdom lost to the ages. Funny enough, rumors have circulated that he has been around since the Han Dynasty! Naturally, I have yet to find any proof that could allow such a thing to be possible. Nevertheless, I am sure he can provide the answers to my questions," he whispered to Shilong. "He almost never leaves the mountain."

"Yes, I think I can somewhat recall one of the abbots of my temple telling us a story of a lonely man at the top of the mountains in Huangshan though I am not sure if this man is the same one you speak of. It is said that he is acquainted with the heavens and that he is hundreds of years old, knowing the secrets to immortality. Not even witches and the sorcerers would dare to challenge him. There is no way that the story is true, is it? He is just a legend," said Zuo Shilong in a skeptical tone of voice.

Famin Jie was laughed heartily. "No, no he is quite real, that I can tell you with certainty. Putting aside embellishments, he is mysterious, yes, but very real and very wise. He is to be treated with the utmost respect and reverence if you wish to meet with him," advised Famin Jie to Shilong. The monk agreed and together they ate their fill for the night and rested in preparation for their ascension to the Celestial Peak. Out from the small opening of the window, Zuo Shilong glanced at the mountains just beyond Xidi. Past the town's charming lights and evening sounds, the mountains were bathed in moonlight and he could almost feel a yearning for that mountain as if what he had been searching for would be found within the Huangshan range. He did not know what to expect at Celestial Peak but the closure he needed would present itself to him sooner than he realized.

When Zuo Shilong and Famin Jie had left Xidi, they came upon a horse-drawn four-wheeled carriage driven by a man with a most friendly disposition. He quickly befriended them and graciously volunteered to take them through the pass towards Huangshan. The man, whom they had just met, happened to be a descendant of the Menggu horsemen and frequented the northern regions of the Middle Kingdom and beyond. His name was Jirgal. He was quite the conversationalist.

Explaining that he had been deemed an outcast among his kinsmen even those who lived in the empire and therefore made a living in the lower provinces conducting business in trade and courier services. Jirgal was a gentle and humorous man despite the story he shared of himself. He was not at all what one would stereotypically expect from a man of Menggu heritage.

"It's darn good to have company. You know I can go for days and even weeks without talking to anyone. I'd strike up an interesting topic of conversation with these two here pullin' me wagon, but uh… they don't say much," he laughed.

"I cannot imagine why," said Zuo Shilong rolling his eyes.

"Climbing Huangshan is no laughing matter. What makes Uncle and stick-wielding baldy want to go there anyway? Naught there but rumors and sightings of heaven knows what. Something has been stirring around the mountains," he continued to say.

"You are right something has been stirring in these parts and not just in our land. My friend and I are paying a visit to an old friend in search of some answers," replied Famin Jie.

"Wait, someone actually takes up residence there? That is incredible! Travelers and monks have been noticing strange things happening over that mountain," cautioned Jirgal.

"What do you mean 'strange' things have been happening?" inquired Zuo Shilong.

Before Jirgal was able to answer, a large and terrible beast leaped from the brush in the distance. It had the appearance of an oversized ox with the ferocious features of a lion and it bellowed a boisterous, terrible noise that spouted what looked like sparks of ash and hot coal from its very mouth. The monster resembled a Nian, a legendary creature of myth not seen since the dawn of the imperial era almost two thousand years ago.

Alarmed and very startled, the horses galloped to full speed and Jirgal was unable to regain control of them. The carriage shook and rattled with the acceleration as the Nian made chase.

"Bad luck! You should've never asked that question, monk!"

shouted Jirgal as he haplessly tumbled backwards into the carriage.

"A demon fast approaches! We must kill it," yelled Zuo Shilong. Famin Jie struggled to sit upright as the carriage careened through the rough and winding dirt road.

"No… really? We should make friends with it and tell it nicely we do not taste very good," Jirgal jested as he fought to regain his footing in the bouncing carriage. He fumbled through some crates searching for his old hunting bow which was conveniently stuffed under skins and furs. The horses raced forward through the rugged road but the Nian was slowly closing the distance enough for them to hear its rumbling, huffing, and puffing. The powerful creature dug its broad hooves into the ground kicking up dirt with every stride pushing every inch of muscle in its body to close the distance between it and its prey. The very impacts of its gallop echoed like war drums.

Jirgal brought his bow to bear. "Maybe I can poke it in the eye or something," he said fumbling to get his weapon ready. Jirgal raised his bow, drew an arrow and pulled it to maximum tension. He aimed for the Nian's face and let the arrow loose. It flew fast and true but harmlessly combed through the Nian's thick mane. He fired a second third and fourth shot all of which penetrated the beast's thick hide and tough flesh reacting with no more than a mere flinch.

The creature leaped right onto the carriage and tore through the wood twisting through the iron frame and axle. The harnesses of the horses snapped free and the carriage along with its passengers came crashing into a heap of wood and twisted metal debris.

Zuo Shilong shook off the disorientation and fought to regain his footing. He grasped his staff and launched himself towards the monster, staff twirling in the air. The beast effortlessly swiped him away and tumbling into the ground unconscious. The beast redirected its attention toward the remaining two men as Jirgal drew the final arrow.

Famin Jie rose to his feet and stood tall and calm before the monster which proceeded towards them step by step.

"You are a creature of the depths and I rebuke you! You have no business here!" declared Famin Jie with an unexpected presence of command that made even Jirgal stop in his tracks.

The creature briefly hesitated as if taken aback by Famin Jie's stand but nevertheless continued forward planting one step with another step. The sage raised his hands and looked high into the heavens.

"Leave us at once and go back into the darkness to await the eternal damnation that is fated for thee and thy masters. Thou hast no power to oppose the Will of Heaven, beast. Leave and be gone!" The earth trembled and a rumble echoed in the wind as Famin Jie's mighty declaration burst forth upon the beast which, unable to face the truth in the rebuke, turned away and scrambled for the hills out of sight and far from Huangshan.

Jirgal still sitting on the ground and gripping his bow was quite stunned and speechless at what he had just witnessed. He shook in his boots and did not realize he was holding his breath the whole time. He grabbed his own jaw and pushed it up closed.

"That was," he said catching his breath, "that was incredible! How did you – Where did the – why is – how??" he asked with his hands dug into his hair. "Are you supposed to be some sort of wizard?" Jirgal took two steps back while the events that had just taken place were beginning to register in his mind.

"Nothing of the sort, my friend. On my own I am nothing. I am powerless. Shang Di has called me to this journey and so I know He will see me through it." He looked up at the majestic mountains and then turned to gaze into the horizon behind. "A great conflict of our age is fast approaching. There will be great suffering. That creature was only a symptom of a greater disease. We must get to the Sanctuary to find out what is happening and why," Famin Jie said anxiously.

He approached Zuo Shilong who lay on the ground out cold. Famin laid hands upon him feeling for injuries then pressed several vital points in his body. This caused the monk to sit up and awaken with a start.

"The creature, it is coming; we must flee!" he shouted in a panic as he spun his head around in search for any sign of the monster.

"Fear not, friend. We are safe. The beast has fled to the hills," said Famin Jie reassuringly. "Come now, we must head for the Sanctuary."

"The beast has left? What? How?" Zuo Shilong whimpered as he rubbed his aching head. Jirgal stood staring into the horizon in shock and awe still unable to fully comprehend what had just taken place.

"That's what I said. You should've seen it, monk. He just stood there and told the beast to take a hike and it just left! Your old friend here has got some recognized authority, eh?"

"Huh?" said Zuo Shilong staring at Jirgal blankly.

"Well, I just spoke the truth and the beast understood but could not handle it. Nothing too miraculous," replied Famin Jie meekly. "I am truly sorry about your losses, my friend," he said apologizing to Jirgal and surveying the wreckage. "There is no way we can repay you at the moment, but we would be delighted if you would accompany us to the Celestial Peak. There is much food and good shelter in our destination. It is the least we can do in exchange for your losses."

Jirgal looked around at the wreckage and sighed. He holstered his bow and gathered what little he could salvage and fit them into one pack. He fastened his thick fur cap and looked to the mountains. "I might as well. No use in walking all the way to the next township or city from here. My horses can take care of themselves," replied Jirgal.

Zuo Shilong rubbed his bald head, still apparently unaware of what he had really missed while he was unconscious. He stood to his feet and flexed his joints.

"Well, at least I did not break any bones. I have never seen such a creature in my life. I know of lions and tigers but never would I have thought such a beast like that exists," he said surveying their surroundings.

"It was massive. Do you think it will follow us here, teacher?"

"I think not. It understands and knows it cannot touch us now.

But I will tell you, I think it is the first of many. These encounters will only become more frequent in the days and weeks to come," said Famin Jie. He did not have a hint of worry in his words. Zuo Shilong found that to be quite intriguing. A simple old man that did not worry or fear even after encountering such a creature was truly impressive and admirable. Jirgal gathered his belongings and picked up a walking stick.

"I believe I'm just about ready for a good hike and climb into the mountains. May Tengri help us," he said concernedly looking up at the tall, intimidating mountains. The trio proceeded onto the pass at Huangshan and traversed narrow and rocky paths that meandered between the peaks, fog, and steep terrain.

The journey was marked by locations full of breathtaking scenery most of which did not go unnoticed by Jirgal who had not seen anything quite like it before. The path to Celestial Peak was not for the faint of heart. It was unforgiving and left no room for survival for anyone with even the slightest of injuries. The trio treaded with great caution, navigating a stone path carved right out of the side of the mountain and crossing an ancient stone bridge that hung precariously between steep cliffs.

Zuo Shilong, being the agile and nimble warrior monk, effortlessly crossed over and climbed the ancient stone steps that snaked along the side of the mountain like it was a common city street, while Jirgal and Famin Jie lagged behind struggling to match his pace.

"I am not as young as used to be," Famin Jie chuckled.

"And I am fatter than I used to be," wheezed Jirgal dramatically. "The loss of my wagon may yet have been a blessing in disguise. Driving all these years has made my heart weak and my legs stiff!"

The trio's laughter echoed through the mountains and canyons beyond the mist and fog as they drew closer to the Sanctuary where the answers to Famin Jie's questions may be found. The hostile path through the mountains was a mere foreshadowing of the path they would have to undertake in the coming days and Famin Jie knew it.

They journeyed for two days with minimal food and water fighting treacherous winds, the rain, and the blistering cold of night. As they neared the their destination, an old welcoming tree gently swaying with the cold breeze arched over the path as if to signal that the long and treacherous road to the Sanctuary had finally come to an end. Nestled at the mountain's breast stood the Sanctuary – a safe haven and stronghold monastery of lost knowledge with halls of study and enlightenment for those who wished to rediscover it.

"Amazing," said Jirgal and Zuo Shilong simultaneously.

"What more can you tell us of this place?" Shilong asked.

"Erm… does anyone else know that this is here? I mean, who would've thought!" Jirgal added. Famin Jie kept his gaze at the Sanctuary in the distance and breathed in deep the cool misty air. They proceeded to make their way to the foot of the mountain.

"When the first emperor united the Nine Domains of the Warring States, some say he had gone mad with power and challenged the mandate of Heaven calling himself 'Most High'. He then sought to secure his new position by eliminating all he perceived as a threat to his reign. History has called it the Great Book Burning and the Burial of Scholars. Countless ancient texts were destroyed along with the works of the One Hundred Schools of Thought founded by the great philosophers who sought the restoration of the Way that once prevailed in the society of ancient times. The followers and students of the schools were therefore captured and buried alive. Thousands of years of transcendent wisdom and the histories of a legendary age were all burned into ash with the swift command of a tyrant. There were those however, who remained faithful to the laws of Heaven and had resisted the emperor in secret. They were the few who remembered the Way that had been lost and remembered that it awaited 'restoration'. These very same scholars had managed to elude the emperor's capture and avoid the mass executions. Though they were very few, they united to create the Sanctuary at the heart of the Huangshan range, hidden in plain sight yet far from the reach of tyrants in order to save and preserve the last true copies of the ancient texts and enlightened teachings of antiquity. It is hoped that the restoration of the Way would yet continue in a different age. Today, only a few are aware of the Sanctuary's existence and even fewer have the discernment to navigate the perilous unknown paths and rugged trails through the mountains that lead to its anterior steps. It was in the Sanctuary that the knowledge of the ancients could be rediscovered and pieces of timeless wisdom bestowed by Heaven could be learned. If there was any hope of restoring the Way to the whole of the Middle Kingdom, it would start in the Sanctuary at the time of Heaven's choosing. Since then, it has survived the coming and going of the dynasties and known only by a few."

For Famin Jie and his companions, the Sanctuary was shelter from the mountain's unforgiving slopes and an avenue to save the Middle Kingdom. They had yet to realize it. The gears of time and destiny have begun to turn once again and everything was in place to be set in motion. So it begins when the trio finally approached the gateway of the Sanctuary, exhausted, yet relieved.

"The Keeper of the Sanctuary awaits us, friends," said Famin Jie as he caught his breath in the cold air. "He will welcome us with shelter."

"And I hope his tables will welcome my sorry belly," remarked Jirgal with urgency. The wind howled and threw blistering cold rain into their faces.

"The Keeper is very old and very wise, Jirgal. I urge you to speak to him with great care and humility," advised Famin Jie.

"Okay, okay, but we really should hurry because my stomach does not recognize or give respect to anybody!" moaned Jirgal. "See? It growled at you just now."

The Sanctuary was a sight to behold as it sat majestically against the mountain's breast where the main hall stood at the center of a compound of tall structures and buildings. Surrounding the Sanctuary was a covered walkway that formed an enclosure around the monastery. Two tall watchtowers stood on the right and left corners of the fortress overlooking the mountain range and the sea of clouds that engulfed it below. At the center of the compound, a large iron statue stood as the centerpiece of the Sanctuary. The image was of an ancient philosopher in long court robes solemnly observing the heavens and holding above its head a wide scroll that faced toward the sky. It was a befitting statue, one that presented the purpose of the Sanctuary: to seek the wisdom and will of Heaven fervently, humbly, and sincerely. Such was the reoccurring theme of the thinkers of old who sought to restore the knowledge of the Way to all people. Past the gated archway it was one hundred steps to the giant red wooden doors. With a knock of three and but two moments later, the door groaned and creaked open. A small elderly woman beside the door greeted them with a bow and a smile.

"Welcome, masters. Your arrival has been anticipated. Please, this way," she said with a small quivering voice. Jirgal and Zuo Shilong looked at each other with surprised expressions and shrugged simultaneously. The trio walked through the main halls passing rooms and studies up to the next floor where they were requested to wait in a library. The place felt quite lonely, antiquated yet elegant. The high ceiling and gray outdoor light beaming through the fabric-covered windows instilled a feeling of awe and mystery that left Zuo Shilong and Jirgal quite mesmerized by its sheer scale.

"Do you have any snacks??" Jirgal did not feel intimidated by the place as he thought he would have, but felt rather protected and welcomed. Zuo Shilong once belonged to a monastery of a different sort so he was quite curious about the Sanctuary and its secrets yet was unsure of the questions that had long riddled his mind.

Exhausted from the journey, the three of them sat still in silence seemingly too tired to produce even the simplest thoughts. After

Jirgal stuffed his face with last piece of bread the trio had almost fallen asleep until the silence was finally broken when the Keeper of Sanctuary entered the library to greet them. Famin Jie met him with a warm embrace as would old friends who have not seen each other for many years.

"I have missed you, my friend but I know you did not come for a mere holiday visit either," said the Keeper smiling. "You too have seen the coming darkness. Such is the gift discernment."

"I have come to find answers. I seek your counsel, wise Keeper. This impending darkness has been troubling my soul of late. I was confronted by a witch in the woods and a foul beast attacked us on the road," said Famin Jie urgently. The Keeper, seeming to not have been listening, turned to Jirgal and Zuo Shilong to extend his welcome and was delighted to have such unique and unlikely visitors. He studied them both.

"You should have seen it! The ugly thing was massive. Monk here tried to fight but he was knocked out cold," Jirgal exclaimed.

"It is strange that a warrior monk and a man of the Menggu would find their way into these halls! But then one would not expect less from my dear friend Famin Jie who seems to be quite adept at making new friends," the Keeper said gleefully with a grin. Zuo Shilong bowed respectfully towards the Keeper.

"I am honored to meet one as esteemed as you, sir," said Zuo Shilong.

"Oh esteemed perhaps, but I really do just live in these halls to make sure they are clean and ready to accommodate visitors like yourselves!" the Keeper replied with humility as he giggled with satisfaction. Though he was very old, Keeper carried with him such contentment and peace. Despite his frailty, he conducted himself in a way that blessed others with his presence alone, for he was a blessed man with a humble spirit and his face glowed with a youthful energy.

"Um… sir, if I may. I'm not so much a warrior as I am a horseman, and even then the only horses I've ever owned pulled my wagon," Jirgal remarked as his face gloomed. "I no longer even have that, thanks to that accursed beast that charged us from the hills."

"No worries, friend. All that you have lost will one day be returned to you in abundance through ways you would not expect," consoled Keeper. "Although it seems that the ancient creatures have begun making more frequent appearances of late. An impending doom we have not foreseen is upon us. It will be an event so monumental that even legendary beasts are answering its call."

"Which is exactly why we have come to you, Keeper!" said Famin Jie urgently. "Yes, I know, but who am I?" replied the Keeper concernedly. "Come, there are serious matters to discuss." Together, the group made their way to another hall in the Sanctuary where they dined and cleansed themselves. There, in the corridors and sparsely occupied chambers, rooms, and libraries Zuo Shilong spent his evening exploring and discovering the Sanctuary. Jirgal had found a bed and slept in an instant.

"Keeper, I have come in search of answers because I feel Heaven's will has become difficult to discern. I feel the negative changes all around me but I do not know whence it came," Famin confessed. "Have you heard the news that not long ago strange men have arrived on the shores of the Middle Kingdom? It is true. Though as men they are not like us at all. They are pale in appearance and offer good tidings and enticing propositions for the people. Very dark clouds hang above them. I have discerned it. I also believe they are the cause of the imbalances we sense," said the Keeper as he pensively combed the fine strands of his silky white beard.

"Pale men? Here? What business do they have in the Middle Kingdom?" questioned Famin seriously.

"Their business is unrighteous, driven by the very same darkness that causes greed, malice, and death," he replied.

"The cause for distress is not so much in the physical destruction these Pale men will bring, Famin Jie, but in the eternal separation from Heaven that many people shall suffer. That, my friend, is the greatest despair that can befall the people in eternity."

In the lowest levels of the Sanctuary's main hall, upon the foundations mighty stone and wood was a message carved upon rock. The Keeper led Famin Jie down a steep staircase beneath the compound. What they read was a mysterious warning was given by the ancients. The Keeper revealed it to Famin Jie and he brought the inscriptions to candlelight. It said: "The Way is salvation. Only Heaven can spare nations from calamity and bring deliverance from all injustice. Turn to Heaven and restore the Way to resist darkness and promote righteousness."

"This is the answer to the impending trials we will face, is it not?" Famin Jie asked.

"We are arriving to a time of great testing when the people must choose their destinies for themselves whether it be of Heaven or of this fallen world," the Keeper answered. "It has been 4,000 years since the Sage Kings of old led the people in the knowledge of the Way. That knowledge has been lost to the ages. I am afraid that the favor of Heaven no longer rests upon the Middle Kingdom and now our trials have finally begun."

"But the people will take arms against the invaders. The Ming is the strongest of all the nations. They will fight to the death." Famin remarked assuredly.

"And death is where it will ultimately lead. It is where it will only lead. Without the grace of Heaven and the restoration of the Way, the people in their own strength and will are powerless against the might of the darkness the invaders bring. If our people will not die by it, they shall succumb to it. City by city, province by province, in the Middle Kingdom and the lands beyond the seas and mountain peaks, the people will fall, enslaved by the accursed power of these foreign beings. I know this to be true. I have heard all the news and have meditated on it day and night." Worry overtook Keeper's face. "I have always known the great defining war of our age would come but never within the span of the years of my life." Famin Jie stood before the engraving in deep thought trying to comprehend the magnitude of what was unfolding.

"I answered the call to serve many years ago leaving behind a life of material wealth and comfort to learn and discover the Way while awaiting the instruction of Heaven," said Famin Jie solemnly. "Until now I still wait for direction even after the darkness had begun to rise. What are we to do against this invasion? For so many years I have waited patiently and yet have I to gain students nor has the Way been restored to the people. I feel I have become lost."

The Keeper stood silently with his hands in his sleeves and closed his eyes. "Even in the moments of silence, there is ever the Grand Orchestrator, preparing the people for the fulfillment of His will. Silence does not mean Heaven has ceased to speak, but rather that you must draw closer so that you may hear and listen," Keeper told Jie.

"The imminent conflict we are about to witness in the Middle Kingdom is but a mere physical manifestation of a great war in the realm of the unseen and we are very much participants in that unseen battle whether we choose to engage in it or not. The outcome of the battles of the invisible shall be the outcome of the battles throughout the realms of the Middle Kingdom." Famin Jie pondered on these words and sighed as he anxiously paced around the room distressed at what was unfolding. He did not know his purpose and why he was not able to accomplish what he had hoped for all these years. His message of Truth had returned void in every challenge he undertook. The people were not ready to accept what he had to teach and Heaven seemed to have not favored his attempts to serve. Uncertainties and doubts overwhelmed his soul for without the Way, the Middle Kingdom will fall.

"I will fight for the cause of the people and for righteousness. It is time that we emerge from obscurity to finally spread the Word of

Heaven, Keeper. For years our message has yielded very little fruit but now the time has come. You are familiar with the dealings of Shang Di. Surely you can tell me what I must do, Keeper" he said fervently.

"That is something you must discover for yourself, for indeed the time has come," he replied. "When the Way prevailed over the land, the people knew the Will of Heaven. When the Way was lost, the people called upon the kings and emperors to mediate. A burnt offering was made at the Border Sacrifice on behalf of the people symbolizing the cleansing needed to be right before the presence of the Most High. Though the Emperor performs the Great Sacrifice to this day, the people of the Ming do not remember Shang Di or his perfect mandates. There are very few like ourselves who have submitted in obedience to the Way -the only path to the Most High. You must go to the Secret Place to humble yourself and be still and meditate upon the mandates of Heaven as revealed in the texts. Neglect the needs of the body so you will not lose sight of your purpose, and to commune in spirit with that which you cannot see. Heaven honors sincere and earnest searching. The correct path will be revealed to you, Seeker."

Famin Jie heeded the Keeper's words and proceeded into the Secret Place – a private courtyard enclosed with stone inside the head of the mountain located behind the Sanctuary. It was where a disciple of the Way and a seeker of Heaven would cleanse the spirit, meditate, and study the truths as revealed by the ancients through sacred scrolls thought to have long been destroyed. For three days and nights

Famin Jie did just that, neglecting rest and bodily nourishment to center his mind on that which transcended the physical and the natural. In the torchlights of the Secret Place, he meditated and read through the transcendent inspiration of the sages through the preserved written declarations and teachings of the partial revelation. High above the walls of stone through the narrow opening above the courtyard, he looked up at the night sky and beheld the innumerable host of stars and was in awe. He praised Heaven. The Darkness bore witness to his communion in spirit and was disturbed by it. It descended upon the Seeker and oppressed him…

The wind blew through the balcony where Zuo Shilong stood. The wind carried a faint yet audible moan, like a distant bellowing of a large bear , and it brought chills down his spine.

"The wind brings a fell cry from the south. It is not from a man," commented Zuo Shilong as he leaned his ear towards the wind with great interest.

"Ah, yes. Even the Yeren can feel the disturbances caused by the unnatural. They are most sensitive to the changes in the delicate balance of nature and they cry for it," said Keeper.

"Ye-ren?" asked Zuo Shilong with a raised eyebrow.

"The Yeren are as old as the Middle Kingdom itself, inhabiting the forests, valleys, and mountains of the central and Northern provinces for many thousand years though they were rarely ever encountered by travelers. They tended to shy away from the approaching footsteps of people. They were very large two-legged creatures of massive strength, taller than the tallest man, covered in long shaggy hair, and were heavier than even the largest bears. Though fierce in appearance and imposing in stature, they were known to be meek and pacific in nature. One can sometimes hear their howls, whoops and grunts echoing for miles across the valleys."

"Such a creature exists??" Zuo Shilong was in disbelief.

"Indeed. Here in Huangshan, one tends to see and hear things no one else would believe."

"I hope to see this 'ye-ren' one day."

"What brings you to the Sanctuary at Huangshan, my monk friend?" asked the Keeper taking on a more friendly tone. "More specifically, what compelled you to accompany Famin Jie on his journey?" Zuo Shilong paused for a moment to gather his answer in his mind though he himself has forgotten how he managed to embark on this journey with the teacher.

"Before my meeting with the teacher, I spent my days wandering from town to town searching for any place where I can help the people. Yes, that is my desire, to help the people and to protect them from harm. That is all I have ever wanted to do. I do not care for great rewards or recognition, though I try to accept the benevolence of the people with humility and great gratitude," said Zuo Shilong innocently with passion. "The generosity of the people has never left me hungry."

The Keeper smiled. "That is a very noble pursuit and I commend you for taking up this selfless path. What of your brothers in the monastery at Shaoshi Mountain?" asked Keeper curiously.

"The longer I stayed at the Temple, the more questions plagued my mind. I searched and searched for answers. What is destiny? What is meaning? What is the standard of righteousness and evil? Why are we here? The masters that raised me at Shaoshi Mountains had grown weary of my questioning and came a time that I offended them. A fellow monk confronted me and in defense, I struck him with my hands. He nearly died. Such a deed was unforgiveable. Thus, I was banished. Since my inability to find answers greatly frustrated me, I occupied myself helping people across the lands to distract my mind from such queries. When I met the teacher, I believed I seemed to have met someone with the wisdom and insight I sought after. His teachings were profoundly wise despite being opposed to my own opinions. I recognized this immediately so I have agreed to follow him."

The Keeper grinned at Zuo Shilong's story and was pleased that his path had crossed with Famin Jie. *Their meeting was no accident*, he thought. "Those who seek truth with seriousness and sincerity while keeping an open mind soon find their answers revealed to them," said Keeper . "There have been a few serious seekers just like you who have walked through the halls of this Sanctuary over the years and to my delight, they have found the answers to their questions! It is not by mere fate that you have found your way here, Shilong. Peace and clarity is what you will find soon enough, for Heaven directs the paths of those who follow righteousness and earnestly seek the truth," Keeper said.

For the first time in a long time Zuo Shilong the warrior monk felt the flame of hope rekindled in his heart. There in the halls of the Sanctuary where sparse groups of academics tread to and fro, the monk and the sage talked of things of great depth and meaning – food for Zuo Shilong's hungering spirit.

Jirgal approached them from the other end of the hallway and was apparently in a good mood. "Hello, Mister Keeper. Hi, Monk! I must say this place is amazing, and I am truly impressed with how you're all able to dish out a living up here in the middle of nowhere! How on earth did they manage to build this place on a mountain? The logistics must have been a nightmare. Oh, and the study halls and libraries are very lovely," said Jirgal gleefully nodding his head in approval.

"That is pleasing to hear . Have you found any interesting material?" asked the Keeper.

Jirgal scratched his head saying "Oh, no, I can't read."

****

In the Secret Place, the oppression of darkness was more powerful than that of the witch he encountered in the forest. It had come upon him with the tremendous burdens of guilt, anger, doubt, and despair in an effort to cast his very being far away from his meditation. In the throes of the oppression befalling him in his solitude, Famin Jie cried out in anguish as the images of his past were whispered into his mind and soul, like smoke snaking through every crack and crevice of a burning house.

"Oh, Heaven who is called Most High, if you find favor in me, I only humbly ask that in thy mercy thou would freest me from these burdens and cast them as far as the East is from the West!" As quickly as the pain and anguish engulfed him, so too did it dissipate and cease altogether. The Darkness and the hosts that delivered his oppression had fled. All had gone quiet and the deafening silence that had befallen the Secret Place faded away.

Yet another figure steadily approached Famin Jie from the winding stairs that descended sharply from the mountain's peak. It stood before him and its voice called out to Famin Jie from a dim corner of the Secret Place. He had the appearance of a mighty warrior with eyes that could pierce the strongest shield and he wore long garments of white embroidered with shades of gold and other such colors he had never before seen. Jie was terrified and fell on his back trembling in awe and fear of this mysterious figure who wielded a powerful presence. "There is no reason to fear, Famin Jie for Shang Di knows your virtue and has heard your pleas. I am here to deliver a message of great importance to you," the figure told him.

"You know my name. Whom among the creatures of this earth do you favor?" Famin Jie asked sternly though he was fearful.

"There is none on earth whom I favor. The tasks of Heaven are what occupy me alone," the figure said with a resonating voice. Famin Jie then sat on his knees and from the respect and reverence of his heart, he bowed and pressed his head against the ground ready to receive the instruction of Heaven. The words of the visiting figure poured forth the instruction, peace, and assurance that Heaven alone could bestow.

"You are to go to the Capital and proceed into the court of the one who holds Heaven's Mandate," the figure said, "and let the ears of all who will listen hear the truth of what is and what is to come. This message which you know well in your heart shall go forth to the nations over the mountains and the seas."

"The emperor's court? I am but a lowly hermit of dusty rags and an unknown name. It is hard for me to understand, but lo, my ways do not compare to Heaven's ways." Famin Jie whispered to himself. The figure answered. "The path before you has been set. Your tongue will be blessed and your body will be strengthened for the hardship to come. The heart of the emperor is prepared and the people must make room for the return of the Way for it shall be the light in the coming darkness. Your companions shall continue to accompany you so that they may bear witness to the deliverance of Heaven over all the people. They too shall be instruments for the cause of righteousness. The battles that will ensue over the corners of the earth are one in the outcome of the battles you cannot see," the figure declared lastly.

"This servant has heard the messenger's words. May it be as Heaven declared," he acknowledged. The messenger then looked up into the sky intently and slowly stepped back as he proceeded to exit.

"The forces that dominate the skies above you have tried to impede me during my approach and have finally returned," he said lastly. The figure proceeded back up the winding stairs that led to the mountain peak and rounded the corner leading to the other side of the slopes never to be seen again.

After all that had transpired, Famin Jie's meditation in solitude had finally come to an end. Famin Jie sat in silence overcome at what he had just heard. The supernatural encounter was the first he had ever experienced but he found tranquility instead of anxiety. 'The Guardian of Celestial Peak the figure was called'. Thought to have been only a myth, Famin Jie has now confirmed otherwise. Legends tell that there had been only one other instance where he had been encountered… and that was many centuries ago.

At the gate of the Sanctuary before the emergence of sunrise, a veteran walked the front steps leading to the large wooden doors. He was cloaked tightly with a hooded cape and hastily made way towards the Sanctuary's entrance to seek shelter from the cold. When the old woman let him in he removed his hooded cloak.

"Well hello, Master Lo. It has been quite some time," she said in a quivering voice.

"Yes, indeed," he replied with a bow. "It is good to be back in the place where I was reborn."

九

# REVOLUTION IN THE FORBIDDEN CITY

THE SCHOLARS AND ONE HUNDRED Academicians made haste towards the capital on the warship the Phoenix Spirit at a speed unmatched by any other vessel in the Ming Imperial Navy. The open sea was quite a relief from the hustle and bustle of the city and the stale ocean breeze was refreshing in comparison to the dust and grime of the streets. These simple pleasures were most appreciated by Lu Guanying who looked forward to their arrival in Beijing so they may coordinate with their comrades in Hanlin Academy – the institution with which the League was well-connected. The Yellow Sea has always been known as the 'peaceful' ocean but was no longer at peace. The waters near the eastern shores of the Middle Kingdom have become a highway for pirates for many years and have grown even more rampant since a severe restriction on ocean-going navigation had been imposed on sailors many years ago. Hostile ships still managed to slip through the seas unchecked.

This fact did not go unnoticed by the Scholars and the crew of the Phoenix Spirit who came upon a pair of pirate ships far towards the East sailing and rowing south at a quickened pace. They bore the banner of Mizushima the pirate lord who had recently had a duel with Sun Xin that ended in a bare stalemate.

"The pirates sail south downwind. It seems they are assembling…amassing. There is naught but scattered islands in the south of the Yellow Sea," commented Shang Jian as he peered through his spyglass.

"I suspect those islands harbor a pirate bay or two. Should we test the weapons system on the ship to see if Big Bang's claims will hold?" Tian Qiu asked.

"Not today, brother. Our priority is the capital. We cannot afford any delays or distractions at such a crucial time, regardless of our ship's superiority. The pirates will definitely be dealt with later," he replied sternly. As soon as he had finished speaking, puffs of blue flames erupted from the box-shaped pirate ships and explosions rang around the Phoenix Spirit's port and starboard and soaked the deck with foamy sea water.

"They're coming about!" shouted one of the crew.

Big Bang came running out from below deck shouting and challenging the pirates to a fight. "You want to fight, do you!? Come get a taste of my very own arsenal, you savages!" he shouted with crazed laughter and excitement as he pounded his chest.

"We are out range, sir!" cried one of the crew members as he clung to the railings bracing for another impact.

"Get the missiles ready now!" Shang Jian barked. The crew brought forth a set of fierce long-range weapons from iron cases. They were two-stage missiles twice the length of a man's arm and powered by a set of rockets on either side. It was elaborately called Fire Dragon Issuing from the Water, and appropriately so, for the anterior of the missile was carved to liken a face of a roaring dragon which unleashed a barrage of fiery arrows should the rockets burn out before reaching the target. The ordnance can be fired into the air or cruise above the water for up to two li. However, with Big Bang's personal improvements, they were able to reach further distances.

A second volley erupted from one of the ships but the projectiles missed by a small margin, again soaking the deck and the crew.

The missiles were mounted on their platforms and primed to launch when the enemy ships fired a second volley with one of the flaming rounds grazing the rear of the vessel. The ship listed slightly with the impact. One of the Academicians grasped the rotating tiller with all his might and spun it around into a hard right that brought the ship ready for retaliation. The shafts and gears that connected the modified tiller to the rudder groaned with the strain.

"Launch the missiles now!" shouted Big Bang with a war cry. The rockets ignited and launched simultaneously with a boisterous rumbling roar that sent the five missiles racing towards the pirate ships as the crew dove away from the back blast. Two missiles scored direct hits on the nearest vessel and engulfed it in flames instantly. The remaining three destroyed the sails and punctured the hulls of the second ships with fiery explosion. Still, the pirates' oars continued to row even as the flames spread.

The Phoenix Spirit circled around the pirate squadron before it could maneuver for a third volley.

The cannons were primed to fire with the crew and Academicians waiting to ignite the fuses. Shang Jian waited for the Phoenix Spirit and enemy ships to get into position.

"Hold, hold!" he shouted. As soon the enemy ships lined up, "Fire! Fire all!" he cried.

With a series of consecutive 'booms', the cannons fired away and unleashed a thunderous salvo of shells that arced over the water and with remarkable accuracy slammed into the hull of one pirate ship, shredding it and sending planks and splinters in all directions. Clouds of white smoke crawled over the deck.

Through the lens, Shang Jian observed the pirates then crashing into the water with some sinking to the depths under the weight of their own armor. Others clung to wooden planks and debris as their very own ships burned away or disappeared beneath the waves.

Shang Jian retracted his monocular and rubbed his chin in satisfaction and winced at the ringing in his ears.

"Aha! Take that, you arrogant buffoons!" Big Bang scorned at the pirates. His unique maniacal laughter continued as the crew cheered for their seamless victory against overwhelming odds thanks to the heavy armaments he had personally engineered and supplied.

"I am quite impressed with your new designs to these armaments," commented Tian Qiu to Big Bang.

"Of course you're impressed! I live for this stuff! Besides, you saw those pirates can't aim if their lives depended on it!" Big Bang replied enthusiastically. The pirates were no longer a threat and were unable to make chase.

The Phoenix Spirit continued towards their rendezvous near the capital and the closer they approached Beijing, the more anxious the Scholars became. They were about to answer the greatest call of their duties. Soon after their escapade against the pirates, the Phoenix Spirit raised its four large battened masts to sail close-haul in a general northerly direction. The rest of the trip was rather uneventful save for the rare sightings of large sea creatures along the way. Days of continuous sailing led the crew of the Phoenix Spirit near the northern mouth of the Grand Canal – a vast and very long artificial river that ran along half of the Middle Kingdom's east coast and far from the sea as it cut through the thick landscape, meandering between several towns and cities. It first began construction nearly two thousand years ago and underwent a restoration under the administration of the Ming Empire. Not far from the northern entrance of the Grand Canal, the Scholars docked their ship at a private harbor where horses and supplies were provided courtesy of the Hanlin Academy.

There, they were greeted by representatives from Hanlin who would escort them all the way to the capital. The crew of the Phoenix

Spirit stayed with the ship and the core Scholars accompanied by one hundred armed Academicians and a light detachment of soldiers belonging to General He Jin proceeded to ride to Beijing.

Far into the distance stood the mega metropolis that was the capital of the Middle Kingdom. It stood proud and strong behind mighty fortress walls surrounded by imposing guard towers armed with cannons and scores of soldiers. Small communities and townships surrounded the capital and endless waves of people made their way in and out of the city. Security at the gate had become heavy and the presence of troops lined the roads leading to the gates. It was but the Hanlin Academician and the banner of General He Jin that allowed the League of Scholars to enter the city without fret.

"It was wise of us to not have taken the route of the Grand Canal," whispered Shang Jian to the others as he observed the security. "The hassle of all the checkpoints would have led to many unwanted delays."

Beijing was grand, being the capital city after all, and as such featured a very bureaucratic infrastructure. Its streets were endless and the buildings were innumerable, but for all its size and grandeur, it lacked the Southern cultural charms of Guangzhou. The entourage plowed through the thick crowds which parted to make way. Curious onlookers from second story balconies waved hand fans and kerchiefs.

After completing the arduous task of navigating the busy and often dusty city streets, the Scholars arrived at the headquarters of Hanlin Academy where they were promptly received by Chancellor

Wu Chan who was evidently relieved with their arrival.

"It is a great pleasure to receive the League of Martial Scholars, Headmaster Lu," said Wu Chan with a salute. "Your timing is impeccable because I believe our great civilization has just entered a crisis."

"That is why we have emerged from the shadows to liberate our nation from the clutches meddling barbarian foreigners," affirmed Lu Guanying. After the formalities and greetings, the Scholars of both schools assembled to discuss matters concerning the Ming and its relations with the pale foreigners who have been discovered to have called themselves "Terukk". Their presence had already become quite apparent in the capital as they have been seen frequenting government headquarters and paying their ceremonial respects to the authorities. To the dismay of the Scholars, the Terukk have already installed outposts and settlements outside the city walls and at the mouth of the Grand Canal. Though their numbers were quite few, their presence was strongly felt as they carried themselves with arrogance and evident overconfidence. The Terukk have been seen frequenting the gates of the palace conducting business with the palace officials to investigate terms of trade and political relations.

"Though in light of recent events, evidence gathered by those within and outside the inner circle of the Hanlin Scholarship showed that colonization and indirect conquest is what truly lay at the heart of their agenda," Wu Chan expressed.

"Our own investigations conducted recently in Guangzhou have led us to the very same conclusions," said Zhang Sunzan.

"I have personally observed interactions with them. They are deceitful and will outwardly show you esteem and respect, but their hearts are full of ill-intent and if we do not act quickly we will find ourselves in a situation with which escape would be most difficult," said Wu Chan. The Scholars present all nodded in agreement. "The easy access Hanlin Academicians have to the Emperor and the politicians of the court have been of great importance to our initial investigation, brothers," he added. "Despite this privileged access, there is not much I or the Hanlin Academy can say with certainty concerning the loyalties of officials in and out of the palace. However, it has become apparent to me that the Emperor has been left in the dark concerning the true state of affairs within the very empire he rules. His health has been in poor condition of late and I fear that many conspire against him in fear of their corruption being discovered. For if the emperor were to know the truth, many government positions would be left… vacant." The meeting room was silent and anxiety filled the air as Academy Chancellor Wu Chan continued.

"A thorough and secretive investigation must be carried out for the following days to see who is conducting illegal business with the Pale Foreigners granting them unfavorable trading rights and diplomatic privileges." He then also presented to the Scholars a small pile of light yellow dust wrapped in paper. "This mysterious substance was seized some time ago by our very own Wei Qiuyuan, currently imprisoned in a government dungeon. It was found in the quarters and offices of several eunuchs and key ministers who have been gaining more political influence than they should." The mysterious substance was passed around among the Scholars who examined it and sniffed its potent odor.

"By its scent it seems to be some sort of drug, one that can be easily abused," remarked Tian Qiu as he passed it slightly beneath his nose. "Even with a small whiff of its toxic fragrance, I am beginning to feel its seemingly euphoric effects. I am not fond of it," he continued to say as he turned his head away from it in distaste.

"You are correct, comrade," said Wu Chan. "In recent days, several of us at Hanlin have been secretly observing its influence on the users. The substance has very addictive effects, and we can confirm that those who are under its influence do not only crave more, but have become susceptible to the Foreigners' bidding. This alien drug is altogether evil."

"This explains many things, including their access to our land, their ridiculous trading privileges, and apparently their influence upon our politics," commented Lu Guanying.

"Specifically what sort of privileges and favors have they been granted?" asked Shang Jian.

"As you know all foreigners from kingdoms near and far conduct limited trade in the southern ports. All transactions are under a conditional level. In other words, the Ming is doing them a favor simply by allowing them any sort of trade and commerce at all. Sad to say, our ancient foreign policies have always been lopsided where the terms were largely in favor of the Middle Kingdom's dynastic rule and the other party is often belittled and exploited.

Trade with the Middle Kingdom has always been treated as a tremendous privilege granted to nations the capital esteemed. In exchange for this favor, the foreigners would pay a handsome monetary and symbolic tribute to the emperor representing their 'inferiority' before the Middle Kingdom." Wu Chan paused for a moment to catch his breath.

"Go on, Chan" said Zhang Sunzan eager to hear Chan's address.

"When these Terukk arrived in relatively small numbers several weeks ago, they proceeded with the same caution and meekness all foreigners were expected to follow. The authorities were not pleased at all that they have anchored along the northeastern coast which was uncomfortably near the capital. However, curiosity quickly overcame reason and the government was enamored by them and soon they were granted permission to move further inland. They kowtowed before the Forbidden City palace, paid their tribute in gold ingots, and addressed them with the proper rites. As the weeks went by however, our government began to favor them moreover than the other foreigners who hail from south overseas. Those of us in the Hanlin Academy's inner circle have grown suspicious of them compelling us to conduct an investigation concerning their activities."

"Soon enough, we uncovered under-the-table negotiations between several officials within the Six Ministries, and handfuls of eunuchs close to the emperor. It was not long until we have also discovered the true extent of the use of bribery with this drug," said Song Yuan, a fellow Hanlin Scholar. "It has an unprecedented ability to twist the mind. Those who take more than what is prescribed experience episodes of hallucination and unexplainable behavior, not to mention slight changes in their physical appearance. Our spies have witnessed their effects immediately after it has been administered," Wu Chan told them sadly.

"This scandalous behavior runs deep, brothers. We are on the verge of losing our great nation to these inhuman corpse-looking Foreigners because of some drug," said Tian Qiu.

Thus was the topic of discussion amongst the Scholars of Beijing and Guangzhou who have now become increasingly alarmed at the nation's state of affairs. The Hongzhi Emperor, who has proved to be more virtuous than his predecessors, has been thoroughly deceived and kept in the dark concerning the conspiratorial events taking place within his own court. To ensure that the emperor did not pose a threat to the Foreigners' agenda, corrupted eunuchs have been serving him a special 'medicinal' brew that causes increased illness that has rendered him unable to fulfill his duties and most importantly, unable discover the truth of what is taking place. The righteous officials in the palace were unable to make a stand in fear of being discovered by those who have fallen under the wiles of the Pale Foreigners. The line between friend and foe has been severely blurred in the imperial court. In fear of neutralization, the righteous officials backed down and were obliged to tolerate the radical changes taking place within the Ming court.

It was not long until Zhang Sunzan discovered that his friend and trusted investigator Fox had been executed on the spot upon the discovery of his investigation. He was proceeding to embark on a ship to Nanjing via the Grand Canal but was somehow caught and arrested just before he could board the ship. Others who have been discovered to be in opposition of recent happenings have also been imprisoned and tortured for "slander and high treason". Zhang Sunzan, inconsolable over the death of his friend grieved for three days. It appeared that even the very own Censorate, created to prevent corruption and bring justice to the corrupt had already fallen to the Terukk's wiles.

After the Scholars had finished discussing matters, they devised a plan to rescue the emperor from the cunning of the corrupted eunuchs and officials and to start a government take-over that will allow them to by force expel the Terukk from the court and from the country. The first order of business was to gain an audience with the emperor in secret and away from the creeping eyes and ears of the palace walls. It would prove difficult as the emperor's strict palace policies prohibited any official or scholar from seeing him outside the appointed times of the day. Second was to discover those of who were still loyal among the key officials in order to coordinate their assault against the opposition. There were many among the secret police, the Jinyiwei, who have proved more loyal to the eunuchs than the emperor himself. A physical confrontation with them would be inevitable.

Over the course of several days, the Scholars of Hanlin in coordination with the League acted as spies within the bureaucracy and the Six Ministries of government to uncover the real depth of the corruption. The investigation was long and tedious, but was nevertheless executed with careful maneuvering. With diligent documentation of the officials' comings and goings across the city, along with the thorough examination of their documents, books, and papers, the Martial Scholars worked long nights, sleeping little and eating even less.

Such was the intricacy involved in exposing the conspiracy, for the palace itself was city within a city with many watchful eyes and ears, and full of rigid ceremony. Even as Hanlin scholars, it was imperative to move with caution. Nothing would stay hidden for very long. It was called the Forbidden City for it was quite possibly the largest palace in the entire world and was the home the emperor, his family, his attendants, and the working place of all officials. To the Scholars conducting their investigations, much of what they were uncovering was indeed, forbidden. Hanlin continued going about the palace gathering information and separating allies from the enemies.

A special observation was placed upon the outposts of the Terukk who remained mysterious in their comings and goings and their activities amongst the palace and the city. The people of the city have become suspicious of their presence in the capital but have remained quite curious about their business. What was rather most insulting was their freedom to build their structures and occupy space that encroached on the Ming Dynasty's sovereignty over the land. The very authority of the empire and the rights of the people were being defied. Overturning the government and defying the presence of the Terukk would be openly declaring war upon them and so this was the full intention of the Scholars.

After the Scholars and Academicians had taken the names of the traitors and have gathered evidence against them, Lu Guanying and Wu Chan maneuvered to gain an audience with the Emperor Hongzhi at the dead of night way past palace curfew despite his weakening health. They met in the Imperial Garden which sat in seclusion within the walls of the mighty palace and was one of the very few places that was remotely safe to speak in private…given that nobody had spotted them on their way to the garden. The emperor emerged before them, though ill, his chin was held high, his shoulders broad, and eyes as focused and determined as ever. A young man who has lived just a few winters beyond twenty stood before Wu Chan and Lu Guanying as the most powerful ruler in the known world.

"I certainly hope there is a rational reason as to why we are breaking protocol at such an hour so late… and in an evening so dark," he said looking down at them both directly from his erect posture. His commanding presence was further reinforced by his reverberating voice and flawless diction.

"Imperial majesty," they said as they transitioned their bow to a kow-tow, their heads pressed firmly against the ground.

"Get up, get up. We can dispense with the formalities and honorifics. This is an unofficial meeting and I am too pragmatic to care about such vanity," he stated. "Chancellor Wu Chan of Hanlin Academy – I suspect this meeting has nothing to do with your secretarial duties? I hope they do not overwhelm you."

"Your imperial majesty, I must introduce you to a most trusted friend and a staunch supporter of your rule – Lu Guanying a great scholar as much as a warrior and Headmaster of a highly respected school in Guangzhou." He kept his eyes to the ground and his posture slightly bowed toward the emperor.

The emperor redirected his gaze to Lu Guanying. "Outsiders in my palace… were it not for the Chancellor I would have already called for my Capital Guards to cut you down, not that I would have needed help. This had better be worth my time. Go on then. Speak." He commanded.

"We come before you today with grave and alarming news regarding the new pale foreigners with which the court has been treating…"

That night, they revealed to him all that was transpiring in secret within and beyond his own court and named to him all who had betrayed the nation and his trust. Thanks to the aid of Zhang Sunzan's allies Fox, Wei Qiuyuan and Zhou Liang –the two vice-censor-in-chiefs of the Censorate, he was also presented with documents that outlined the deals done with the Terukk and a record of all their transactions serving as proof of the Pale Foreigners' sinister and subtle colonial and expansionist agendas. They told him that a coalition of seven eunuchs and other officials led by a certain Liu Jin was at the core of the corruption that had taken hold in the court and spy agencies.

"Long before the arrival of the Terukk, Liu Jin has had a rather long record of greed and fraud which did not go unnoticed by the Scholars and other key officials. Such a fact was what led us to suspect Liu Jin of illegal dealings with Terukk in the first place. He and his allies were instrumental in the spread of corruption and greed within the court and within the provincial-level governments throughout the eastern coast of the Ming Empire," informed Wu Chan.

"The arrival of the Pale Foreigners has also caused a drastic decline in the Ming's relationship with its tributaries as trade and communications with other nations have been neglected or altogether severed by the palace officials. Tributes have not been received since the Terukk have grown unchecked and unbalanced as they monopolized all trade, commerce, and have meddled in the political affairs of the nations and kingdoms over the mountains, deserts, and sea," added Lu Guanying.

Upon receiving the disturbing news and hearing the truth from the findings of the Scholars, Emperor Hongzhi became outraged and distraught at what had become of his reign. The very eunuchs that served him had plotted against not only his family and throne, but his life by keeping him ill with a mystery concoction that had left him bedridden and delirious.

Emperor Hongzhi's fists shook. His entire body trembled with anger. "How could I have been so blind to confide in those eunuchs without doubt? Never before have I been made such a fool but now, they will feel my wrath!" he declared. "I have suspected the Terukk the moment they presented themselves before the palace gates. There had not been one moment where I found their presence and their ways the slightest bit pleasurable. Because of what I had felt about them, I acted upon my instincts and ordered them to leave and never return. However, not even in my wildest dreams would I have ever thought that events would unfold the way they have. The Terukk will be punished for not leaving our lands and shores as I have commanded on the very first day. Heaven has witnessed that I have only ever held my position with honor and truth. All those who have played a part in all of this must be dealt with immediately!" he shouted.

"Summon all the officials and eunuchs of the court and gather them to the palace square," suggested Lu Guanying and Wu Chan. "You now have the evidence and multiple witnesses. Call out the guilty from amongst the crowd of eunuchs and officials of the Six Ministries and confront them regarding their traitorous actions and punish them however you see fit. I must add, that although your Capital Guards may remain loyal to you, some agents of the Depots as well as the secret police may reveal their true colors. If they choose to be against you, our Academicians will ensure your Majesty's safety and security."

Emperor Hongzhi agreed to the Scholars' advice and the next day summoned all the officials inside the palace and those serving in the city and they stood before him at the Forbidden City's main square. With the careful and diligent aid of the Martial Scholars and Academicians, the emperor forsook the strict rites and schedules of the palace and straightaway made the preparations necessary to make his address. Representatives from the Terukk delegation were present among the officials as well. They stood tall and arrogant and no longer observed palace rites such as kowtowing before the emperor when he stood before them. It appeared that they too sensed something within the palace had changed. The emperor glared at them with malice evidently infuriated by their very arrogant presence. He nonetheless proceeded to address the crowd assembled before him. He began with a simple speech by preaching to them the purpose of government, the values upon which their civilization stood, and the causes of the poor political situation in which the Ming government had now found itself. Finally, he revealed his recent knowledge of the scandals and conspiracies taking place right under his nose –knowledge provided by those who were still loyal to the throne. He called out the accused from amongst the crowd separating the guilty from the innocent according to the League of Scholars' thorough investigation. There were dozens from the Six Ministries and many more from the Eastern and Western Depots and the Jinyiwei officers with whom they coordinate. The drug that the corrupt officials had been abusing had side effects that over time became quite apparent. One was the trembling of the hands and the other was a discoloration of the chest right above where the heart rested.

"You have committed the greatest of crimes against the Ming Dynasty and the entire civilization of the Middle Kingdom! You have willingly sold our land and our sovereignty over to the Foreigners who want nothing more than domination and conquest of what Heaven has granted to us for over four and a half thousand years! You are all fools for failing to realize these foreign devils will grant you nothing; all they have promised you are but lies and deceit. They are all FALSE, just as the effects of the drug with which you have been bribed!" The emperor was infuriated and the tension within the palace square ran extremely high amongst all who were present.

"Most of all, you would attempt to murder me. ME! The one who holds the Mandate of Heaven! This is beyond treason. This is an offense against Heaven itself!"

After the emperor had finished his address, the Terukk delegation present in the square made a hasty exit, seamlessly bypassing the secret police that stood by the gateways and paths. It appears that the guards had already had themselves sold to the Terukk.

The emperor frowned but continued. Upon commanding the guilty to segregate themselves from the rest, Liu Jin and his coalition jumped out from the rest of the guilty.

"You are wrong!" shouted Liu Jin defiantly. "The Terukk will bring unity, peace, and salvation to the world. They have power and wealth beyond our wildest dreams and they have graciously offered them in abundance to those who would are willing to join their campaign against all who refuse to see the truth!"

"You know nothing of truth, you vermin. You and your kind are ignorant, blind and stupid for you have lost all sense of reality. Guards, seize them at once!" the emperor barked, at the Jinyiwei. The guards however, were hesitant to obey and remained at their post. The evil eunuch then rallied the guilty dozens to riot against the throne and summoned the officers of the fallen Jinyiwei to defend them. Their loyalties of the officers it seemed already belonged to the evil eunuch and his followers. In that same moment, the Scholars present at the square summoned the martial Academicians to come to the aid of the emperor's personal guards and to the remaining loyal government officials and eunuchs. Hundreds of Jinyiwei and the hooded Academicians from both schools stood facing each other in the square tensed and ready to battle for the sovereignty of the Ming's governance over the Middle Kingdom. Dozens of the emperor's personal Capital Guards formed up alongside the Academicians.

The battle began with the unexpected entrance of Big Bang who, with a war cry, fired a mortar onto the Jinyiwei. He shouted and cursed at them.

"Take that, you accursed traitors!" he screamed. The first battle of the Ming's first civil war was taking place within the emperor's very own palace. Swords, shields, and polearms clashed as the highly skilled combatants on both sides battled to the death. Lu Guanying and the remaining Martial Scholars joined the fray. Government officials, clerks, and other eunuchs who have not been charged with a crime scrambled in different directions to take cover in the nearby structures and offices.

The battle lasted many minutes without either side gaining a decisive foothold over the other. At last, when the timing was most crucial, Big Bang tossed several powerful explosives into the side of the traitors. Bodies flew in every direction and leaving many others disoriented or paralyzed. Big Bang's attacks consequently turned the tide of the battle in favor of the Scholars. After the Jinyiwei had surrendered or fled, the guilty parties were seized from escape as the Academicians and the loyal Capital Palace Guards secured the victory for the emperor. Liu Jin and his seven accomplices including many scheming officials however, had slipped past their grasp and immediately made their way out of the palace and mounted up in haste to their new masters the Pale Foreigners elsewhere outside the city. The victorious Scholars then imprisoned the survivors and the defeated Jinyiwei into the lowest dungeons then proceeded to secure the entire Forbidden City.

The Scholars and their Academicians were now officially the emperor's new trusted advisors, protectors, and attendants. Those loyal men working within the palace expressed their gratitude and great relief for what had transpired. It was most unfortunate however, that the vast majority of the government's secret police force had seceded to the enemy or had long since disappeared into hiding.

The Terukk were most cunning indeed, being sure to win over the emperor's trusted officers of the Depots and secret police to their devious agenda. No bother. The Martial Scholars and Hanlin Academicians more than sufficed to fill the gap left behind by the Jinyiwei and the traitorous officials. Unlike their traitorous counterparts, the Academicians were highly educated and intelligent in more than just warfare. Each of the initiated would have passed the Imperial Examinations to the highest degree so the emperor was far better off under the protection of the Martial Academicians despite being much fewer.

"Many of us here knew what was happening behind the walls and closed doors of the palace. We did not know whom to trust and where each of us stood. The Foreigners are extremely clever and would have most surely brought death and ruin to us all," the remaining palace officials expressed to the League and the emperor.

"We commend you, brothers, for what you have accomplished for the emperor and the Ming Empire!" The Hongzhi Emperor sat upon his throne still clearly distressed and bereaved. He grieved not only for his administration, but for the utter betrayal he and all the people suffered. He was nonetheless grateful to the Scholars and Academicians for what they had done though he expressed mixed emotions concerning the existence of the League from Guangzhou and the brotherhood they had forged with their Academician warriors.

The Middle Kingdom had just declared war on the Terukk and the Scholars would do all in their power to fight alongside the Emperor to protect the nation. Censors Zhou Liang and Wei Qiuyuan were found in a pit beneath the Jinyiwei headquarters starved, tortured, and near death. They were transported to the palace for recovery and rehabilitation. Chancellor of the Hanlin Academy Wu Chan approached the Emperor and assured him saying,

"As Chancellor of Hanlin, good Emperor, I am able to ensure that the palace and the central government are in the most capable hands and minds. All the key Scholars of both Academies are not only masters of the civil service examinations, but polymaths, men and women of superior skills and intellect most qualified for aiding the emperor in the management of the government and the strategizing of war." The Emperor gazed at him without blinking an eye. "Of Hanlin I know this to be true but then little did I know of the true extent of neither its capability nor the number of the initiated within your inner circles. What is of great bother to my already-anguished mind, however, is the discovery of yet another order – a League of Scholars that has existed beneath my sight and the sight of my fathers' whilst operating freely with a hidden army outside the parameters of the government for many years. The existence of such a secret society that occupies itself with campaigns that belong to the government alone is punishable by death. You as well, Chancellor, are not innocent of this withheld knowledge," said the Emperor seemingly testing the response of Wu Chan.

"Your Excellency, the League at Guangzhou is but an association of professionals, the wealthy, and highly educated. They aim not to defy the authority of your government by working behind it, but rather take action in favor of the empire and its emperor for the preservation of the culture of the Middle Kingdom and the protection of the commoners from outlaws and rebels throughout the provinces. Their services are but great gifts to your very throne and the thrones of those who came before you. They exist in secret only so that their actions would be swift and to be of great effect as they are able to bypass what they would deem are bothersome, time-consuming politics. In fact, I should add that it was through their work that the Wo pirates of Riben have been kept at bay and rebels in the outlying regions have been subdued. Their actions are selfless and rarely do they ever receive reward for their work. They will prove to be more capable and trustworthy than the traitors we had just eradicated. Their services would be invaluable for our campaigns against the Pale Ones," assured Wu Chan.

"Your words will be taken to consideration. Other pressing matters require my attention for the time being. I will deal with the League of Martial Scholars and decide their fate after this is ordeal with the Terukk is over," answered the emperor.

He was compelled to agree with Wu Chan's justifications on behalf of the League of Scholars. He had little choice but to accept their aid. They had, after all, saved his administration from the destructive corruption and betrayal of the powerful eunuchs and their puppet officials. Now, he needed the Scholars to free the Middle Kingdom from the bonds of the deceitful and cunning Terukk. A dozen members of the Scholars from Beijing and Guangzhou took their seats within the ministries and conducted their duties according to court tradition and laws. Wu Chan and Lu Guanying were now the emperor's closest advisors.

****

The evening after the battle within the Forbidden City, Big Bang and a strike team of Martial Academicians with a light detachment of imperial troops led an attack to destroy the Terukk outpost which stood not far outside the walls of the capital. The Terukk leadership had already fled the premises before the team arrived leaving only handfuls of Jinyiwei defectors dressed in Terukk uniforms to defend the compound and encampment. Resistance was minimal and all defectors within the secret police who defended it were eliminated. By dawn, what was left of the Terukk outposts were but rubble, splinters, and ash. The compound had already been emptied of its supplies and materials leaving nothing for the Scholars to investigate. The great conflict of their age had officially begun. Much blood would be spilt and in the mind of Lu Guanying, he aimed to make most of that blood from the Terukk themselves.

The emperor and the Scholars had to act swiftly. The Terukk were just beginning to leave their mark upon the Ming Empire and would no doubt be infuriated at the unexpected turn of events that have reversed the tide against them in the Middle Kingdom. The rise and the defiance of the Scholars were unforeseen and greatly unexpected by the corrupted eunuchs and the Terukk. The true extent of their capabilities had finally been revealed and with one swift act, the pale devils have become unwanted guests. Through the efforts of the new government, every province along the coast would have the alien visitors expelled and destroyed by the command of the Hongzhi Emperor. In the following weeks, an imperial decree then spread across the governments across the provinces and prefectures commanding all righteous magistrates, grand coordinators, governors, and prefects to cease all diplomatic relations and treaties with the Terukk. All Pale Foreigners were to leave at once never to return should they face the full military might of the Ming Empire.

All their structures and settlements were to be dismantled or be destroyed. Thousands once loyal to the Jinyiwei fled to unknown regions of the empire and stayed low among the ranks of the Underworld only to regroup elsewhere, ready to finish what the foreigners had started.

The emperor and the Scholars knew this task would not be so easy and neither would every one of the government officials, guards, and soldiers, across the empire remain loyal to the throne. Their defecting would have unforeseen and inevitable consequences as their knowledge of the empire's strengths and weaknesses were now at the disposal of the Terukk. This did not dismay the capital as the emperor and his new administration were more determined than ever before to rid the foreign scum from their shores and their seas. The attack led by Big Bang and the Academicians were similarly repeated by the provinces on many other Terukk outposts in the major cities and towns along the eastern and southern provinces. The strikes were led by loyal and capable military officers whom the Terukk had not yet had the opportunity to corrupt. So it was with the angered Terukk who did not take kindly to these new actions and changes.

Therefore, they sought to defend their right to stay in the Middle Kingdom based on their self-imposed feelings of superiority over the people in as much the same way a master was to his slave. Many of their ships were anchored in the island of Dayuen and south of the Yellow Sea. Their eunuch puppets rallied many from within and from abroad – a force one hundred thousand strong. Within a fortnight, defected Jinyiwei officers, slaves, and defected Nuzhen and Menggu horse warriors from the fringes of the steppe all assembled under the command the enemy. They established several outposts and one major encampment on the Peninsula of Liaodong. The Terukk regrouped along the northeastern coastlines and in the waters of the Gulf of Beizhili within reach of the most eastern border garrison of the Great Wall in an attempt to stand their ground and perhaps take back the capital. The bulk of the Terukk forces had retreated to island kingdoms south of Dayuen Island leaving their new minions, some so-called "mages", and a few dozen of their commanders to deal with the fighting in the Ming Empire. No longer were the defected Jinyiwei officers clad in the uniforms of the Imperial Police.

All such reports and more were gathered together by the court through the aid of the Martial Scholars, Hanlin, and all the Academicians working in tandem with the bureaucracy.

"They are likely to start with a hasty invasion from the North and the burning of the Forbidden City palace. Their true colors have finally been revealed to all the Ming people who at first looked upon the Terukk with great curiosity and esteem. In the recent weeks and days, several fierce and isolated clashes between government troops and the forces of the initial Terukk occupation have already been reported to have occurred in Guangzhou, Nanjing, and in several townships in the south and in the east during the Terukk oustings. Many of their districts have been left smoldering in ruins or ashes. The expelled Terukk now regroup with their kin who have taken to the seas and along the shores of the Penghu Islands off the coast of the island the natives called Dayuen, in the archipelago kingdoms to the south, and in coastlines of the neighboring sister nation of Joseon in the northeast. They too have begun to resist the Pale Foreigners not long after the Ming's expulsion of them," reported the Scholars to the emperor.

But for how long would they be able to resist?

"These are an unexpected turn of events for the Terukk. All that we have done is simply cause them to prematurely initiate the second stage of their grander plan – and that is war," said Shang Jian. "What they have been unable to accomplish with the use of deceitful diplomacy and politics they shall achieve with force."

****

The sun arced and neared its dip into the horizon when Sun Xin had been sitting in meditation under a small pavilion overlooking his master's estate. His mind still grew clouded and restless. The rains had just about come to a complete stop and through the mist and drizzle, the afternoon sunshine bathed the wealthy village in golden rays as if to signal the end of his time in quiet solitude. Meiling approached him from behind holding a parasol and a tray of hot tea, her dress gently swaying in the breeze. Xin opened his eyes and stood from his stiff seated position and turned to face her.

"It's a pleasure to see you before all other things, Meiling," said Xin as he emerged from meditation with a slight smile in his eyes. She blushed and although she tried to hide it, it pleased Xin to see her still fond of him. They sat together as the smile on Xin's face faded into a solemn reminiscing. "My deeds and accomplishments through all these years have not left me fulfilled or any closer to finding peace. I have absolutely no sense of my destiny, Meiling," confessed Sun Xin humbly. "Though I have done much, my deeds have achieved the very opposite of what I have intended. Where one would expect a decrease in criminality and corruption, I instead find a significant resurgence of darkness as if in retaliation to what I have done." Meiling sat and listened intently as Xin continued to pour his thoughts and inner disturbances. "I am continually haunted by the lives I have taken. They haunt me in my thoughts and in my dreams, as if slaying them was a much greater injustice than their crimes. I do not understand it. It makes no sense. Seven years ago, after a prolonged manhunt I had finally tracked down one of the Ming's largest crime lords. After I had slain his companions, I pursued him across the province and tracked him down to his large estate, which I knew was acquired by ill means. When I had finally landed the killing blow, I saw a woman and a young boy glaring at me in horror at what they had just witnessed," Xin said as his face writhed with the memory. "He held documents in his hand granting him full pardon for his crimes in exchange of the services and charities he offered for the local and imperial governments. I had read through them, smearing the blood blotting out the letter proving that he was transitioning to legitimate and lawful enterprise… for the sake of his family. Right before the eyes of his family I killed a man who sought reform." Xin and Meiling kept silent for several moments as they absorbed the depressing story. "Now that I think about it, he tried to tell me he was a changed man, but I denied him that chance." He closed his eyes and turned away feeling remorse for what he had done. "Now his son has grown much in the past several years and has rallied his father's allies to hunt me. I cannot blame him and I cannot find it in myself to confront the boy. I have spent most of this past year trying to elude them". Meiling summoned the courage to tell Xin what she thought.

"Perhaps it is time that you put your sword to rest from these sorts of contracts. Truth and reality are often times far more complex than we realize and the permanence of our actions produce finality we can never retract. A peaceful life is nothing to be looked down upon," she counseled Xin.

"I am ill at ease knowing my skills are put to no use," he said.

"The skill and strength of a swordsman goes far beyond mere fighting, Xin," she preached.

"In the journey that is life, the sword is but a tool used sparingly and with extreme discretion; it is not a measuring rod for judgment." These words left a mark in Sun Xin's heart and mind as he lightly smiled and nodded to her words.

Meiling had become wise as much as she had grown fair. An honorable and principled young woman was she, far from the playful and mischievous girl she was ten years ago.

"Your reminders have humbled me, 'Ling," whispered Xin. Together under that pavilion they had tea While Xin continued to speak of his travels and adventures throughout the provinces, to the lands across the sea, and the kingdoms beyond the deserts to the west. Upon searching for Master Lo he was told that he had left for some time to attend to certain personal matters of particular importance far away from the village. No one was certain as to where he had gone or matter it was that he had to attend. The estate and the woodshop business were left in the care of Meiling and the workers, so there Sun Xin took up the work alongside them just as he did during the days of his youth. For the first time in a long time, Sun Xin felt at peace and a sense of belonging he had not felt since the day he allied himself with the League of Scholars. He wondered however, what they were doing at that moment.

\*\*\*\*

News of these drastic and world-changing events have finally reached the ears of Sun Xin who had all that time been working and staying in his master's woodshop alongside Lo Meiling, his master's daughter for the past few weeks.

"Have you seen the notice board's announcements in town? It appears my comrades in the League of Martial Scholars have been busy in my absence," Sun Xin said to Meiling. "I feel I have abandoned them as well. It's time I go back to them in the capital to give my support."

Meiling looked down and fell silent at the news. "I will not stop from doing what you feel is your duty, Xin," she muttered worriedly. "It is right that you fulfill your oath to your allies. If you must depart, may it be by the will of Heaven," she told him as her eyes watered with tears.

"I am sorry that I must leave you again, but I promise I will return, Meiling. When all is done, I would lead a new life of peace with you and Master. Tell him that this time I will return regardless of what he thinks," he said assuring her. He gathered his belongings and secured his sword to his hip once again. "I have spent many years putting down those that would do harm to others all over the land and all throughout that time, I have felt my deeds have been insufficient and would never ever suffice. Now that these beasts have come to threaten our very civilization, I am finally presented with a chance to fight where my actions would actually be of an honorable cause. At long last, the results would be meaningful and long-lasting."

"Then go. You always were destined for great things, Xin. This I have always known since the days of our youth." With these words having been said, Meiling mustered the confidence to tenderly embrace him farewell. From atop the hill and under the pavilion, she watched him ride north in haste towards the far, far away capital until he disappeared behind the hills and trees. Her father's home and town was far from the conflict and hidden from the sight of the Pale Ones. This gave Sun Xin a small measure of peace leaving behind Meiling as he made the long, arduous journey north. He was sure to avoid the main roads for there were many from his past that still sought the bounty upon his head. He would cut through to lesser known roads that leaned northwest passing the Wudang Mountains were the mystical priests have lived peacefully in temples and dwellings along the misty peaks. His journey would yet reveal to him something else the Scholars and the Emperor have not foreseen. It would only hasten his pace towards the capital.

# THE PIECES IN MOTION

WHEN THE SCHOLARS HAD FIRST arrived in the Ming Empire's capital, Famin Jie had just concluded his communion in solitude inside the Secret Place. Within the walls of the Sanctuary at the top of the Celestial Peak in Huangshan mountain range, Master Lo too had arrived in the very steps of the monastery.

"The prompting in my heart has led me back into the halls of the Sanctuary. I have many fond memories here for it is where my life in the knowledge of truth first began many years ago," said Master Lo delightedly. "My arrival is even more blessed that I am able to see you again, my dear friends," he said to the Keeper and Famin Jie.

"Disturbed has been my spirit of late and my dreams have become dark during the night. I have returned in search of the answers to the disturbances of my peace, but good to see you it is, friend," said Famin Jie.

"It is indeed truly a delight to see you again, Master Lo, and very timely as well," said the Keeper. "I am also certain that the promptings within your heart are of reasonable cause. Divine orchestration has brought us all here in preparation for what has and is to come. Such is the nature of Heaven, to direct the paths of unlikely individuals to do mighty things," he said with a smile.

"As much as I am overjoyed to see you once again, we must be focused upon the task that has been entrusted to us. In my solitude in the Secret Place I meditated and cried out for the revelation of Heaven's will. My cries… did not go unanswered," said Famin Jie to the group which looked to him eagerly in anticipation of what he was to say. "Believe me when I say that a figure with a powerful presence descended from the top of the mountain. It appeared before me with instructions from Heaven. He said that the time for the restoration of the great Way is nigh, and the orchestration of key events present and future are in place to see it done. The only thing required of us now is obedience… by journeying to Beijing to meet the emperor," said Famin Jie earnestly to everyone listening.

"A mysterious figure descended from the peak of the mountain you say?" said the Keeper. "None inhabit the mountain's peak. But if what you say is true, then that presence, which has not revealed itself for a very long time, is a sign of a great time of testing. Truly our situation has become momentous," he said deeply whilst stroking his silky white beard. The rest merely looked to each other and shrugged.

"Well, I'm not sure how in the world we're going to manage to get to Beijing and meet the emperor, but seeing as I have no place else to go, I will go with you. It'd be a long journey, but Beijing seems like a good destination," remarked Jirgal.

"I see the nobility of this cause and long have I searched for a meaningful undertaking since the day of my banishment. I too, therefore, will accompany you there," pledged Zuo Shilong.

"I have been brought here for good reason and in obedience, I will be with you through this great task with courage and faith," said Master Lo with assurance and encouragement.

"It is done then," remarked the Keeper. "The sages of old have long sought the restoration of the great Way and Heaven is finally fulfilling that same dream we share to this day. Go forth in peace and let not the darkness cause you to stray." To Zuo Shilong, the Keeper presented a long metallic rod of elaborate engravings. The mid-point of the staff was carved with an ancient writing style that could be most closely read as "Never for self-gain, but for the benefit of others". It was heavy but wonderfully balanced and adamantine.

"This once belonged to a great fighter who also found his way here many years ago. Before he passed away, he requested that the staff be gifted to whoever was of worthy character," said the Keeper. "I believe I have seen that worthy character in this young monk. It wields the power to stop a tiger with one swift blow. May it serve you well in the cause of righteousness." Zuo Shilong graciously accepted the gift which the Keeper wrapped in cloth and tied with silk cordage.

"You honor me with this tremendous gift, Keeper. I feel unworthy, but... I shall wield it skillfully and virtuously," said Zuo Shilong. He did not question the decision of the wise Keeper. With these words, the group proceeded out of the Huangshan range through a broad path behind the Sanctuary that led directly North towards the capital. The restoration of the Way over all the Middle Kingdom now rested upon a humble teacher, a meek sword master, a fallen monk, and a wise-cracking nomad descended from the horse masters of the steppe.

The distant howls and cries of the Yeren continued to echo through the valley and the mountains in response to the great disturbances in the delicate balance of the metaphysical realm which they painfully feel within their very own life force.

\*\*\*\*

After hiring a boatman to ferry him across the river, Sun Xin pushed his mount towards the mountains of the Wudang located to the north of Huguang at the border of the province. The thickness of the forest and the steep uneven terrain was cause for the slowing of his pace lest the horse slip and become lame. At the edge of the mountains, a multitude of people scrambled hurriedly through the woods. "You there, stop!" he called out to one of the fleeing townsfolk. "What has happened?"

"Marauders have overtaken the village and burned it to the

ground!" she cried. "We tried looking for soldiers to help us but we couldn't find anyone! Please save us. They're still hunting us down!"

"Everyone, make your way to the Wudang temple. Make haste to the foot of the mountain!" Xin said to the people.

The people listened and redirected their route toward Wudang Mountain to find refuge among the warrior priests and nuns of the temple.

Looking to the east, Sun Xin observed a company of figures clad in black robes and demonic war masks pursuing the villagers with great speed. They wielded sabers, ropes, and pikes of sorts which they used to cut down stragglers. As the people cried and fled in a panic, Sun Xin dismounted swooped in with his sword drawn to meet them head on.

He crossed blades with the first two attackers but it became immediately apparent that they were no ordinary fighters. They were much stronger and faster than those from their counterparts and quickly he found himself becoming unable to compensate. The first attacker was surprisingly resilient and able to withstand several fatal blows before finally succumbing to the attacks. The second stood his own against Xin's techniques with unexpected reflexes and strength. Xin strained to take him down as well. A series of rapid fire kicks and open hand techniques were necessary to keep him at bay and finally defeat him. After the second fighter fell, over one dozen of the other attackers charged with great speed towards Xin.

He grew alarmed and was forced to retreat uphill to lure them away from the townsfolk. His strategy was simple and classic. The fastest of the group would charge ahead of the rest. He would then turn to slay him and then fall back to repeat the process. Despite his reputation for having great speed, Xin had difficulty maintaining his pace ahead of the vicious pack as their snarling and growling became audibly closer and closer. Eleven remained and Xin judged that he should stand his ground against them. They surrounded Xin with weapons at the ready. Some perched on branches directly above poised to strike at any angle. Their breathing was eerily labored. With a loud screech they attacked, but all of a sudden, out from the brush and foliage canopy, several Wudang priests leaped at the occultists, striking them down with their blades using the fluid techniques for which they were renowned.

Xin eased his stance and watched as the Wudang priests bring down the attackers methodically and gracefully. The battle lasted only several moments and one managed to escape into the thickness of the forest. The priests turned to attend to the refugees who have already begun the climb up the mountain to the temples at the peak. One of the priests approached Sun Xin and greeted him fist in hand.

"It has been a long time, Xin" she said, her voice warm and tart. Xin recognized her as one of his old training partners during his brief stay at Wudang. Her name was Yang Mai and had been a close friend to Xin during their younger days. Her beauty had matured since they had last met but her round face retained its smooth and fair complexion.

"It has indeed been some time, good friend," replied Xin as he returned gesture. "I am afraid there is not much time for pleasantries for I am on an errand of great urgency." They turned to examine the bodies of their defeated foes. "There is something very dark at work in our lands and that this in accord with the arrival of our new enemies the Pale Foreigners. It is of no mere coincidence," he said.

"Yes, I too have recently heard much of these mysterious visitors from an alien land. They bring malice and ill-intent. I connect their arrival with the sudden surge of activity among the sects," said Yang. Xin leaned over one of the dead and removed the ghastly mask on the body's face. What he saw was not pleasant in the least. The occultists face had deformed to abnormal proportions that no longer resembled a man. His skin was a pale blue and his pupils were near white. The others also possessed the same mutations. The sight of it startled Yang.

"What foul alchemy could have caused this?" she asked in disgust. On the belts of every occultist hung a small calabash canteen that contained a bitter-smelling black potion.

"I believe this is the source of their new-found abilities and fierce physical appearance," said Xin as he poured the gourd's contents.

"Even its odor is evil. The sects have been experimenting with elixirs and potions of long lost alchemies. I am not surprised," she said. "This sect has been Wudang's rival for many years. They are the antithesis of Wudang. Their wiles rarely succeed, though."

Xin and Yang then proceeded up to the mountain following the refugees and the other priests that escorted them up the precarious and ancient moss-covered stone steps towards the palace of temples at the top. The Wudang monastery was nestled cozily upon of the mountain as it had always been for hundreds of years. It was a very sacred spiritual place for the priests who spent their days venerating many deities whose images stood as the centerpieces for many of the temples throughout the monastery grounds. The mountain was covered with thick forest and was continually shrouded in gray mist and clouds which further added to the mystical aura for which Wudang Mountain was well known. Hours of climbing steep stone steps led to the very top where the Purple Cloud Temple stood majestically at the heart of the complex themed with bright red walls and forest green rooftops surrounded by towering trees and shallow cliffs covered in lush vegetation. At the base of its steps in the small yard and beyond, the refugees hustled together for warmth as the priests distributed what little food and blankets they could provide. Many of the priests were delighted upon Sun Xin's unexpected reappearance.

Together with the elders of the priesthood they gathered around Xin to hear what he had to say. He told them that the attack upon the villages and how the noticeable rise of terror organizations and secret societies across the land was merely the beginning of their woes. He warned them that safe havens like the monastery were under imminent attack from such secret societies that would only likely grow in strength and frequency. He had told them what he knew concerning the arrival of the Terukk and the unfortunate turn of events that has caused their initiation of hostility with the Ming.

"This sudden act of hostility is but a taste of the hardships to come for us and the people. The arrival of the Pale Foreigners has initiated a movement amongst all followers of the dark but I have yet to discover whether the Foreigners are directly responsible for these uprisings," Xin told them. "Of this we can be certain: the forces of the Underworld are rallying against us and we must be ready to take a stand for our own survival." He had also respectfully requested, that though the priests of Wudang were exempt from militaristic services, they would still be called upon to defend their homeland in aid of the Scholars for the Ming's struggle against the Foreigners was now also their very own as well..

After he had given the Wudang priests these warnings and requests he bid them farewell and good fortune for any impending battles they may have against the enemy.

He left the mountain the following morning with great speed some few hundred li up north towards the edge of the province where yet another sect of great warrior monks have established their domain in the mountains of Shaoshi. After days pushing his mount to full gallop for days of expedient travel through the old roads and beaten paths of the provinces, Sun Xin stumbled upon a large clearing in the forest far in the distance. From the elevated beaten path where he had directed his horse, he saw legions of men encamped in valley.

A thousand trees had been cut and thousands more tents had been erected at this large gathering of men dressed in black robes similar to those he had defeated at the foot of the Wudang Mountains. An army of dark occultists and rebels from the secret societies were being united under a common banner and was amassing at the very doorstep of the civilized world. Herds of foul Nian-like beasts gathered in the makeshift stables of their remote encampments. A very tall and imposing figure at the head of the encampment was stirring up this dark army, their thundering shouts and chants echoed across the valley and reverberated through the trees. What they were shouting and chanting was unclear but it became apparent that the words were not of the Middle Kingdom for it possessed a negative power that weighed heavily upon Xin. Large vessels were erected at the rear of the camp and emitted large plumes of steam with a hue of blue. Companies of men made their way through them entering on one side, and exiting out the other. What it was he was observing, Xin could not be certain but the very arrangement looked sinister.

"Who're they?" he asked himself. "Black Dragon School? Eye of the Serpent and Crimson Moon? An alliance of the three?" These questions aggravated the sense of urgency he developed since leaving Wudang Mountain.

He could not observe them for more than a few moments as he was no longer able to tolerate the oppression he felt from their accursed shouting and chanting. Xin discovered he was not alone in his oppression when he heard the painful howls of the Yeren in the distance.

From the west, yet another creature of ancient myth emerged from the woods and gazed upon the black army in the valley. Far into the distance, Sun Xin observed that it had the body of a lion, the face of a dragon, and the long pointed horn of a unicorn. It was perhaps the legendary creature Xiezhi –a beast supposedly possessing supernatural instincts with the sole purpose of dispensing justice and punishment against wrongdoers. It appeared that it was poising itself to take aggressive action whenever it would happen. He sighed and shook his head before massaging his eyes. He looked into the distance once again and saw it gone.

"I need to get it together. I'm starting to see things," he told himself.

Bearing witness to all these things further hastened Sun Xin's steps towards the capital. He reared his horse and galloped north towards the Shaoshi Mountains to seek more urgent aid for this new domestic crisis. The monks there knew of him and were on good terms with him despite how much they disagreed with his methods. Their support would prove to be indispensable to the Scholars for the great battles ahead.

****

After the party of four had left the Sanctuary at Huangshan, Zuo Shilong passed the time by engaging in deep conversation with Famin Jie whom he had been calling "teacher". He wanted to know so much about this "Way" that Famin Jie continually spoke of and what it meant for people and society. It was unlike anything he had ever heard and it greatly intrigued him though he struggled to comprehend it.

"The Way *is*. It is Heaven's revelation to man and the transcendent moral path given to us so that we should live in accordance with it. This is what it means to be in harmony with the Way. It is infinite; it is timeless, eternal. It is from the immaterial and transcendent Way that the cosmos and all of physicality were birthed. It nourishes all things with power, balance, harmony, and fine-tuned perfection. It is inseparable with Heaven for they eternally existed in the beginning. Being the cause of the infinitely complex universe, the Way is the source of all truth, wisdom, and knowledge. It is the only window into knowing the character, nature, and power of the Most High. Those who live in accord with the Way obey the will of Heaven and those who obey Heaven's will are therefore in harmony with the Way. Thus it is the standard of righteousness and the key to the perfect civilization. The Middle Kingdom has thrived for thousands of years because our ancestors obeyed Heaven and because the Way prevailed over all the land. It was sufficient so that even long after it had been lost and forgotten, Heaven's blessings continue to this day… though I am afraid that the Spirit has retreated from us in these times," Famin said sadly. He looked ahead in deep thought as Zuo Shilong continued his queries. His mind struggled to comprehend such questionable beliefs.

"How do we know if we're living in accordance with the Way?" he asked.

"It has been written since time immemorial and preserved through the ages. The Way is this written Word."

"Where is it?" he asked.

"I will reveal it to you when the time is right," Famin Jie answered.

Zuo Shilong continued to listen nonetheless.

"The ultimate expression of the Way is Love. This makes it the greatest of all the ethics! The Old Master said 2,000 years ago: 'I have three treasures in me. The first of these is Love.' Therefore I can say that Love is synonymous with the Way of Heaven."

"How can the Way of Heaven be love? Death, disease, famine, and war abound. If it were indeed 'love', Heaven would not allow such afflictions to fall upon the world? Evil men would be instantly struck down and suffering in any form would be no more," said Shilong passionately.

"Many men have chosen the path of wickedness and that choice is theirs alone. However, the standard of Heaven is perfection in all things, and therefore by that same standard it may seem, no one is worthy. It is by divine mercy that we have not all been 'instantly struck down' already. We are given much time to change our ways to choose righteousness. All people will be judged and those that deserve punishment will be granted it. Both the worst and greatest of men are short of Heaven's standards. Even if one bridge is far longer than the other, it is for naught if it cannot reach the other side. By man's efforts alone, the other side is unreachable. How do we reach the other side? It is by only the Way."

"That is a profound teaching, teacher Jie. But I am still not satisfied. What about the millions of suffering innocents all over the world inflicted with disease, hunger, and death? Why should not

Heaven miraculously catch someone falling from the mountain to save him from death?" asked Zuo Shilong meaningfully.

"Why stop there? Why should not Heaven restrain your foot to keep you from stumbling over a rock or catch your cup to keep the tea from spilling? What you are asking for, friend, is a reality other than humanity. We cannot know why there is so much pain allowed in the world, but we can bear witness to the grand orchestrations of Heaven navigating through the darkness so that we may experience the ultimate victory that comes with choosing love and choosing to walk in righteousness despite the great tribulations we face. In the end, we will realize there are reasons why we are not always rescued from disaster and suffering: so that we may also see the sovereignty of Heaven… and the triumph of truth and light overcoming deceit and darkness," Famin Jie preached.

Zuo Shilong looked ahead with a blank stare while massaging his bald head. He was trying to grasp the profundity of what Famin Jie had shared. Jirgal had been at the rear of the group and was listening intently.

"My head hurts," he said.

"So… how did you discover the Way in your life?" Zuo asked. "Learning the Way is a continuous undertaking that requires eternity. Just like you I had begun asking many questions in my life. Though I was young, I had wealth, land, influence, and a promising career. I did not care for the philosophical or of the spiritual. I was enthralled with what the world had to offer," Famin's face turned gloomy as he collected his memories. "Life for me then was like climbing a mountain where my ultimate goal lay in reaching the peak: wealth, power, and land. When I had finally reached the peak did you know what I found?" he asked Zuo Shilong seriously. "Nothing. I found absolutely nothing."

The rest of the group kept silent except Jirgal. "Well that's quite encouraging," he quipped sarcastically with noticeable discouragement.

"Reaching my ultimate goal only to find nothing was at the top tore me apart. I searched desperately for what it was that was missing in my life. My spirit grew much clouded and my mind was full of noise. In my arrogance I had failed to listen to wiser counsel and in one night, I lost everything I had worked for. I was a broken man. For many months I wandered the wilderness in my grief until I had stumbled upon the Sanctuary. The Keeper took me in as his brother and loved me. It was in the Sanctuary I had found rehabilitation and my journey of discovering the Way first began. First I humbled myself and acknowledged the sovereignty of Heaven. Second I became still and quite so that I could listen and not just hear. Third, through humility and stillness of mind and spirit, I cultivated a passionate and sincere search for the truth. Heaven saw me and answered the longing of my heart. Thus began my journey of discovery of the Way."

"How then can I begin my discovery of the Way?"

"In meditation, surrender yourself completely to Heaven and open your heart to receive Heaven's Way. With a genuine conviction, release yourself from carnal pursuits. Follow the Will of Heaven and love your neighbors impartially," answered Famin Jie plainly.

"Just who exactly are my neighbors?" Zuo asked. Before Famin could produce a response, a large, muscular man sitting limp and bloodied on the back of his horse approached them from the north. Master Lo caught him before he could fall.

"My men... all killed. They killed them all!" he mumbled, barely able to neither speak nor open his eyes. "They ambushed us out of nowhere, those beasts of the night. I can still hear their screams and their blood, but I made it out. I tried to fight but, but, they were everywhere," the large man rambled before he slipped into unconsciousness. On his horse was slung large long-handled saber – the crescent blade that Zuo Shilong immediately recognized. "That is Buff Baby. He is a bandit of the mountain whom the teacher and I encountered prior to our arrival at the Sanctuary," said Zuo Shilong.

When the sun had set, the group set up camp while Famin Jie and Master Lo nursed Buff Baby's wounds by the campfire. The smell of Famin's herbs inside the bandages filled the air as Master Lo treated him with fine acupuncture needles to relieve the pain.

"Earlier you had asked who were your neighbors," said Famin Jie to Zuo Shilong. "The true question is: will you be a neighbor to all people?" Zuo Shilong pondered upon the teacher's words for the rest of the night. He could not reconcile treating the wounds of a man that would have killed them before. By dawn the group had awakened to the moans and groans of Buff Baby who was emerging out of his unconsciousness though was apparently still in pain. He had fully awakened soon after Famin Jie and Master Lo had administered additional treatments. Buff Baby had remained silent throughout breakfast barely blinking an eye or bothering to look at the others around him. It was when they were making preparations to leave that he finally spoke.

"I… uhm… I thank ye masters for coming to my aid. I would've perished on my own," he said in the low tone of his deep voice.

"What happened to you and your merry band?" asked Famin Jie.

"We had been pursued for days through the woods and mountains by attackers dressed in dark robes and masks. We had fought as hard as we could, but alas we were separated. I suspect I am the sole survivor. I took my mount and fled for the next few days before finding you all." He paused for a moment and looked down. "They were not human. Their strength and ferocity was that of a beast," he recalled. After he had finished telling them his story he grabbed his share of food and stuffed his face. The rest of the group looked at each other in concern of his story and whether or not they would suffer a similar end while en route to the capital. Safety was now their priority and avoiding conflict was of utmost importance.

"We can expedite our journey if we head northeast to the Grand Canal towards the city of Hangzhou and cut through Shandong province on a ferry," said Master Lo as he surveyed an old map. "I also know of old unknown roads that would help ensure our safe passage where ambush would be most difficult."

As soon as they had prepared to leave, Buff Baby kowtowed before Master Lo and Famin Jie in deep gratitude for saving his life. While on his knees he pledged his allegiance to them and begged forgiveness from Famin for their earlier hostile encounter. "I pledge my services to you, Masters for saving my life despite my unworthiness and my crimes. From this day forward until my death, I pledge my skills and my blade for your protection and for the battles you will engage," declared Buff Baby before them.

With a gentle smile on his face, Famin picked him up from his feet and reassured him. "The biggest battles a person will face are of the mind and of the spirit, my friend. I have forgiven you on the very same day we made our first encounter. I am overjoyed at your repentance but there is no need for such passionate pledging. However, we would be delighted if you would join us. We have more than enough provisions to make room for one more," said Famin. Buff Baby was overwhelmed with gladness upon receiving the offer and grabbed Famin Jie and Master Lo off their feet in a bone-crushing embrace.

"We do not doubt your great strength that you have recovered so quickly, sir. Put me down now," said Master Lo as respectfully as he could. Buff Baby let them down gently and laughed in embarrassment. Zuo Shilong observed him not sure whether or not the bandit was to be trusted. He'd be sure to keep an eye on him.

"Do not think for a second I will share my rations with you so easily, big guy," joked Jirgal. "No, really, I will not."

Buff Baby released a hearty laugh though he stopped and winced when it aggravated his injuries. So the company of five continued their trek north towards the capital taking the roads and trails that leaned to the east. Despite fancying himself as a "notorious" bandit,

Buff Baby was quite child-like, loud, and a bit talkative as he often bragged about his adventures or exploits in the brief time he was a rogue, if he legitimately ever was one. Zuo Shilong shook his head while Jirgal just rolled his eyes.

"I certainly hope you do not harbor hard feelings over our previous encounter, monk," said Buff Baby. "It is never easy to accept that there is someone who in truth is more skilled in combat than you."

"Oh, is that why after the end of our fight you were the one asleep on the ground and I remained uninjured?" said Zuo Shilong with a smirk.

"Do not think for a moment that your lucky hit proved anything, for luck was all it was, and luck it shall always be for you!" Buff Baby spat.

"Care to test your theory?" Both warriors jumped from their horses ready to brawl when Master Lo jumped in between them and scolded them for acting like children. Jirgal sat in the background laughing apparently entertained and thoroughly amused at the friction between the monk and the bandit.

"The last time some tough guy challenged me to a fight..." he gestured aiming a bow, "I just shot him in the foot." He giggled with satisfaction at the memory. Famin Jie just shook his head at their silly behavior.

"Humility is the key to resolving conflicts with your neighbors before they even start," he told them. Buff Baby and Zuo Shilong remained silent for the rest of the day while Jirgal whistled and hummed, carefree as he usually was.

*****

After nearly a nonstop journey cutting through the province of Huguang, Sun Xin finally made it to the Shaolin monastery at the heart of Shaoshi Mountain. He dismounted and rubbed his stallion's crest.

"Good boy, Cloud," he said as he brushed the mane. The horse breathed deep and heavy but still managed to nibble the treats from Xin's hand.

The entrance upon the red buildings of the monastery had two stone lions on either side, the ferocity of their faces representing the explosive combative arts for which the warrior monks were most renowned. He was greeted by one of the students who immediately recognized him and welcomed him inside the temple grounds. There, in the courtyard, he watched the monks practice their forms in unison, shouting with each defining technique. They were fast, precise, and powerful, masters of many weapons. Their skills were able to impress any warrior of the highest caliber. Just like the Wudang priests who practiced the internal combative arts, Xin had also good relations with the Shaolin sect, masters of the external combative arts. On more than one occasion he had come to their aid in battle and had earned asylum within the monastery. There in the stone Pagoda Forest near the temple, he spoke with the monastery's abbot and Master dressed in yellow and red robes and held a long staff called a Xizhang that featured a large ornament with hanging rings on the top end.

Sun Xin explained all that was happening to the country and what he had witnessed on his way in an effort to convince the Master that the very temple of Shaolin was in grave danger.

"We of the Shaolin Monastery abstain from worldly pursuits and the affairs of men. But it seems we will not be able to avoid this coming threat. We will take up arms for the emperor just when the time is right," they pledged. They and several of the elder monks devised various contingency plans should the worst come to pass.

Xin assured them that the Scholars and the Imperial Army would come to their aid should they come under serious attack and advised them to retreat to the capital should the monastery be overrun by the Underworld amassing in hidden place across the provinces. The warrior monks were not unfamiliar with battles against overwhelming odds. Their one thousand year history had been marked by continual warring with rival sects, bandits, and invaders.

By law they were subject to the emperor and were required to serve militarily if they were called upon during times of crisis. The monks knew that time was imminent and assured Xin that they would be ready to act should anything happen. They proceeded to contact the other schools of the Shaolin sect to coordinate with them and make arrangements for the time of crisis.

"I must ask you, Swordmaster, if upon your travels you encountered a wandering monk from this temple," asked the abbot.

"His name is Zuo Shilong. He is most inquisitive and rather naïve concerning life," said the abbot.

"I'm sorry, I have not. I would have most definitely remembered him," Xin answered.

"If you should find him… tell him to take care and be watchful of the paths he treads." Sun Xin agreed and after he and his horse had eaten and briefly rested, he continued his rugged journey to Beijing ferrying across the Wei River and passing many towns and villages. His heart worried for the innocent people of these places who lived quiet simple lives. Many lay undefended now that the imperial forces were being called elsewhere in light of recent events.

The people were the most vulnerable to threat upon the Middle Kingdom. It was for them that he decided to take his sword to the wilderness in the first place. Remembering this hastened his journey.

# THE EMPEROR'S UNEXPECTED GUEST

WITHIN THE WALLS OF THE Forbidden City, the Hongzhi Emperor and his officials in the Ministry of War as well as the scholars of both academies stood anxiously in anticipation of what was unfolding within the empire. Academician scouts have reported a large encampment of mostly former Jinyiwei and steppe nomads to the northeast on the Liaodong Peninsula near the border of the nation of Joseon. Many of the Foreigners' ships have also just anchored along both the Liaodong and Shandong peninsulas guarding the broad entrance to the Gulf of Beizhili which led directly to the shores not far from Beijing. There were other ships sailing directly from the nations and islands to the south and have arrived in response to their kin's call for aid. Upon receiving the report, the

Hongzhi Emperor immediately issued orders to summon the troops from garrisons across all the neighboring inner provinces with the top commanders, captains, and officers whom the Terukk have not yet had the opportunity to corrupt.

"What is it that the wretched traitors are doing on the Liaodong Peninsula? They are delaying their attack as if in waiting for us to amass our forces," observed the Hongzhi Emperor.

"When a powerful force adopts a foreign new army, it would take the time to indoctrinate them, train them in their art of war, all to become more like them. Even as we speak, the pale devils are providing your once-faithful imperial guards and the northern barbarians with their dark armors and weapons and even going so far as to change their bodies," said Shang Jian, a professor in the art of war. "We have witnessed the physical effects of this drug the traitors have been prescribed. There is a sinister reason for that. In confidence of their victory they fear not that we amass our forces."

"I cannot help but become anxious with our lack of knowledge of the enemy," said an official from the Ministry of War. "We do not know the extent of their military capabilities nor of the technological advantages they possess. We can no longer boast of our advancements. Our superior numbers are all we may have."

"There is an overwhelming possibility that we are alone in this conflict. Our 'lesser' neighbors and allies may have already been fully subjugated under the will of the Terukk and know not the better of it," continued Shang Jian. "Our decisive victories would be at sea for if we regain full control of the waters around the empire, we control the Foreigners' accessibility to our land. Our current standing navy may not suffice against our enemy. In the meantime, it is logical to assume that the bulk of the expelled Terukk forces would regroup and amass in their colonies in the south and in the archipelagos in the warmer seas."

"Then we shall restore the naval might we once possessed under the reign of my ancestor the Yongle Emperor Zhu Di. The might naval shipyards at Nanjing shall be reawakened. I pray Heaven grant us the time to gather our forces," said the emperor.

Word of the emperor's declaration spread quickly through the government's communication network connecting from town to town all the way to Nanjing's shipyards. Along with the emperor's declaration were the blueprints and manuals containing advanced shipbuilding techniques long forgotten since the glory days of the Treasure Fleet. The once great Treasure Fleet would be awakened as the Ming Imperial Armada. Thousands of carpenters, shipwrights, sail wrights, smiths, and laborers from various districts immediately gathered at Nanjing to begin the rapid construction of the Emperor's new navy. The appearance of this new fleet would be largely unexpected by the Foreigners who have mistakenly deemed the Ming Navy as largely unmaintained in size and effectivity. The emperor ordered the current fleet of veteran warships to sail as soon as possible from Nanjing and head directly north towards the Gulf of Beizhili while a smaller fleet would sail from the shipyard near Beijing to meet the few anchored Terukk ships simultaneously, in an attempt to pin them from two sides. Such was the strategy of the emperor –

one that would only work if the Foreigners continue to delay any aggressive action towards the Ming for the next several weeks. Such a premise was highly unlikely. Until then, their surest defense would be on land where Imperial troops would make a stand should the traitorous Jinyiwei initiate an attack or if the Terukk were to storm the shores. Over the next several days troops from various garrisons began setting up camp outside the capital awaiting orders for deployment from the emperor. Smithies and factories from the districts then began the mass manufacturing of new weapons such as swords, spears, cannons, bows, and hand guns. Smoke rose from rooftops all over the mega metropolis.

The Commander of the Imperial Army was the highest ranking officer of the Ming Military who answered only to the emperor himself. Coming from the outlying provinces and frontier areas of the empire, he arrived in Beijing with a force of 16,800 soldiers he had personally trained from garrisons of the inner central and northern districts adjacent to Beijing. His name was He Feishen, the elder brother of General He Jin and he was a highly decorated and accomplished soldier known for his mercilessness in battle, effective leadership, and fighting prowess. He was best known for his astonishing record and despite his age, was at the prime of his life. He conducted himself with precision and was well known for his strictness and harsh disciplinary methods… and he hated the Terukk much more than he did the other foreigners who esteemed themselves equal or superior to the Ming Empire. His majestic armor was worthy of his rank and he wore it proudly as he rode his steed through the gates of the Forbidden City to personally report to the Hongzhi Emperor. Upon questioning the sudden change in security throughout the palace, he had been completely informed of the situation he had largely missed during his campaigns in the West and the training of troops in the outlying provinces. After hearing the news he grew red with anger and swore to destroy the traitors and eradicate the barbarous insolent foreigners, as he had said in his own words. The pieces were set and the time for war was nigh. Imperial Commander Feishen had fully come aboard in the war against the Terukk.

\*\*\*\*

Near the southern tip of the Grand Canal, the group led by Famin Jie and Master Lo arrived at the small bustling port city of Hangzhou in search of a ferry that would take them near the capital posthaste via the Grand Canal. Towards the east near the sea, large structures of foreign architectural styles were being burned and demolished.

"It appears that the Foreigners have attempted to complete the first stage of their colonization of our land," commented Master Lo.

"Their agenda goes far beyond mere colonization for what they seek is in direct opposition and defiance to Heaven," added Famin Jie. They made their way through the narrow streets until they came upon a large tavern that sailors and boat captains of the canal frequented. If they were to find a captain that would be willing to take them up the Grand Canal, it was at a tavern.

"I will go inside to find a boatman for us," said Master Lo.

"You must be careful, sailors are an unrefined and shifty lot," said Buff Baby.

"I have dealt with their kind without incident many times before." Upon entering the tavern, Master Lo found himself audience to a drunken brawl. One young man in particular was effectively fending off several others with his bare hands and fists. Tables, chairs, and furniture were the sorriest victims of the brawl as the beaten men crashed upon them by the unconventional carefree style fighting displayed by the young man. After the fight was over, he stood alone over his defeated opponents rather unscathed as he chuckled with a smug smile on his face. He took a drink from his canteen like nothing had happened. Master Lo approached him with hands relaxed behind his back.

"That was quite an entertaining display of fisticuffs," he commented to the young man.

"What is it, Pops? Do you want a piece of this too?" he said holding up his fists.

"I am not much of a pugilist, I'm afraid. I am looking for a boat driver willing to ferry my companions and me to Beijing. We have ample coin," replied Master Lo with a raised eyebrow evidently unamused.

"Ah, well why didn't you say so?" he said. "I have the fastest boat in the Grand Canal!" He tossed a small bag of coins to the owner of the tavern and walked out with Master Lo. "That ought to cover the damages, mate," he told the tavern keeper. Right outside the tavern, he greeted the group with a hand gesture. "My name is Fang Jiang and I will be ferrying you towards Beijing... I am headed to a town in that direction anyway," he said. He guaranteed he had the fastest boat around and claimed to be well known (or most probably infamous) in almost every town or city along the Grand Canal.

The group struck a deal with him and pledged full payment upon arrival. Jiang was barely in his mid-twenties and was dashing, rugged, and charming. He was the kind of man who did not live by many rules or principles. He did whatever he needed to survive and live for the moment and he loved the life he lived.

"I've heard of this guy before," whispered Buff Baby to Master Lo and Famin Jie. "He's a smuggler, no better than a pirate."

"Smuggler??" said Jiang clearly offended if not annoyed by the comment. "I take offense to that label, you bear man. I am no crook. I do whatever I must to get by. Whatever it is that people pay me to deliver is none of my business. I just deliver and I get paid."

"I hear you there, comrade!" said Jirgal. "Although, I almost blew myself up when I was hired to deliver a shipment of explosive powder to a wealthy noble. Then I started to care about what I delivered." The group laughed as they finally approached Jiang's boat. It looked rather old and had several hastily-applied patches along the length of its hull.

"I mean no offense, sir but you said your boat was fast. This barge does not look fast at all," commented Zuo Shilong scratching his bald head.

"The thing's a piece of junk," commented Jirgal.

"Do not be so hasty to judge for there is more to this barge than meets the eye!" Jiang assured them. He removed the tarp that covered the barge's mid-section revealing two paddle-wheels directly linked to a set of gears and a pair of treadmills propelled by a crew of four. It served to supplement the boat's two battened sails. Jirgal tried his best to hold back his laughter and instead released a loud snort that he quickly covered up with "coughs".

"We have fresh clients, mates! We head to Beijing immediately," said Jiang. The crew departed from Hangzhou and began the three and a half thousand li journey through the length of the Grand Canal passing several ancient towns and cities making only short stops for supplies and for Jiang's personal matters. Buff Baby had remained rather silent throughout the lengthy journey, unable to rest properly, and ever more troubled. Trauma of his recent experiences in the wilderness and the loss of his men had been haunting him and although he had tried to hide it, his countenance all the more revealed his troubled and angry soul.

"The ones who attacked us—they were not men. I witnessed one of them become pierced by three arrows but still managed to kill two more before he fell to the weight of my blade. After I had dispatched two others, more descended from the mountain like a plague of death. I cannot live with the fact that I alone survived while none who were under my command had lived. I feel like I had betrayed them. For all my strength, I could not save them," said Buff Baby to

Famin Jie as he trembled in anger and grief.

"Dark times have descended upon us. Do not feel guilty for the loss of your men. The evil that had taken their lives was not of your doing. It was also not fate that had allowed you to live so that we may find you on the road," he said. "Fret no more, for now you are in the company of friends." Upon passing into the border of the province of Shandong, the company bore witness to the passing of a city in smoldering ruins. Its smoke could be seen from afar. People fled the town from both sides of the shore many crying and injured. As the barge sailed closer, the wreckage of many other boats littered the canal with some still burning as others managed to paddle and row past.

"That is Jining city, or may have been," said Jiang as he observed the rising smoke.

"Turn back! Flee! Devils have come to end the world!" cried the men of the boats and barges that paddled past them. When Jiang's barge entered the waters of Jining, the company beheld many hosts of men in dark robes and strange armors occupying the city's smoldering ruins. They marched about and glanced at Jiang's passing barge silently if not but communicating with whispers carried into the wind. Without warning, a flurry of arrows stormed over and onto the barge some tearing holes into the sails and piercing the deck. Jiang shouted to the crew to turn the crankshafts and run the treadmills to power the water wheels. To the rest, he distributed crossbows. A second volley of fiery arrows rained down upon the barge's deck and into the hull in which Jiang immediately doused with blankets and buckets of water. Other arrows were parried and deflected by Zuo Shilong and his new metallic staff. Jirgal readied his own bow and began to return fire on the black clad archers on the shore. He sneered when his bolt directly hit the chest of one archer but did not fall.

"You like how that tastes? Well, have some more!" he shouted. He aimed but a hair higher and launched a bolt right into the archer's helmeted head. He laughed with satisfaction as the shooter fell into the water.

From beneath deck, Jiang produced an antiquated mortar along with a crate of iron balls. He fired the mortar and decimated the line of archers on the shore. They scattered and repositioned themselves.

On top a broad pavilion, a tall figure stood upright and motionless as it glared at the passing barge. It wore a ghastly mask and a head covering adorned with what looked like large nails. The figure's robes of black and red swayed gently in the breeze as he eerily observed the curious company of men passing by in the water. Famin Jie stood erectly on the barge's bow seemingly unaffected by the fighting going on around him. He glared right back at the dark mysterious figure declaring an opposition and defiance to his presence -which did not go unnoticed by others. Jiang ordered all fire be directed upon the mysterious figure. It became apparent to them however, that none of the arrows, bolts, and mortars was able to land their mark. Every shot went unexplainably wayward, many times missing their target by mere finger lengths. The figure remained standing completely indifferent to the attacks being directed upon him. Even a small ballast stone that Jirgal hurled in frustration landed harmlessly at the foot of the figure.

"Oh, come on, you cheating filth!" he shouted angrily slamming his fist onto the deck. When the barge had finally passed the waters of the ruined city, Jiang stood in bewilderment unable to reconcile what he had just witnessed. Though the crew and company were left virtually unharmed and minimal damage had been inflicted on his vessel, he was in disbelief of not only the fate of the ancient city of Jining, but the dark figure's ability to avoid harm. These disturbances did not go unaired to the rest of the company whom he felt knew more than he about the present situation.

"It's obvious to me that these foreigners who haven't even been here long shan't be willing to be ousted so easily. But what is happening has to be of another source, a different cause!" Jiang exclaimed.

"The destruction of the city and the creature dressed in the dark robes are one in purpose with that of the Pale Foreigners. The rise of the darkness within the Ming Empire and the presence of the invaders along our shores are intrinsically linked." said Famin Jie and Master Lo. "What we have witnessed is merely the beginning of a larger uprising. It was but a taste of what should befall the entire Middle Kingdom."

"What of the tall man we saw standing there? How did he avoid harm without moving? Such a feat is impossible and unheard of even amongst the greatest warriors and masters!" Zuo Shilong exclaimed.

"Whether he was a man, I have doubts. I discern that he is one of the many Foreigners rallying evil in secret across the empire. He is a conjurer of a foreign and powerful magic. It is accursed and altogether a potent evil," said Master Lo, his eyes narrowing in thought. "He is more than flesh and blood that we can destroy. Darkness sustains him."

Jirgal moved about on the deck collecting the arrows that had stuck to the wooden planks. He secured them into his quiver.

Beneath the deck of Jiang's barge Master Lo laid down on the mats restlessly. He had grown worrisome and greatly anxious.

"What is troubling you, brother?" asked Famin Jie.

"Evil is rising across the provinces. I fear for my daughter and all who take refuge in my home. Who shall defend them when the soldiers of darkness would descend upon my home?"

"It is by your obedience to Heaven that you sit in the bowels of this boat and it is also through obedience that you place the safety of your home through faith and trust in Heaven," said Famin assuring him. "You are right. I am wrong to fear."

The final stop of the Grand Canal ended at the district of Tongzhou on the south east edge of the capital. Many days of sailing have finally brought the company to Beijing and Buff Baby's sigh of relief could be heard by everyone as they departed the barge. Fearful of leaving the security inside the city limits, Jiang and his crew of four agreed to keep their barge harbored in Tongzhou's port where a heavy military presence patrolled the streets. Alas, weeks of journeying have brought them to their destination and Famin Jie and Master Lo gave thanks to Heaven in the streets as onlookers scratched their heads. The immensity of the capital lay before them and was as it seemed a sea of streets and large buildings.

"The endless sky can only be seen in glimpses from the streets. It does not feel natural," said Jirgal who was most accustomed to the countryside where the full expanse of land and sky had become most familiar to him. A large and thick gate of solid wood stood between the company and the city proper. It was guarded by lightly armored Academicians and by soldiers loyal to the emperor. Famin Jie's company looked most peculiar and with some effort they bypassed the hassle of being stopped and questioned by blending with the crowds that squeezed through the busy gates.

Within the bowels of the city, the curious company meandered through the busy streets careful to avoid the attention of prefects and soldiers patrolling the blocks. "We are famished. Let us station at one of the inns for food to regain our strength," they said. It was after they have had their fill that Famin Jie alone decided to approach the heavily guarded gates of the Forbidden City palace on his own and would call for them should he be successful in speaking with the emperor. He himself was not sure how he, a lowly man advanced in years would ever gain such access to the emperor. His only concern at this moment was obeying the command that was given to him and trusted the rest would fall in sequence according to Heaven's Will. It had been less than half a day that the gates that opened up to the avenue leading to the palace was finally in view. Famin Jie marched carefully towards the first main gate of the majestic and awe-inspiring palace grounds.

"Never before have I seen such a tremendous display of wealth and power. Oh how great is the favor of Heaven upon the fathers of the Ming," he whispered to himself. As he approached the gate a troop of soldiers led by an Academician stopped him mid-stride.

"Do not approach the palace any more, sire," said the Academician. "Are you lost?"

"I mean no harm, young man. It is very important that I speak with the Emperor for I have a message from Heaven that he must hear during these extraordinary times," Famin Jie replied. The soldiers looked to each other puzzled and laughed.

"You are confused, Uncle," the soldier said without intentions of mockery. "No one but the Scholars and royal officials are to see the emperor. Come we will take you home to your children."

"My mind is clear and what I bring holds the fate of the empire. You must listen!" said Famin. The soldiers just shook their heads. He continued to plead to no avail. They proceeded to escort Famin Jie away from the palace premises. Just as he began to lose hope, the rhythm of hooves pounding the road quickly approached the guards and the rider presented forth to them a badge as proof of his comradery with the League of Scholars.

Sun Xin dismounted from his horse and approached the guards. "The teacher is my friend and ally. I am to meet with the Scholars immediately and he shall accompany me there as well," Sun Xin declared to the guards. They looked to each other and shrugged. With approval from the supervising Martial Academicians, some of whom recognized Sun Xin immediately granted them access and escorted them through the Forbidden City's grand entrance. It opened up to a long, awe-inspiring ceremonial avenue which led directly through the palace's three monumental gates –the largest of which was the majestic Meridian Gate which served as the main entrance to the palace. It was not long until the 'Hall for Venerating Heaven' stood before them and it was there they would find the emperor. The Academician guard greeted Xin as he passed.

"I never would have expected to see you here of all places, teacher. It is truly a pleasant surprise though I have many questions as well," said Xin delighted to see the man who saved his life many weeks ago.

"Neither would I have expected it!" exclaimed Famin Jie. "Oh, how amazingly Heaven orchestrates the events of our lives!"

"Indeed… if that is how you see it, I suppose," Xin replied respectfully. "As I have mentioned before, I am in close comradery with the Scholars that now… *appear* to administrate this court and assist the emperor. I've arrived to fulfill my duties to them… and warn them of the imminent threat that has been encroaching on these lands upon the arrival of the Foreigners."

"Yes, I too know of the darkness you speak of for I have borne witness to it during my journeys from the south. It is vital I can gain an audience with the emperor concerning the matters that occupy the nation. The message I bring can determine the fate of the empire," said Famin Jie.

"I believe you, friend. I shall vouch for you," said Xin. The Forbidden City was a tremendous sight to behold and it captivated the awe of both men who had only heard of the palace's splendor. The structures of vermillion and the rooftops of gold on the monumental halls testified to the power and wealth of the Ming Dynasty.

Shortly after their entrance, Sun Xin was united with Lu Guanying and the rest of the core members of the Martial and Hanlin scholars. He had told them of where he had been, what he had done, and what he had witnessed during his travels and told them of the Underworld amassing secretly in the forest to conspire against the Ming Empire. The news was of the great disturbance to the Scholars had not foreseen such an uprising occurring within their doorstep.

Word was immediately sent to the Hongzhi Emperor who received the news with a great pain. "I have brought with me the hermit teacher from the South who had saved my life not long ago. He has proven himself a true friend and a wise ally," said Sun Xin to the emperor and the Scholars. "He claims to have a message of the greatest importance that must be delivered immediately to the emperor. I am compelled to believe that what he should say would be most valuable."

Famin Jie had been standing in the square outside the Hall for Venerating Heaven where the emperor sat on his golden Dragon Throne. When he had been summoned he kowtowed before the Hongzhi Emperor with great respect and humility. He rose, and while maintaining his bow, prepared to deliver the message of Heaven to the emperor and to all who would listen within the court.

# THE FIRST STRIKE

"A THOUSAND BLESSINGS AND MANY THOUSAND more be poured upon thee, thou who art the reigning Son of Heaven," began Famin Jie along with other honorifics addressed to the young ruler of the Middle Kingdom.

"The loyal subjects of this court have told me you deliver a message of divine importance, one that would determine the fate of my empire and its entire people. Take great care with the words that would roll from your mouth for the time that slips away moment by moment is precious and I have not the pleasure of engaging in meaningless conversation," said the emperor with utmost seriousness. Famin Jie bowed once more and began to speak the message.

"Your Imperial Majesty, what I am to tell you is not of my own thought but was entrusted to me by that which is infinitely higher. A time of great trials has come to the Middle Kingdom; it was perceived by those who came long before me. What has unfolded upon your shores and upon your land is but the beginning of our great sorrows. Should this chain of events be left to continue, it would be the end of the Middle Kingdom and the end of all nations of this world. The time for the return of the Way to govern the hearts of men has come, for as the sages of old once lamented its great loss, from this day forth we shall rejoice in the beginning of the path to its restoration. Our newfound enemies are but a worldly manifestation of a great evil that roars in a realm unseen by the eyes of man. In that unseen realm burns a great battle in spirit. Hear this, O great emperor; Heaven had once favored our mighty nation in the days of old, but woe unto us who have forgotten the infinite expanse of the sovereignty of Shang Di! The people most go back to the ways of old, when Heaven's wisdom guided the Sage Kings and when the great Way nourished the people. For in this alone does our hope lie and it must begin with you, Emperor of the mighty Ming Dynasty. The Middle Kingdom must become right with Heaven."

The Emperor rose from his seat and carefully examined Famin Jie who had kept his head bowed throughout the message's delivery. Emperor Zhu Youcheng looked puzzled and somewhat irritated as he massaged his forehead. He descended from his throne and approached the old hermit. "What are you even saying? By what authority can you make such outlandish claims? You claim that Heaven has sent you this to warn me of what is and what is to come.

Prove it to me or you will be punished for wasting my time," he scolded.

So it was for Famin Jie who was burdened with the revelation of truth to the Hongzhi Emperor. Having no power of his own, he did the only thing he could do. He closed his eyes and under his breath whispered a prayer of petition. He whispered it inaudibly.

"Great and mighty Heaven, open the eyes of the man whom You have ordained to serve," Famin Jie prayed. The dark clouds rolled in the following moments as if brought forth by a mighty rushing wind. Thunder and rain set over the capital and a powerful supernatural vision came to the emperor, and it brought him to his knees as he began to weep. What he saw was of a great mystery to everyone who stood in his court as they watched in shock of the Emperor's dramatic response. The vision shook the emperor to the very core of his being. His face shifted drastically from one expression to another changing swiftly from astonishment and awe to fear and trembling. The final expressions to come across his face however, were peace, assurance, and great relief. What he had seen was beyond what could be written with words, but Famin Jie knew that what the emperor beheld was a majestic revelation of truth granted to his eyes – a divine response to the sincerity of his heart to seek the truth.

It was a supernatural occurrence that Scholars present in the court could not understand. They were rather alarmed at the emperor's unexpected reaction to the hermit's words. Shang Jian looked concernedly at Lu Guanying and was eager to arrest Famin Jie for the disturbance. The Capital Guards turned their heads in unison to the commotion and even lowered the stance of their weapons. They were hesitant to take action without a command from the emperor.

The emperor could not even begin to open his eyes for they have been saturated with the supernatural revelation as it passed over them. Full expression with mere words is vain but although his experience took place within court, he was taken as it were, to the beginning and the end of things, the outcomes of righteousness and evil, and to the infinite expanse of the cosmos and dominions in the planes that could not be seen by human eyes alone.

"I am Zhu Youcheng!" he cried as he tore the golden robes upon his chest, "the emperor who has undeservedly called his reign Hongzhi, the Good Government! I am overwhelmed with such unimaginable awe for I have seen that which man has not the capacity to behold with mortal eyes! I am but a flake of dust in the presence of a mighty mountain. Let me be an instrument for the obedience to the transcendent will of Heaven for there is no greater purpose for man to pursue." He continued to weep utterly humbled by the vision that was granted upon him though he could not completely comprehend it. "The whole empire must know of this truth: Darkness has descended upon the world and Heaven is our only hope for deliverance. The devils that lie in wait for us must be destroyed through our obedience to Heaven."

The Scholars were dumbstruck at the emperor's proclamation and were most curious with had just taken place. They rushed to his side to help him off his feet while he was yet able to see. Shang Jian ordered the guards to arrest Famin Jie.

"Guards, arrest the intruder for acts of sorcery against the emperor!" Shang Jian cried.

"No, release him for he has committed no crime. His coming is not an accident. I have seen the truth of our crisis and now the truth alone. From this point forward, this man shall have a place by my side in the court," declared Emperor Zhu Youcheng.

Though concerns among the Scholars grew, they were satisfied at the moment to know that their emperor was bent on destroying the Terukk once and for all. With Famin Jie however, they have become greatly suspicious.

"I want that Famin guy under strict surveillance. From this point forward I demand a record of all his comings and goings. Assign a Senior Academician to keep eyes on him at all times. Tell him, it's a personal guard," ordered Lu Guanying. Lu Guanying and Wu Chan were greatly distrusting of Famin Jie for they did not understand what he had "done" to the emperor to invoke such a dramatic reaction. They had no choice but to honor the emperor's wishes and were compelled to comply with the developments happening in the court.

Of all the ceremonies an emperor performed, there was none more sacred, profound, elaborate and magnificent than the Border Sacrifice. It first began during the Xia Dynasty where the kings of old presented forth lavish offerings and a sacrificial beast as a display of penance, praise, and petition towards Shang Di whom they later called 'Heaven'. The ceremony was essentially a physical outward representation of what occurred in the hearts of the people. On behalf of all the people, kings and emperors performed this ceremony as to daily redeem the nation before Heaven so that favor and blessing would remain upon them. Just as the Way had been lost, however, so too did the meaning of the Border Sacrifice. For almost one thousand five hundred years, long lines of emperors have conducted the ceremony with improper meaning, largely deviating from the way it had been done in ancient times. It was not until the rise of the great Ming Dynasty, that the Border Sacrifice was returned to its rightful form where the supremacy and exclusivity of Shang Di as the Most High over all beings physical and metaphysical had been reinstated. After the Hongzhi Emperor had been granted his vision he became greatly convicted in his heart and thus commanded the immediate conducting of the ancient ceremony of the Border Sacrifice. He summoned loyal government officials of every level and warriors of the highest ranks to the complex known as the Altar of Heaven in preparation of the grand ceremony. There were those amongst the Scholars such as Lu Guanying and Wu Chan who protested to its arduous undertaking for the enemy was assembling at their doorstep and the forces of the Ming have yet to fully assemble.

"We do not have the luxury for a glamorous day-long procession while the enemy moves to strike us down, your Majesty," said the Scholars to the emperor.

"If there is one thing of greatest importance that we must do to prepare the defense and security of the empire, it would be this. For of all the great ceremonies performed in the Middle Kingdom, there is none more important than the Great Sacrifice," the emperor answered. The Scholars looked upon Famin Jie with a hint of disdain for causing what they had considered was a distraction. Famin Jie nonetheless remained silent in humility.

"The offerings of jewels and silks and the beasts prepared for sacrifice were merely symbols," said Famin Jie to the emperor. "When you proceed with the ceremony, and present the jewels, silks, and beasts, present most especially your heart, for Heaven's desire does not lie in materials but in the hearts of the servants."

And so it was that at the wake of war where enemies grew stronger and drew ever closer to the capital's doorstep, that the emperor began his processions for the Border Sacrifice and it would be the ceremony of ceremonies in all of the Middle Kingdom's history. As in accordance to the Statutes of the Ming Dynasty, he fasted and practiced abstinence for three days, denying the needs of the body to symbolize cleanliness when he approached the altar on the day when the sacrifice was to be performed. When the day had arrived, there was not one person in the capital's streets. All citizens of Beijing were to cease all activity and close themselves inside their homes on that most sacred day. The emperor began the ceremony with his proclamation before the vast spiritual hosts on earth and in the sky alerting them to bear witness to the honoring of the great name of Shang Di who dwelt in sovereignty in the heavens.

"Bear witness spirits of the lights, spirits of both the day and the night, spirits of the skies and earth, ye who have dominion over the mountains, the seas, and the rivers – bear witness for this you must know that I shall lead my people in honoring the name of Almighty Shang Di," he proclaimed. The long procession continued throughout the complex of the Altar of Heaven where many songs of praise were sung with the highest reverence and praise to Heaven and proclaiming the goodness and power of Shang Di. The songs were sung with the court musicians singing,

"By the decree of Almighty Shang Di, heaven, earth, and man were called into existence… You, O Lord are the Ancestor of all things… Di has promised to hear us like a Father to His child… Your love is abundant. How great is Your name…"

When the time came for the offering of the burnt sacrifice a perfect, spotless bull was slain and offered to Shang Di and the emperor made a new proclamation on behalf the officials and civil servants, the warriors, and all the people. In accordance with the Statutes of the Ming Dynasty, the emperor recites:

"Unworthy and insignificant as we are, by Your grace and mercy O Di, You still care for us. Though the people have departed from Your ways and Your mandates, thy blessings have continued to shower over all the lands. How boundless is Your Love, Almighty Heaven, the source and standard for all goodness and righteousness. We come before you now Lord, with our spirits broken and our hearts contrite. We give all our essence to your Spirit so that we may stand against the enemy that converges around us. With my utmost sincerity, though petty as it may be, respectfully beseech you, Heaven, restore us as Your children, and let the Truth and Light renew this land for Your glory!"

The ground shook, more than it had before, and the clouds beneath the heavens stirred in a mighty way and with a loud crack and tear, the clouds parted over the altar. All present beheld, a winged beast, a large raptor likened to a phoenix plunged through the parting clouds and soared over the altar, the shadow of its massive wings passing over the entire procession and onto the armies that stood in wait near the capital.

It seemed, at least to the emperor and Famin Jie that Heaven has heard the emperor's woes and has answered his petitions on behalf of all the people. To them, the "phoenix" signified the dawn of a new age and the people's hope of deliverance from a great enemy.

It was in that moment that the emperor was bestowed with the heavenly favor once gifted to the Sage Kings of old. This phenomenal occurrence was of great shock and mystery to the Scholars, officials, and military personnel present in the ceremony. Those who were not terrified of the supernatural signs were left in great awe or curiosity.

"What on earth was that?" Tian Qiu asked with skepticism.

"A large bird flew overhead. Looked like a phoenix to the rest. Perhaps it was merely an oversized golden eagle that swooped in from the Menggu steppe," Lu Guanying answered him.

"Strange that a golden eagle rarely sighted in these parts would appear here of all times," Zhen Shu stated.

"Rare but not impossible," said Tian Qiu.

"Is no one going to mention how the clouds rolled in with the thunder and rain just as the ceremony began?" said Shang Jian.

"We've not the time to discuss these trivialities. There is far more important work to be done," said Lu Guanying as he proceeded to exit the premises.

In their minds they somehow knew that the things they could not see were as true and existent as the world with which they interact. Now it may seem that the people of the Middle Kingdom would no longer be alone in their conflict with the Pale Foreigners. The Scholars of the League and of the Hanlin Academy, being men of reason, logic, and science, could not seem rationalize what had just taken place in the Altar of Heaven complex. They had attempted to dismiss the event as the work of natural causes occurring coincidentally at the same time as the ceremony. However, they could not deny the profundity and the deep religious symbolism the ceremony held for the Middle Kingdom. They felt that perhaps there was more to the ceremony than met the eye and maybe accomplished a higher purpose they could not yet see that would eventually define the outcome of their woes.

War was brewing on the gulf of Beizhili and on the peninsula. Now, renewed with hope and divine assurance, the emperor would make the first offensive move against the Terukk. After the troops from the neighboring garrisons had assembled at the foot of the capital, the Scholars coordinated with the emperor for a preemptive first strike against the enemy who has established an unlawful occupation of the shores in the Shandong and Liaodong Peninsulas.

Scouts have further reported recent activity concerning enemy movements. The fallen Jinyiwei and foreign tribes allied with them, it may seem, were beginning to assemble their divisions from the east and the south in preparation for an immediate invasion and takeover of the capital city.

"Though they are numerous in number and wear a new armor unlike anything we have seen, there is strangely no visible evidence of artillery or any form of cavalry. They are preparing to march on foot. All highly unlike the Nuzhen and Menggu method of conducting warfare," the imperial scouts said. "There is one other element of concern we must mention. Plumes of ominous blue clouds encircle the encampments of the former Jinyiwei and emulates from unknown mechanisms or vessels from inside their camps. We are not certain what is causing them nor can we guess the purpose of this occurrence." The scouts' reports immediately caught the attention of Sun Xin.

"I have seen the very same clouds of blue dust deep within the forest of Huguang where the dark armies have begun to assemble," Xin said.

"Clearly, the pale devils are planning to use the traitors and the barbarians as grunts to weaken our defenses and exhaust our resources. Or perhaps test us. Evidently, this is but the first stage of their larger strategy," Shang Jian said. "We should utilize superior weapons range against them to minimize the loss to our forces in close combat."

"It is vital that we do not underestimate the Terukk's recruited forces for we know close to nothing of their capabilities and tactics on the battlefield," advised Lu Guanying.

Imperial Commander He Feishen was to lead his army of twenty thousand strong to meet the enemy at the valley under the slopes of Tai Shan. The other officers present at the capital proceeded towards the eastern most border garrison Liaodong along the Great Wall near to the north to repel invaders that may march around the Beizhili Gulf to attempt a siege on the capital. The remaining forces stood guard along the passes and roads leading to Beijing in the neighboring provinces to the south and west. The first fleet of thirty warships of the Imperial Ming Navy from the south had anchored at the tip of the Hai River near the evacuated city of Tianjin at the western edge of the Beizhili Gulf.

Sun Xin together with Big Bang and a team of Academicians were chosen to infiltrate enemy lines for a reconnaissance mission to discover the enemy's activities and current status and to investigate the blue smoke seen to have been rising from their camps. They were to proceed as soon as Imperial Commander Feishen would lead his forces against the Pale Foreigner's newfound army. The garrisons scattered throughout the empire as well have been set on high alert and maneuvered to secure the towns and villages under their jurisdictions. The pieces were set for the Ming forces to go on the offensive. They presented these plans to the emperor and he granted them permission to strike. The Hongzhi Emperor addressed the army that was to depart southeast to meet the incoming enemy troops. He had about him an aura assurance and wisdom not had prior to his experience of revelation and enlightenment. He imparted these words to them.

"We will make these demons know that we are not so easily treaded upon. Though we have been defeated and overtaken by barbarians before, this time Heaven goes before us." Famin Jie personally had a word with Imperial Commander Feishen.

"We will be victorious against our demonic foes as long as we are sure to not claim any glory and honor that rightfully belongs to Heaven. Beseech Heaven and give praise to Shang Di alone and you will find abundant power and grace in your midst!"

He Feishen took Famin Jie's words to heart though he himself did not fully understand.

"Thanks for the advice, but I've seen my fair share of battles. Been on many campaigns as well. This ought to be interesting," the Imperial Commander said. A great eagerness oozed from his countenance. His walked with an imposing presence that commanded respect from all men; especially those who were not even soldiers. The Imperial Commander was not only the highest ranking officer in the army, but was perhaps the Middle Kingdom's most capable leader and warrior since Yue Fei of the Song dynasty. Thousands had perished under his sword and all the soldiers within the Ming army knew it well.

An army of roughly ten thousand of the fallen former Jinyiwei officers, slaves, and steppe 'barbarian's marched northwest towards Beijing from Shandong Peninsula as Imperial Commander He Feishen led an army double the number to meet them. Confident in his superior numbers, he refused to bring heavy artillery that would otherwise slow his advance. He had made an exception for a few cannons that would serve to protect his strategic position upon the battlefield. As his army drew closer to the valley, scores of fleeing refugees made their way to the safety of Feishen's troops. Many empty villages in the path of the fallen guards were burned to the ground. "Unstoppable, tireless, demonic," the refugees called them. Hearing the plight of the villagers greatly angered Feishen and his officers as they quickened their pace towards the field where their imminent battle would take place. In the vast open plains under the shadow and clouds of the colossal Mount Tai, the two armies met face to face with nearly two li of flat land laid between them. The plain geography provided very little tactical options for the soldiers but Commander Feishen was confident in his superior numbers. The enemy, it may seem, had not anticipated the astonishingly expedient assembly of Ming forces around the capital.

They stood before Ming forces completely motionless, silent, and encased in angular metallic armor – mass manufactured and cheaply made. They were it seemed, noticeably larger and heavier than their former selves. Upon the hill, adjacent to the enemy army, stood a tall figure clad in long robes of black and red. The army of the fallen looked to the figure to await their next order. In one swift unified motion, the pawn army of the Terukk readied their spears and assumed the stance for a charge. Imperial Commander Feishen ordered his combined force of 6,720 archers and gunners front to answer the incoming initial assault. With a thunderous roar, the enemy initiated and the battle began with a ground-shaking charge. Little by little, they came within range rapidly approaching the arrow marker on the ground. The instant the enemy crossed the marker, a swarm of 6,720 armor-piercing arrows arched high over the battlefield like a dark cloud. With the sound of a great wind, the arrows rained down mercilessly upon the charging enemy. Few fell to the first salvo while the rest merely regained their momentum and continued to charge though their armors had been riddled with protruding arrow shafts. A second salvo fell like a hailstorm upon the enemy this time accumulating the damage done by the first volley. To the troops' dismay, the arrow volleys achieved little of their desired effect and were not sufficient to hurt their numbers. The archers withdrew behind the spearmen as 2,240 gunners brought their three-barrel hand cannons to bear and fired at the incoming army. With bright flashes and the sound of powerful thunder, the balls of heavy lead launched out from the barrels with great velocity, slamming into the incoming enemy. The second and third hand cannon barrels were ignited in sequence and many hundreds fell to the hailstorm of bullets. Unfazed by the effect of the projectiles, the remaining enemy troops maintained their charge as the gunners withdrew with the rest of the archers to reload their weapons while the Spear and *Sword and Shield* divisions marched front to confront the enemy in hand to hand combat.

Commander Feishen grimaced at the resilience of the enemy to withstand the arrows and bullets. He perched erectly on his mount, surrounded by officers and personal guard while overlooking the battlefield. The ground rumbled and the sound of reverberating armor and pounding boots filled the air. With a loud crash of steel, the enemy juggernaut army slammed into Feishen's forces and engaged in full hand to hand combat. The fighting was ferocious and violent as the fallen soldiers, resembling very little of their former selves, clashed with the Ming troops with beastly ferocity. They were powerful and tireless as the refugees had warned. Shouts, cries, and the sound of steel grinding steel by the tens of thousands echoed across the valley and dissipated over the plains.

"Fire at will, aim through their helmets!" shouted one of the field commanders. Squads of archers and gunners assembled in various formations on the edges of the battlefield firing and shooting in directions wherever the enemy would cluster. The Terukk pawn army nevertheless pushed forward against the tides of Ming soldiers fighting to repel them. Many of the injured or disarmed among the Ming began to retreat. After all ammunitions were exhausted, the archers and the gunners drew their broadswords and were ordered to charge onto the flanks of the enemy formation but the enemy hordes proved their flanks to be nearly impenetrable. The fighting prolonged as the Ming's superior numbers were proving ineffective against the enemy's tireless onslaught. The longer the battle raged the more of his men were being slaughtered. The enemy troops were simply too ferocious and maddeningly violent despite the Ming troops admirable and courageous efforts to forge on. It did not help that the enemy was most resilient to attack and were surprisingly impervious to stabs, slashes, and piercings that should have been lethal. It took the effort of an entire squad of Ming soldiers to effectively cut down one or two. Feishen grew increasingly frustrated at the battle's progression and decided to jump into the chaos himself.

His high ranking officers followed close behind to support the troops. He charged through their thinning front ranks trampling over several of them and severing a few heads with his longsword before getting dismounted. He stood and readied his primary weapon –the spear. Feishen wielded his spear with great skill honed through years of training, battlefield experience, and martial examinations. It was like an oversized steel dagger attached to an extended wooden shaft the height of a tall man. He continuously thrust and stabbed his spear into the charging enemy cutting through their cheap, mass-produced armor. He was sure to aim for the heart, neck, and head to ensure his kills especially after knocking some to the ground with aerial kicks. His men fought with renewed vigor after seeing their Commander pushing back the enemy next to them. He swung his spear left and right slashing, cutting, and impaling all who would run into it. Glancing blows from their crude weapons scraped against his heavy mountain scale armor leaving only dents and jagged scratches. His officers fought nearby effectively cutting down the Terukk's pawns one after another. The strength of the enemy became apparent as one of them lunged itself at Feishen, knocking him off his feet and crashing to the ground. They grappled for a dominant position as Feishen experienced the raw brute strength of his monstrous attacker. The Terukk pawn grabbed his chest plate and threw him to the ground again like an adult could to a child. It charged again at

Feishen, who then swiftly ducked low, grabbed him by the legs, lifted him above his head, and slammed him to a part of the ground riddled with protruding stones. Its armor bent and buckled and the bones underneath it cracked and crunched. It did little to stop the monstrosity from continuing to fight. It quickly rolled back onto its feet and swung a gauntleted fist at Feishen's head. He blocked the blow and countered it with a powerful straight right punch into the opening of its helmet. The enemy soldier staggered with nose crushed and front teeth missing. The mutant was hardly able to stand and was completely disoriented from Feishen's concussive blow. As the soldier finally fell to the ground, Feishen unsheathed his longsword and thrust the blade into the creature's disfigured face. The chaos of the battle continued all around him as he witnessed his men falling to the enemy's tireless onslaught.

Something had to be done to turn the tide of the battle. In the distance, Feishen observed the black-robed figure upon the hill. It now stood arched forward with hands raised towards the armies. Accursed incantations rolled forth from its mouth and a dark life force emulated from its body and it oppressed Feishen. It no doubt also oppressed his troops in the field, weakening them whilst strengthening the mutants. He ordered his three cannons to bear and aimed it at the figure's position. With deafening explosions, the mighty cannons fired onto the hill where the figure stood. Chunks of dirt flew into the air as the bombs landed upon the figure and nearly flattened the hill. When the dust had settled, the figure remained standing completely untouched by the bombardment.

"Impossible!" spat Feishen. He retrieved his spear, mounted, and kicked his horse to full gallop. He was determined to win this battle and he knew slaying that dark figure would do much to grant him that victory. He rapidly charged towards the figure as he could feel the oppression grow stronger the more he closed the distance. With a war cry, he readied his spear and skewered the heavily robed figure right through its chest. As it attempted to stand, Feishen dismounted, drew two-handed his longsword and beheaded it with one downward stroke. The burden of the oppression was immediately lifted as he removed the spear from the headless body and spat. He looked to the ongoing battle and immediately, his men had already begun to push the enemy back to a stalemate, although this time, the former Jinyiwei had lost their previous ferocity and were becoming tired… but so were his men. Something else however, caught the ears of the Imperial Commander.

From the south, a thousand thundering hooves rapidly approached the battle. Dust rose from the incoming force – unexpected reinforcements were making their entrance. A commando cavalry formation of one thousand led by Feishen's younger brother General He Jin decimated the enemy lines. Mounted lancers and archers shot down, impaled, and trampled what remained of the enemy forces.

Some of the commandos dismounted and finished them off close quarters, with blows that guaranteed a kill.

Feishen and several of his commanding officers grouped together to join the assault. None were allowed to retreat and those that had tried were swiftly cut down. The battle lasted for another several minutes as the numerically superior Ming soldiers pushed forward through the pawns finishing off whatever remained of them. The victorious survivors cheered and cried in relief at the unexpected turn of events. The high-ranking military brothers greeted each other with a tight embrace.

"We probably would have suffered greater losses had you not arrived, little brother," said Feishen to Jin.

"I was marching a respectable force to the capital to join you as the emperor had ordered. When I had heard a battle was being fought here, I immediately lead my cavalry to your aid," said Jin. As the soldiers searched for survivors and scavenged the dead, General He Jin removed the helmet of one of the fallen Jinyiwei. Its face was mutated, resembling almost none of his former self. The skin was rough and a pale blue and purple. Its teeth were sharp and his body significantly more muscular than average.

"Sorcery has turned the traitors into brutes," observed Feishen. "Though they retain none of their former martial skill, they fight with unsurpassed ferocity, and massive strength. It's truly a savage transformation."

"This very same sorcery has been inflicted upon the terrorists of the Underworld amassing in the provinces as I've heard. A small contingent of them ambushed me and my men not long after our departure. Their bodies have been morphed the same way," said General Jin. They approached the headless body of the figure that had led the army to the battlefield. Upon unmasking the head, they discovered it to be one of the Pale Foreigners.

"He is likened to a priest," said Feishen. "I had felt him chanting in a foreign tongue with evil so great, it weighed heavily upon my spirit."

"Foul alchemy created these mutant armies. Black magic fuels them," Jin added.

"Heaven has orchestrated our victory today, brother," said Feishen. Jin nodded in agreement although did not expect his brother to make such a statement. Together, they began the long march back to Beijing to report all that had transpired at the battle.

\*\*\*\*

Before Feishen's battle at Tai Shan or Mount Tai began, Sun Xin, Big Bang, and a light company of Academicians ferried in secret over to the northeastern coast of Liaodong Peninsula where a substantially large number of Terukk mutant forces were amassed. They had arrived to investigate the enemy's positions and to learn of their current activities. They set up base camp some distance away from sight and proceeded on horseback to the outer perimeter of the enemy encampment. Big Bang left with a pack full of various devices, supplies and materials for the mission as he was quite vocal about bringing explosives to the mission insisting in his words, "the savages need to be blown up to hell." Stealth and reconnaissance was of utmost importance for the mission and the clanking of Big Bang's gear was a risk Xin did not want to take so he instructed him to wait until a path to their destination had been cleared.

At the outer edge of the encampment not far from the Gulf, watchtowers had been erected ready to sound alarms for any signs of a siege or to eliminate intruders. In the bush, Xin and the Academicians silently took up positions near the guard towers' blind spots with crossbows at the ready. Upon the signal of a faint whistle, Xin and crew eliminated the guards with perfectly-placed head shots – some passing clean through their helmets. The team then proceeded deeper into enemy territory as Big Bang clanked closely behind mumbling to himself. Patrols made loosely knit patrols around the camp and with synchronized maneuvering, were completely eliminated with crossbow bolts and silent takedowns. From a concealed position hugging the face of a grassy hill, Xin beheld a sea of the armies of defected imperial officers and steppe barbarians from various tribes spread out before him, their torches littered the plain like the stars in the night sky. They were vastly numerous, easily 100,000 strong and just like the army he saw in the forests of the South, they too were being led by figures clad in long robes of black and red, fully masked, and dark.

"How could we have allowed them to have amassed in such large numbers?" said one Academician.

"It seems that the machinations of the enemy were a long time in the making. This would not have been possible without masterful planning. The Terukk have outlined their strategy for conquest of the Middle Kingdom a long time ago. What we're seeing now, this army is the result," Xin answered.

The masked and hooded figures addressed the mutant soldiers in a speech that again cast oppression upon Sun Xin. The language was foul and heavy and did much to fire up the troops who roared like animals. It was incomprehensible, riddled with short screeches, groans, and guttural stops.

"Kkenkdit ogekt triklut gatempt lekturr gatempt" The speech was beginning to become unbearable for the spell it was casting began to weigh heavily upon Xin and his allies.

"Let us proceed with the mission and be done with it," they said to Xin. In the distance not far behind the encampment and concealed between the hills and the trees stood heavily guarded structures the shape of towers of many spires had been erected just as he had seen in the forest at the province of Henan, and he saw multitudes of them standing in the presence of the structures slowly becoming enveloped by a fog of misty blue as its gears and cranks began to turn and grind. The fog spread as far as one li and continued no further after which slowly it ascended into the sky. The fumes that were the fog dissipated after many minutes and them that stood within it were revived, strengthened, and changed more grievously than they were before the process began.

Xin and the team waited for the cover of night before they were to proceed with the mission. Together with the Academicians, he drew a map of the enemy encampment and the positions and placements of troops, storehouses, and amassment of weapons. They were to take the war to the enemy by severely crippling them before they could cause damage to the capital.

"Now we see why the savages have delayed their attack upon us. They needed time to prepare turning themselves into these beasts," said Big Bang in one of his rare moments of clarity. He then promptly resumed staring blankly into the distance. After the sun had set and the enemy troops had for the most part vacated the premises of the structures, Sun Xin and the team proceeded to eliminate the guards. It was not an easy task. The "mutants", as they were, had a special resilience against lethal strikes. Anything less than a killing blow to the head or neck did not suffice to kill them. Still, with limited effort Sun Xin made good use of his dagger and crossbow and moved through the darkness like a shadow in the night, as if an assassin on rampage. After he had hidden the bodies, he blazed a trail towards the machines of mutation as Big Bang grew excited in anticipation of finally being able to exercise his role in the mission: demolition. Throughout the night, Xin and the crew assisted Big Bang in the construction of powerful bombs which he had assembled from his oversized back pack and tool belt.

They stealthily proceeded through the exterior of the massive camp attaching the bombs in hidden places against storehouses, depots, and their makeshift harbor, and at one point nearly having been spotted by guard patrols. One guard had nearly alerted the entire encampment were it not for the fact that an Academician loosed an arrow into his head. It was nearly dawn by the time they had finished.

After the slow-burning fuses had been lit, Xin and the team regrouped to the edge of the encampment only to discover a new set of patrols were hastily circling the outer edges of the camp.

"We are about to be discovered," said one Academician. "They have found the bodies."

A blaring horn resounded from the camp alerting all the troops stationed within two li of their position.

"We must leave, and quickly!" commanded Xin. "How much time remains before the bombs blow?"

"Any glorious second now!" said Big Bang. By the time they had reached the horses along the shore, the bombs that were dispersed throughout the camp erupted in quick succession, lighting up the early evening sky. Horns blared for many li throughout the occupied coastlines of the peninsula as the team made a mad dash towards their boat which waited for them at the shore. Big Bang laughed maniacally at hearing the success of his bombs. The enemy had never anticipated such an infiltration and unlikely breach of their security. Sun Xin hoped it would suffice to buy the emperor and the Scholars more time to prepare the Ming military.

Their path however, was blocked by yet another tall figure under the cover of a broad deep red hood that extended to a cape. He stood confidently alone blocking their access to the boat pulled to the shore in the distance. With a gauntleted hand, the mysterious figure unsheathed a long slender blade of dark metallic texture that reflected the moonlight. Sun Xin recognized the figure. It was the Terukk swordsman he had seen entering the government headquarters back at Guangzhou.

The six Academicians unslung their crossbows and fired

simultaneously but every bolt was slashed out of the air in one stroke. Sharp bolt heads and splintered shafts littered the ground as the Terukk swordsman lifted his blade and pointed it at Sun Xin. He was challenging him to a duel. Xin signaled for Big Bang and the Academicians to return directly to the boat and start heading towards the anchored ferry near the shore. The Terukk swordsman removed his hood and cloak to reveal his pale unblemished face and long hair as white as snow. His deep-set eyes shone bright red as it reflected the unusually clear moonlight which cast dark shadows around his high arched cheek bones. Sun Xin loosened the strap on his wide brimmed hat and let it hang behind his upper back. His long blue scarf danced in the breeze together with the tall grass around them.

"You are a cunning one, sword master," the Terukk warrior said with a heavy accent. "I remember your spying on me from the rooftops of one of your great cities… a city which will soon belong to the Terukk along with the rest of your empire. The nations to the South and across the sea already belong to us. It will be just a matter of time before yours will fall as well." Sun Xin remained silent and unsheathed his blade and assumed a low reverse-grip sword stance. The Terukk warrior simply smirked. "Your skills are admirable. I have heard many a great folktale about you but do not mistake me as merely another one of your pathetic opponents. My name is Kurr, and I am here to slay the slayer," the Terukk warrior said arrogantly as he bared his sharpened teeth and spread his arms.

With a blur of motion, Xin initiated the duel with a bursting charge and attacked Kurr with circular strokes and slashes with his reverse grip. The Terukk ducked, leaned, and side-stepped each strike effortlessly. In a swift continuous motion, Xin altered his sword grip and lunged at Kurr with a thrust. Kurr grabbed the blade with his armored hand and yanked it towards himself. He threw a bone crunching uppercut into Xin's abdomen as he stumbled forward. Xin fell to his knees, coughing, hacking, and spitting blood. The pain blared in his body; however, he felt the surge of another powerful force rising into his spirit. The Swordsman's Curse was once again upon him and the fury it brought to Xin was… sinisterly reassuring.

"I can sense darkness within you, sword master . Why would you not welcome it? It might just make our little game more entertaining… for me, at least," Kurr laughed. The sound of it infuriated Sun Xin. Without even looking up, he burst into motion furiously slashing at Kurr from every height and every angle pushing the limits of the speed for which he had grown infamous. Xin's newfound dark strength however, was to no avail. With his every attempt to strike him down, Kurr became more untouchable and impervious, and he continued to laugh in mockery.

"Go on, feed that darkness. It betrays you and will only prove to be in my benefit," Kurr said. He brought his own sword to bear and began to strike back with his black metallic blade. Every parry, every block, and every deflection rocked Xin to the bone; the very force of the swords' impact blurred his vision and numbed his hand. Kurr grabbed Xin's wrist, wrenched it, and twisted his arm causing Xin to flip backwards and collapsing onto the ground. Sun Xin rolled back onto his feet and switched to the offensive. The furious duel had eventually led them to the edge of a steep cliff near the shore.

"I am the incarnation of the very darkness that breathes within your soul. The harder you fight, the stronger I will grow," Kurr proclaimed. He raised his sword for a killing blow.

Unbeknownst to Kurr, Big Bang sneaked behind him with a lit grenade in his hand. He signaled for Xin to create some distance quickly. Xin rolled backwards onto his feet and dove away from Kurr. In the same instant, Big Bang tossed the short-fused grenade right at Kurr's feet. It detonated upon impact sending chunks of shrapnel, dirt, and dust in every direction and with Kurr seemingly falling off the cliff. After the dust and smoke had settled, Sun Xin rose to his feet and peered over the edge searching for Kurr's body, but saw only jagged rocks and foamy water. He turned to give his thanks to Big Bang for the bailout but collapsed at his feet before he had the chance. He drifted in and out of consciousness as the Academicians carried him back to the ferry returning to the capital a few days' journey away. At the shore under the shadow of the cliff Kurr stood watching his opponent sail on the ferry. He smirked with satisfaction as he removed the scorched and torn plates of his armor then made his way back to the camp.

# TURNING WAR GEARS

THE GLARE OF THE AFTERNOON sun beamed through the window in the room of an inn where Xin had been laid since his return from Liaodong Peninsula. He opened his eyes to a room bathed in golden sunlight and to the noise of a bustling nearby street. His body ached and he groaned with the soreness that coursed through his limbs; his abdomen still tender from Kurr's powerful blow.

"If I had not believed in the orchestrations of a higher power , I would say your stubbornness was what has sustained you through the past several hours," said a familiar voice in the room. Xin strained to focus his vision to a figure sitting in a shaded corner of the room.

"Master," said Xin. "What has happened? How is it that you are here?" He struggled to sit upright fighting the heavy weight of sluggishness that had come upon him.

"No, do not force yourself up just yet. Your body's strength was sapped from your battle. Your life force has yet to recover from the exhaustive effects of the Swordsman's Curse," said Master Lo.

"The Curse? I can barely remember. I thought I had tamed that price a long time ago but it has been resurging of late," said Xin as he groaned in discomfort.

"It will always be there deep within the recesses of your soul, for a man you are, and in a man's heart darkness will always linger. You can never fully remove the Curse. But starve it, you certainly must," Master Lo replied. "It is a continual ordeal you will have to undertake for the rest of your life."

"How so, Master? I carry the Curse with a great pain and a high price."

"Only with the Way can you achieve this through the transformation and the renewing of your mind," said Master Lo simply.

"You speak so much like the teacher I had encountered from the far South... and he is here, in the capital. The capital, I must get back to the capital immediately!" exclaimed Xin.

"I know of whom it is you speak for I accompanied him all the way here from the Huangshan. I have received word from him. Your mission in Liaodong has severely crippled the enemy. All that you have discovered there has been reported to the emperor and he moves to strike them down with full force before they can recover from the blow," Master Lo informed him. "Some Scholars from the palace are in the inn's lobby anticipating your presence at the court."

"You are acquainted with the hermit from the south? It is such a coincidence for I had met him not long ago. He had saved my life," said Xin. Master Lo nodded slightly and frowned.

"You did not tell me you were aligned with the League of Martial Scholars. I cannot say I fully approve of this alliance. They make many moral compromises and do not adhere to the teachings of the sages despite the 'good' they claim to enforce. Do not ask me how I know of them but just know that not all of what they do is not in accordance to higher standards."

Sun Xin leaned his head back against the head rest and signed. "The League of Martial Scholars is a noble and honorable band of good men. They may not be perfect in their ways and dealings, but their cause is pure and just according to the standards of the law. That alone will suffice for me, Master," answered Sun Xin. Master Lo just sighed and gestured for him to meet with the Scholars and Academicians waiting on the ground floor. Xin mustered the strength to rise and get dressed. He needed to know the details of what the Scholars and the emperor were planning. Master Lo accompanied Xin in meeting with the Scholars below. Tian Qiu the polymath greeted him with relief and gladness.

"It is a relief to see you on your feet, comrade," he said to Xin. "If I am on my feet I do it with great discomfort. My encounter at Liaodong has left me exhausted. Never mind that. What of the activities in the palace?" Xin asked.

"The Academicians and the demolitions expert have reported

the success of your mission to the emperor. I must say he was quite impressed. He did not believe that you all would have survived, calling 'suicidal'. In any case, the Scholars have received his majesty's approval of a major assault on two fronts through land and sea. The palace anticipates imminent the arrival of troops from several other garrisons. It must be quick; I am doubtful that the Dark Armies amassing in the central provinces will be giving us time for respite after this great battle is over," said Tian Qiu.

Together with Master Lo and the Scholars, Sun Xin reported back to the Forbidden City and received commendations from the emperor.

"Though I am slightly disturbed by your infamous reputation as a vigilante, your selfless actions on behalf of the Ming Empire has made you a hero, and a hero you will be in the eyes of the imperial law," said the emperor. Sun Xin bowed to the emperor and extended his gratitude for the commendation. "The second stage of our strategy is nigh. The garrisons to the west have arrived with many warriors; the industries have delivered many fresh armaments for land and sea, some of which were made with Fung's modifications," the emperor said. "He would be the one whom you all call 'Big Bang', by the way."

There, in the Forbidden City palace complex, the emperor, the Martial Scholars, army officers, Sun Xin, and the company of Famin Jie, who were privileged guests, gathered to discuss the army's decisive strike against the enemy camped on the edges of Liaodong and Shandong Peninsulas. The Art of War and its commentaries have always emphasized knowledge of the enemy. Thus, the information gathered from the covert operation led by Sun Xin was decisive for their strategy. Imperial Commander He Feishen and the master strategist Shang Jian presented the strategy for the battle. A large map of the Northeast Ming Empire was laid out before them and moved the models accordingly.

"Our assault will focus on Liaodong. The armies on foot and horseback will coordinate with the border garrison along the Great Wall and navigate the terrain using old passes that cut around the Nuzhen plain. We may strike the peninsula from the north. Our refurbished navy now harbors at the coast near the evacuated city of Tianjin and is ready to strike from the Gulf of Beizhili. The battleships will initiate the battle and will bombard the enemy encampment with a barrage of missile and cannon fire from a safe distance before proceeding in formation against the enemy vessels blocking the entrance to the gulf. If all goes well, they will converge with the fleet coming from the harbors near Nanjing to attack the Terukk ships from both sides. The improved weapons systems provided by comrade Big Bang will be instrumental in our effectiveness for the assault from the sea. After the initial bombardment, artillery and cavalry units will push the mutants towards the sea. They have made a grave mistake placing their mutant forces in an isolated area. With coordination and a strong will, the battle can be won decisively in a day," said Shang Jian and He Feishen.

"Something does not feel right. It seems all too simple, as if it is a distraction for something greater," Xin thought aloud. "We have shifted so much of our focus on this area of the empire, I'm afraid we are not seeing the darkness rising elsewhere."

"I suspect that this is just a means to study our forces, our methods, and strategies. In this battle we would be revealing much of our capabilities," Lu Guanying said as he rubbed his chin.

"Fear not, Xin. The empire has many capable military commanders scattered throughout the provinces. Many citizens have been placed under special protection and the majority of our vast army moves actively on high alert in the provinces," assured Shang Jian.

"Besides, the 100,000 mutant warriors are a significant threat to the capital at the northern border. They must be neutralized immediately," added General He Jin. "The success of our mission depends heavily on the element of surprise. I doubt the Pale Barbarians have anticipated neither the impressive takeover of the Scholars nor the impressively expedient assembly of our resources and forces, as previously emphasized. They will not anticipate our maneuver on such a massive scale as this."

One of the Academicians entered the room with an urgent report saying that spies have been detected in the capital and have escaped capture.

"They have seen the hidden assembly of our forces and know our imminent attack, but luckily, our tactical teams posted on the rooftops have shot them down," the Academician reported.

"That is good news. However, it does not matter if they discover the plans of our assault. There is nothing they can do to provide an answer for our attack. The army and navy will prepare to depart immediately," said Imperial Commander Feishen. "There is one other important matter I must mention to the rest of you," he added. The congregation gave their full attention in anticipation of what he would say. "The mutant armies are led by figures that are likened to priests. In the heat of my recent battle they recite dark and powerful incantations to as a means to 'bless' their warriors. They must be a priority target lest the Ming forces have great difficulty achieving victory. They are Terukk that wear long black robes with red borders, headdresses of nails, and ominous masks. The Scholars must assemble strike teams to seek out these evil clerical Foreigners and eliminate them if the army is to be victorious."

"A cooperation of my personal commando units together with the skills of the Martial Academicians would suffice to complete this task," said General Jin.

"Sun Xin, are you willing and able to lead this aspect of the mission during the heat of battle? Are you fit to fight again so soon?" they asked.

Xin nodded and was determined to complete the mission. In his heart, he felt that this was his calling, the very thing for which he was born. Buff Baby, Big Bang, Jirgal, and Zuo Shilong volunteered to join the Commandos and Academicians to aid Sun Xin with the operation. Master Lo volunteered to fight alongside his student whom he still saw as his son. He did not say however, that he was joining out of fear for Sun Xin's safety. He wanted to be there to protect him. Such was the fatherly instinct within him.

"I too will accompany you, Commander," said Famin Jie unexpectedly. "We must not forget that this war is but a manifestation of a greater spiritual conflict. I would like to personally oversee this operation to petition Heaven for victory over the spiritual warfare that transpires directly with the one we are about to undertake, for if we proceed without Heaven's blessing, we proceed to defeat."

Commander Feishen agreed to let Famin Jie accompany him as the spiritual leader of his forces. "I beseech you, comrade, to keep your distance from the fighting. If your presence is truly required as you believe, then you must stay away from the enemy's reach."

\*\*\*\*

Though Sun Xin was greatly determined to succeed, his heart grew troubled. The task he would undertake was similar to the one he undertook against the pirate lord Mizushima and the new enemy he had just faced – this "Kurr". His inability to complete that task now clouded his judgment and impacted his confidence. He also grew worrisome over the Swordsman's Curs. It clouded his spirit in the heat of combat. His meditations in solitude no longer sufficed to calm his troubled mind. He sought the counsel of his master. He told him all his woes and troubles and the details of his nightmarish duel with Kurr.

"You and Kurr can be presented as good and evil, you obviously being the good and Kurr being the representation of the latter. The difference between you two is this. You, my student, like all other men, have both the light and the darkness within. The darkness however, most often dwarfs the light; such is the plight of all those who are not in harmony with the Way. The Curse that lives within you is merely that very same darkness residing inside the hearts of all men, nothing more. The catch is that it manifests itself more strongly in your swordsmanship. The more it grows the more you become like Kurr who by nature is pure darkness. Through the Way, light can dwarf the darkness and only then will you be able to stand your ground against Kurr. After all, what is darkness but the mere absence of light? Kurr would not be able to comprehend it." Such were the words of wisdom Master Lo imparted upon his student and adopted son, Sun Xin.

"Show me, Master. Finish my training. I long to overcome the darkness within myself so that I my sword would be not be guided by my fury alone." He kowtowed before him and Master Lo took pity. "I have become lost and my judgment has become clouded by doubt and fear. I no longer confidence in my own discernment. I do not understand what it is that I am missing. I have spent ten long years of life in search of truth and justice but all I have found beneath the sharp edge of my sword was more despair and an endless sea of questions to which I have no answer."

"Come, let us go outside. There is something I must impart unto you," said Master Lo. In one of the Forbidden City's larger gardens Master Lo took Xin for his final lessons in the Way of the Lo

Family's sword art. He began with his introduction of the Way to Sun Xin. "The Way is the cause of all things that exist both physical and spiritual. To have been the originator of the immeasurably complex and balanced reality, it can only be the source of all truth, wisdom, and knowledge. It is Heaven's revelation to us. This is the lesson I wish to impart to you: When a warrior is in the will of Heaven and is in accord with the Way he begins to understand these truths and achieves gifts far more precious than weapons and armor, gold and riches. They are peace, clarity, and effortless action – the Wu Wei of the swordsman. It is by far more effective than sheer force and brute strength fueled by fury with which you have grown accustomed. This is why the sword art of my family rests upon this truth. Without those gifts granted to a swordsman of the Way, victory against the darkness is impossible. Heaven's favor is not upon him. Peace, clarity, and effortless action –are these not the very things that would put your mind and heart to rest, Xin?" Xin pondered deeply upon the words his master had spoken. He did not even know where to begin.

"You said I could achieve this through the transformation of my mind," recalled Xin.

"Indeed. Only Heaven can do that now. If you truly desire to live in accordance to the Way, you must completely humble yourself. Be still and admit your weakness and emptiness outside of the Will of Heaven. Ask with absolute sincerity, and Heaven's favor will be upon you. Do this right, and the light within you will soon dwarf the darkness. Peace, clarity, and effortless action would be your greatest weapons and with the training of the heart, spirit, and body, you can develop them fully. As part of the consequence, you will notice a drastic difference in your swordsmanship, Xin. It would be effortless, free-flowing, and far above your best techniques being that it would emulate the nature of the Way."

It was then that Xin took into full account all that his master had said though yet without full understanding. His heart yearned to know and his genuine desire to follow his master's counsel helped put his mind at ease.

Throughout the eve of the Ming Armies' departure, he meditated in complete solitude in stillness and in quiet. With humility and sincerity within his heart he did plead his case before Heaven. He did not eat and did not drink and he did not sleep. By dawn he felt no exhaustion, no hunger, and no thirst. He cast aside his pride and all his anger and hatred for just one evening so that he could receive but a quick taste of the enlightenment his Master Lo and Famin Jie had already discovered.

"If you are indeed, Heaven, I desire to see the truth. I beseech you to reveal to me the meaning of peace in the imminent battles. Grant me a sign that I cannot deny." When his meditation had come to a close, his countenance emulated a mysterious newfound peace that did not go unnoticed by Famin Jie.

"You are different today, my dear friend. Heaven goes before us, there is little to fear," he said. Xin nodded, the gaze of his steely eyes oozed with newfound determination and focus. He proceeded to join the assembly that accompanied General He Jin and the Scholars. He did realize it yet, but the words Master Lo had imparted to him would forever change how he understood the meaning of battle.

As Sun Xin was meditating in solitude, Famin Jie conversed with Buff Baby under the night sky. Buff Baby was pensive and much quieter than his usual self.

"What is on your mind, friend?" asked Famin Jie. Buff Baby opened up to Famin Jie and shared his story. "I never would have thought I would ever find myself in the Forbidden City. I could not help but think of how my path had just changed drastically in the course of mere days. Before I had resorted to small-time banditry my name was 'Bao' and I was a famous prize fighter and brawler," he said proudly. "I was gifted with incredible strength that had made me both admired and shunned since my youth. I had built my body to the maximum. Of this I was completely proud. Time came when another fighter challenged me in front of my followers. Not only did I lose the fight, I had lost my honor as well. I had lost everything else soon after that. Anger and resentment consumed me and I ran to a different province where I was unknown. After defeating many small-time fighters in other underground tournaments I had gained a small following. It wasn't long before I started stealing from the rich give to the poor whom I saw were oppressed. In the back of my mind I always knew that it would be just a matter of time until misfortune would catch up with me. That's when I had lost all my men, and the lot of you found me barely alive." He tried hard to keep himself from shedding tears. Mourning the loss of his brothers was something he had not yet had the chance to do. "I will avenge their deaths. I swear it."

For all his size and great strength, Bao, now known by his bandit name Buff Baby, was in reality, a kind spirit. Though loud and boastful at times, he was loyal and shone a heart of gold. Famin Jie realized this immediately and did not judge him.

"I can sympathize with your story, Sir Bao, for I too have lost much in life. But the mercy and grace of Heaven has restored much more than what I had lost with things that cannot be measured by earthly standards," said Famin Jie.

"You too can achieve this gift of restoration. I can also assure you that the deaths of your friends were not in vain. What may seem to be a disaster in one day may turn out to be an unexpected blessing in the next."

Upon the arrival of dawn, one hundred thousand soldiers and convoys of supply wagons and artillery carts poured out of the gates of the Great Wall and proceeded to circle around the Gulf of Beizhili to attack the mutant forces of the Terukk from the North. A dozen bands of cavalry forces followed close behind. Not long after the soldiers departed to the north, scores of ships from the Ming Imperial Navy sailed west from the harbor near Tianjin to meet in synchronization with the invading forces at Liaodong Peninsula. A military maneuver of this scale in short time was unprecedented in the history of the Middle Kingdom. Never before has a campaign such as this ever been done. But it was after all, a more desperate time, one where the very survival of the empire hung in the balance and hung most heavily on the commanders —the few chosen to lead the attack on the Terukk priests upon whom the power of the mutant forces depended greatly.

Famin Jie and company rode alongside Sun Xin and General He Jin. They have been outfitted with custom lamellar armor designed by Shen Zhu the armorer of the Scholars. Jirgal was apparently uncomfortable and unaccustomed to armor and he constantly fidgeted.

"I have a terrible itch in my upper back and this blasted armor is keeping me from reaching it for a good scratch," Jirgal complained. Buff Baby let out a hearty laugh and handed him a rough old chopstick which he quickly used as a backscratcher. His eyes came to a near cross as he relieved the horrid itching. Xin has had his eye on Zuo Shilong since their departure and remembered what the abbot of Shaolin Monastery had requested of him. He pulled in close to the monk.

"When I made my way to Beijing from the central provinces I made a brief visit to a certain monastery," said Xin. Zuo Shilong's narrow eyes widened and turned to face Xin.

"The benevolent abbot wishes you well and hopes you are in good health. He has worried about you." Zuo Shilong was not sure how to react but found himself unexpectedly delighted at the news. He too wished for the safety for the monastery and his fellow monks. For a fleeting moment, he actually missed them and the simple life he once lived in safety and seclusion in the temple.

The sea of soldiers navigated across the wilderness with good pace and the sound of their thundering footfalls resounded across the land. They were entering the territory of the Nuzhen nation, a minority peoples that have established a rival nation at the northern edges of the Middle Kingdom throughout different dynasties. They paid tribute to the Ming Empire nonetheless. They have been at odds with their cousins the Menggu warrior horsemen who had occupied the Middle Kingdom for one hundred years. The Nuzhen as well did not take the Terukk into liking and have made efforts to distance themselves and keep them at bay. Commander He Feishen sent teams of envoys ahead of the marching military to notify the Nuzhen chieftains of the passage of the Ming Imperial Army. They had been previously been given notice though due to cultural rivalries have declined to aid the Ming in battle. To the south, the Imperial Navy of thirty war vessels of various specialties and sizes cruised westward, led by the Scholars' warship the Phoenix Spirit and was heavily armed with two dozen cannon and two shielded rocket platforms. At the ship's helm stood Admiral Han Bin –an old ally of the Scholars. Even the Hongzhi Emperor had wished to board but stayed at the palace under the advisement of Lu Guanying and Chancellor Wu Chan.

At ship's stern, Tian Qiu studied Big Bang's update on a hand book of the Ming Empire's latest developments on weapons technology. It was a manual poetically named The Fire Dragon Manual. He couldn't help but marvel at the innovation behind the 'fire and thunder' weapons. They were so simple yet very effective at improving the range, accuracy, and reliability of the Ming Dynasty's trademark weapons. It was also not unusual to Tian Qiu that Big Bang signed his name as "Big Bang" on the book. It was a good day to field test the new weaponry. Towards the north where nearly an eighth of the Ming Empire's forces currently marched, the sun had begun to set once again. They set up camp in a large green field sparsely populated with trees, surrounded by hills and small mountains.

By nightfall scouts report clear passage for another day's march. Commander Feishen could rest with less anxiety as he ordered rotating patrols to keep a lookout on the outer perimeters of the encampment. Sitting around a fire, the company of Famin Jie and Master Lo ate in silence and pondered what the coming days would bring for them. Famin Jie pulled out an antique classical instrument. It was called Guqin —a zither of seven strings commonly associated with artists, poets, and philosophers. He began to pluck and strum the melancholy notes and produced a resonating melody that spoke to the company. "A great responsibility has been entrusted to you, my brothers, but know that Heaven has already prepared the outcome of the battle. Steady your heart to discern the promptings of Heaven and keep your eyes set towards righteousness," he recited. After Famin Jie had finished playing his piece, Xin reached under his garment and produced a bamboo flute and began to play just as he always had during his journeys through the provinces. The message of the music was clear though it had no words. Under the vast expanse of the night sky the flute spoke to all who were near enough to hear it. "From pain, anguish, and hardship we are made strong. Suffering is necessary to find strength."

# RECLAIMING THE PENINSULA

"I DO NOT EVEN KNOW HOW I ended up with you guys. You're all crazy! I should not even be here; I am no warrior. I am a trader! I sit in a wagon all day singing songs and sipping wine!" said Jirgal as he scratched his head. Buff Baby laughed out loud though tried not to offend him.

"Do not worry," said Zuo Shilong. "I will watch out for you."

"You're a descendant of the fierce Menggu horsemen are you not? Where is your conquering barbarian spirit?" said Buff Baby subtly trying to inspire Jirgal's warrior heritage. Jirgal glance at him with a comically resentful look.

"I am not at all like my kinsmen; I am no barbarian and they do not even see me as one of their own. It has been many years since I have experienced the traditional Menggu life in the steppe and I had wrongfully spent all of my father's money in the city until a wagon and two horses were all I had left, until recently anyway. I will just get in your way," Jirgal said. "My saber is rusted, my archery skills are unrefined, and I can barely manage this horse."

"Your instincts will return to you in the heat of battle. Do not doubt yourself, friend. I sense there is more to you than meets the eye... even your own," said Buff Baby encouragingly. "Meeting you all is one of the best things that have happened to me in a very long time. I am truly honored to be with such a unique lot good men." It became obvious that Buff Baby fought the urge to shed a tear in an effort to retain his tough persona but Famin Jie saw right through it and smiled.

"Our union as a fellowship is by no mere accident. There is a grand plan for us and the trials we are to face in the coming days would only serve to make us closer as brothers," said Famin Jie.

"Except him, I think," said Jirgal pointing at Big Bang who sat on a supply wagon full of munitions. "If we get any closer to him an explosion just might blow us all away from each other." There was a second of silence until Buff Baby burst into uncontrollable laughter that could be heard all across the ranks. Big Bang proceeded as if he had heard nothing, apparently still locked away in his own world, looking forward to his next big explosion.

Master Lo leaned over to Famin Jie saying, "You make quite unusual friends, brother. So much rests upon them who seem most unlikely to accomplish much. I cannot help but be amazed at the series of unlikely circumstances that have brought all of us together to end up here at the dawn of one of the greatest battles in history."

"Indeed. It is also in this way that Heaven displays infinite wisdom and sovereignty through the most unlikely of people, even the outcasts," said Famin Jie. "It is in such circumstances that we can observe the supernatural unfold through the unexpected and surprising."

Days of marching have finally brought the army to the far outer edges of the mutant encampment. Scouts returning from their surveillance have reported the presence of guard towers surrounding a large outpost guarded by a light military presence. It was obstructing the main pass that led to the primary enemy installation some several li away. Commander Feishen ordered two dozen of the new cannons to be brought to the front line while General He Jin summoned his cavalry units to stand by the artillery from the rear. The brunt of the army held their position close behind to await orders. From atop a tall rocky hill, Sun Xin observed the movement of the Ming Forces. It was truly a majestic and terrifying sight. Tens of thousands of professional soldiers in armor and thousands more on horseback moved in precise unison, marching in tight-knit square formations spread out across the plain. Their spears were seemingly as numerous as the grass of the fields. From the view of his spyglass he observed the movements of artillery and cavalry units move front over to the top of grassy knolls. Further south into the distance, the forts and towers of the enemy outposts awakened with activity and movement as they desperately assembled to hopelessly defend against the unexpected arrival of Ming Imperial forces.

Field commanders shouted from every direction. Flags were waved and drums were struck. Moments later, the Ming cannons thundered and sent dozens upon dozens of fiery bombs blazing and arching through the air and into the outpost. One guard tower collapsed and the outlying structures were completely destroyed in minutes, obliterated by the bombardment. Fires spread quickly as hundreds of the mutant forces were left in utter disarray running wildly in every direction and unable to properly respond to the chaos. It was hard to think that these very same mutants were once living, breathing people who have dedicated their lives to protecting and serving the emperor in the name of their country. What lies and deceit could have possibly caused almost every member of the elite Imperial Guard to betray the nation and emperor they swore to protect? How many false promises were told that would cause them to give up their very humanity to serve an alien power? To Xin it was incomprehensible. Only the darkness of supernatural evil would have caused such an occurrence. Although the mutants needed to be eradicated, Xin felt regret for their loss.

After the cannons had done their work, General He Jin and his captain swooped in with the mounted commando forces to cut down the survivors still trying to resist the attack. The battle was over in mere minutes. The Ming suffered no casualties. The rest of the Ming forces proceeded to overrun the outpost and begin the attack on the mutant army encamped at the heart of the forested regions of the peninsula. The army passed by ghost villages and townships that had once thrived in the land but now had only charred stone and ash in their place. Skeletons and burnt bodies still lay along some of the streets and the smell of death still pervaded.

"Of all the savages and barbarians in the world, there are none more evil, arrogant, and insolent as the Terukk," commented Commander Feishen angrily. "They will be dealt with a thousand times more severity than what they have granted their victims!" He quickened his pace as the rest of the army hastened their march to keep up.

Sun Xin pulled ahead with great speed to accompany the scouts who raced ahead to survey the terrain leading to the enemy encampment. It was hard to think that it was but a week and a few days ago that he led a mission into the same Terukk encampment to deal a decisive blow against them. He grimaced at the memory of his duel with Kurr. If he is to meet him in battle today, it would be a different outcome. Of that he was sure. He and the scouts dismounted and crawled to higher grounds that overlooked the mutant army. From there, Xin could see much more than he could ever have at ground level and in the cover of night. Countless trees had been cleared and just like what he had seen in the province. Fires of industry burned within the settlement. Many structures with water wheels, cranes, and smithies with plumes of steam rising from their jagged rooftops riddled the landscape. The mutants and their Terukk overlords were hard at work rebuilding what Xin and his team had destroyed several days before. From his spyglass he could still see their handiwork as mutant squads hustled and bustled about clearing debris in an effort to rebuild their structures and machinery. Terukk priests walked about directing orders and managing the mutants' activities. They were completely unaware that a massive army of devastating Ming Imperial forces were about to descend upon them from the north and from the sea a few dozen li south east into the distance. The conditions it seemed were perfect for their victory although Xin and the scouts have yet to spot the arrival of the Ming ships. Alas, scores of red sails soaring sky-high appeared over the horizon. The navy had come just in time. Xin and the scouts made haste towards Feishen's approaching army to notify them of the arrival of the navy. The pieces were set and the time for vengeance was finally come.

"The enemy encampment is within sight, Admiral!" shouted one of the Academicians on the Phoenix Spirit's observatory platform. It was a little more until the first line of ships was ready to turn about and bring the cannons to bear. Meanwhile on land, Imperial Commander Feishen and General Jin led their forces through the broad pass and on to high ground that sloped directly onto the mutant army. Just like they had done to the outpost some distance back, the artillery was brought to the front and angled towards the crowds of unsuspecting mutant army. Cannons however, were not the only artillery present in the field. There was another weapon Commander Feishen was particularly eager to implement in the field – the batteries of rocket-propelled arrows. A set of signal flags and the pounding of large war drums signaled the battle's commencement and the Ming Army's advance. Two dozen cannons nestled at the top of the elevated field fired away onto the large crowds of mutants that had assembled in the forest clearing. Another dozen cannons fired from the other side of the field, their thunderclaps rolled over the forest as the bombs decimated through their nearest ranks and formations. Confusion overtook the mutant army as they desperately tried to regain order and discover the origin of their attacks. Those that were battle-ready were stationed to the rear of the encampment and made haste to meet the surprise assault as their commanders shouted orders with warbled and distorted voices. They braved the raining bombards and brought their forces into a defensive formation. The sound raised alarms filled the air as horns blared all across the landscape. The cannons continued to fire their volleys at the enemy ranks even as they assembled to repel the assault. The mutants did not appear to have artillery present on the field. Superior firepower would greatly be in favor the Ming forces.

    The cannon bombs arced high over the field continuing to pour their devastation. Commander Feishen was sure to apply his artillery to its fullest potential considering how he had witnessed the ferocity, beastly strength, and tirelessness of the mutant forces in the battle under Mt. Tai. They did not feel pain and boasted a high capacity for bodily damage and he had kept it in mind since that day. Many of the infantry units present in the field however, were not raw recruits. He had trained them and fought alongside these battalions for years and has been with him through many campaigns. They were strong physically and mentally, very disciplined, and skilled in fighting, but today of all days, their strengths and experiences would be put to the test. He had personally known some of them over the years and it pained him greatly to know that not all of his men would be going home. Nevertheless, they were ready for that outcome and knew of these risks when they had joined his command. Feishen made an effort to emulate an aura of confidence and assuredness among his troops so they would not easily lose heart when the odds would be stacked against them.

The enemy's first battalions moved up towards the Ming troops and away from the cannon bombardments. Feishen's flags waved their signal and the drums began to pound their mighty beat. Archers, gunners, and shield units moved up to meet the mutants. The two juggernaut armies maneuvered like two large colonies of ants about to settle their rivalries. It was quite a sight to behold.

Out on the gulf of Beizhili, several warships from the Ming Imperial Navy brought about their new cannons towards the enemy position, angled for maximum range. They aligned themselves parallel to the shore and opened fire as soon as they came within range. Flashes of light spouted flames from the ship cannons and dozens of consecutive thunderous booms resounded from the ships. Plumes of white smoke engulfed their decks. The cannon shells and bombs arced over the sea and plummeted further inland. They crashed onto the enemy forces with great effect, decimating their ranks, causing chaos, and sending mounds of dirt flying into the air.

Bodies and debris flew in every direction as fires spread like flood waters while explosions ensued. The Phoenix Spirit continuously fired the six long-range cannons from its starboard and the bombs came crashing into the heart of the enemy's formations. Out from the shore, a series of loud whistles resonated through the air. Explosions detonated all around the ship, soaking the hull and deck, and rocked it back and forth. The enemy was returning fire with primitive mortar shells. It should have been impossible from their range and with such power.

Tian Qiu spotted the puffs of blue flame bursting from the far side of shore. "Aim all cannons onto the mortar platforms!" he shouted. The crew of the Phoenix Spirit swiveled the cannons slightly to the left, reloaded, and fired precisely at the median of vertical and horizontal–the optimal angle for achieving maximum weapons range. The cannon shells hit their mark and the explosive rounds swiftly devastated the mortar position. With the sound of drums and the signaling of flags, the ships spun around in unison and ignited port cannons which continued to dispense devastation into the mutant camps. Though the improved cannons were largely effective, they did not suffice to decrease the enemy numbers fast enough. Yet another devastating weapons system was brought to the deck. Batteries of dozens of powerful rockets were primed to fire. The fuse was ignited and with the sound of a mighty typhoon, the rockets fired away with great velocity and raced high over the sky leaving long trails of smoke. Hundreds upon hundreds of rockets rained down upon the mutants with twice the velocity and killing power of bow-drawn arrows. Fires raged and continued to spread while the trees that had not been felled were utterly splintered by remnant cannon fire.

Commander Feishen brought his own array of rocket-propelled arrows stationed right behind the cannons.

"Bring out the Nest of Bees! Move! Move!" he spat.

In one command, the soldiers ignited the fuse and launched them with great speed. Hundreds more of the hissing arrows descended upon the enemy, administering armor-piercing death.

The tall, black-robed Terukk priests emerged from the chaos and in unison raised their hands to chant the oppressive incantations. With them emerged heavily armored squads of mutants that surrounded the priests with a wall of shields and polearms. After the fires had been extinguished, the mutants as if with a hive mind quickly reformed their ranks, reestablishing their battle formations in the large clearing outside the tree line where General He Jin's mounted commandos were stationed in the shade. Beyond the clearing, over the fields, the Ming Infantry and their officers stood eagerly awaiting Feishen's signal. Archers, gunners, spears, swords and shields, captains, garrison commanders, and lieutenants were about to engage in the battle of their lives.

The war drums pounded their vigorous war beats, signaling the Ming forces to assume their battle formations. Archers, crossbow units, and gunners took positions from various angles from the tree lines and clearings. They initiated with salvos of arrows, bolts, and bullets that pierced through armor and tore through flesh. The mutants retaliated with showers of fragmentation bombs fired from mortars. Harpoon-pointed projectiles launched from spring-loaded mechanisms and flew in a graceful arc over their heads landing directly above the Ming. Dozens upon dozens from both armies fell with each volley as the bombards from the Ming warships continued to obliterate the enemy positions.

The impacts shook the ground leaving behind scorched craters and fiery splinters of wood and chunks of stone. Ming shield units moved front to cover the ranged infantry from incoming enemy fire. Several battalions of lethal spearmen charged ahead of the ranged units as arrows continued to fly over and in-between their helmeted heads. Spears pierced through the enemy formations impaling, stabbing, and swiping through armor and flesh.

The mutants answered with heavy polearms that cut clean through Ming scale and lamellar armor like paper. Many were swept off their feet and crushed while others fell to their knees and into their deaths. The fierce battle became unbearable for Famin Jie to witness. He sat atop a hill overlooking the battlefield. He cried out to Heaven to intervene.

On the outskirts of the ferocious battle, four Terukk priests took positions on elevated platforms and in unison continued to recite their dark mantras with renewed vigor. They cast spells upon their mutant army to enhance their ferocity in battle. The Spirit of Heaven then spoke to Famin Jie and moved him to ascend a hill overlooking the battle. He brought with him his Guqin zither and after he had sat, he set the instrument upon his lap and began to play a tune of lamentation and plea. In response to Famin Jie's spiritual opposition, the Terukk priests increased their incantations. The fighting intensified as sword and shield units charged into the fray. Battalions of mutants at the rear of the battle hastily erected trebuchets and catapults and launched large fireballs into the Ming forces behind the hills and at the ships circling around in the Beizhili Gulf. One of the firebombs scored a direct hit on one of the vessels quickly spreading fire across the deck and pouring over the hull as the crew scrambled to douse the flames. The Phoenix Spirit waved their signal flags and the warships turned in unison and concentrated their fire upon the distant enemy artillery. It was not long however until their concentrated cannon fire had rendered the enemy artillery useless or completely destroyed. The Terukk priests continued pouring forth evil mantras from their mouths as Famin Jie intensified the notes he played upon his Guqin. With the music, he vouched for the troops seeking heavenly help in resisting the terrible opposition the priests were spewing from foul mouths.

Sun Xin and the fellowship of Famin Jie led several companies of one hundred twelve Academicians each to destroy the Terukk priests who stood exposed, albeit surrounded by heavily armored mutants with long Terukk spears. Cannon fire, bullets, and arrows aimed towards the priests completely missed as if deflected or diverted by rogue winds. Before Xin could reach the priest, the company of mutants tightened their formation to defend him. They locked their shields creating an impervious wall of iron with protruding polearms. Sun Xin dismounted to engage them directly while the Academicians and Master Lo followed close behind on foot to join the fight. Jirgal and Buff Baby charged at the next nearest priest and so did Big Bang and Zuo Shilong with the last priest who stood at the far end of the ranks. He was rushed by powerful cavalry led by General He Jin and a detachment of his mounted commandos who trampled over , impaled, or slashed at the mutants. They lobbed short-fused grenades up and over the mutant armor formation. They landed right behind them and detonated in an instant devastating their shield wall and rendering their defenses broken. General Jin and his mounted commandos proceeded to finish them off with their lances and glaives with devastating effect. The mutant soldiers were by no means mere grunts and their resilience to lethal strikes became apparent to Sun Xin who bobbed and weaved his way through the horde while cutting and stabbing through openings in their armor. They were incredibly strong and fearless and easily tossed the Academicians like little children. Some had their swords broken while other Academicians were grappled and fatally struck with armored fists. Master Lo as well exerted extra effort into the fight trying to stay a step ahead of multiple attacks from the enemy. Sun Xin pushed his way through mutant horde and positioned himself for a swift assassination maneuver. He stepped up from the back of a mutant and leaped off with great force to land an aerial assassination on the priest. His blow however, was swiftly deflected by a familiar dark metallic blade. Kurr had made his reappearance.

Up from the left, Master Lo charged in and engaged Kurr into sword combat. "I will take care of this demon, Xin. Destroy that devil of a priest!" shouted Master Lo. Kurr rushed in to defend the priest and engaged both swordsmen. He laughed menacingly and grinned with a sinister look upon his face. "This is going to be quite entertaining," he quipped.

****

"RAH!" Big Bang and Zuo Shilong struggled to fight as well. Zuo Shilong spun and slammed his iron rod into the mutant hordes smashing in helmets, shattering armor, and breaking bones. Very few could handle a staff with the same mastery displayed by Zuo. Big Bang stayed close behind though heavy-laden with gear, weapons, and ammunition. He lobbed grenades wherever the mutants clustered in large groups. He also brought with him an oversized hand cannon which he fired from the hip. It knocked him off his feet whenever he fired it all the while maniacally laughing in the process. It was not long before he resorted to insults and swearing upon the realization that the priests were immune to ranged weapons fire. The oversized hand cannon apparently also came in quite handy as a club which he used to great effect during close encounters.

The Academicians kept the mutants occupied as Zuo Shilong swooped in to engage the devilish priest in hand to hand combat. His swings were evaded as the Terukk priest ducked and side-stepped his strikes even as he continued to recite the incantations. Shilong found himself quickly heavy-laden in his spirit and fought hard to ignore it. Not far from the others of the company, Buff Baby muscled through the fight using his massive strength to overwhelm the mutant hordes.

"Aha! You are strong but there are none here stronger than I!" he boasted loudly. He violently swung his heavy glaive, tearing through flesh and armor as if it were paper, and slashed away mutant brutes by the handfuls. Jirgal stood some distance behind him picking away enemies one shot at a time with a high-resistance recurve bow.

"Curse this weapon, my shoulder is starting to cramp and my neck is going stiff!" he whined. He unslung his crossbow and continued to fire methodically at the heads of mutants engaging Buff Baby and the Martial Academicians. A large dagger was attached to the front end of the weapon which he used effectively.

The incantations of the priests grew louder and more powerful as Sun Xin and Master Lo engaged Kurr simultaneously. Kurr laughed in mockery as he ducked, dodged, and parried their sword strikes with little effort. His blade resounded like a heavy bronze tuning bell every time it clashed with their steel. Master Lo took to the offense and engaged Kurr head on, with no restraint. Their blades were a blur, each strike already anticipated the next. Master Lo managed to land a large cut across Kurr's chest armor. Another strike cut into an exposed area of his arm. Kurr had enough and spat.

"So that's how it's going to be, old man!?" he exclaimed. He feigned a forward thrust and launched a spinning back kick that sent Master Lo flying backward and tumbling into the dirt. He was barely able to stand.

"You must kill the priest!" he shouted as he coughed up blood. Xin quickly reached into the compartment of his belt and tossed several smoke bombs into Kurr's position blowing up into large plumes of white intoxicating smoke. Xin refocused his attention on the priest and dashed to perform a second assassination attempt but was immediately thwarted by the spinning blades that Kurr had tossed into Xin's line of attack. It nearly cut through Xin's neck. The blades then spun back towards Kurr who arrogantly grinned as the blades spun back to his hand; he refastened them onto his hips.

Xin knew that he was never going to be able to kill the priest if he could not get passed Kurr. If he continued to fight the same way he had always been, this duel could either end in yet another stalemate or in defeat. He then remembered the words of his master. His sword was still guided by brute force, power, and anger. It was the style that had failed him twice already. He remembered, however, that what truly prevailed in a battle such as this was the sword of effortless action which emulated the nature of the Way. Xin completely relaxed his stance and instead of being consumed by the darkness within himself, he allowed the peace, clarity, and control that come only from Heaven fill his spirit in its stead. He did not expect it but he welcomed it nonetheless. What he was experiencing was brand new but he decided to trust it. So, he completely relaxed himself, breathed, and assumed a low defensive stance. Kurr raised an eyebrow and was visibly puzzled by Sun Xin's response to their encounter.

"You are different today, Master Swordsman, but I seriously doubt this 'new' approach will stack the odds in your favor," he said maliciously, once again baring his sharp teeth with a grin.

"In our first meeting, I failed realize that you were not my greater enemy. But because I had dealt with what *was*, I realize that I can now deal with you," Xin said in a new voice of steel that can unnerve even the most hardened warriors. Even he was surprised by it. Kurr growled and burst towards Xin now gripping his black metallic sword with both hands.

Upon the top of the hill, Famin Jie continued to play his Guqin vigorously in an effort to equalize the priests' incantations to buy the company more time. As long as he kept playing, he thought, the Ming forces would not become overwhelmed by the mutant hordes being fueled by the dark sorcery of the Terukk. Though his hands began to stiffen with the pain that surged through them, he strummed the seven strings with passion as he continued to pray to Heaven.

After he had forcefully forged a path through the mutant hordes, Buff Baby struck down the Terukk priest with a sweep of its legs and a powerful down stroke for a swift beheading. Zuo Shilong and Big Bang as well had successfully cleared the area of mutants as Ming troops and Academicians swooped in to secure their position. A large mutant soldier in particular charged at Buff Baby in an attempt to grapple him to the ground. The force of the impact knocked Buff Baby's weapon from his grasp though he instantly regained his footing and sprawled to counter the tackle. His feet grazed across the ground raising clouds of dust as he was shoved back several strides.

He counter-pushed the mutant's charge and with a pivot of the hips, Buff Baby tossed the mutant to the ground. Now, the two wrestled for leverage. Buff Baby grasped the mutant's wrists in restraint and slammed his forehead onto its nose then proceeded pound its face with his bare fists until its head had turned to a pulp.

"Is there anyone else who would dare challenge me in hand to hand combat?" he shouted with a fiery vigor. A stone's throw away from where Buff Baby continued to fight, the Terukk priest facing Zuo Shilong had finally ceased his accursed chanting to divert his full attention onto his attackers. Upon his hand materialized a long-handled cleaver with a serrated edge forged with the same black metallic alloy used in the sword of Kurr. He swung decisively at Zuo Shilong's neck but the monk dove beneath the attack with a forward roll and thrust the end of his staff into the priest's abdomen. As the priest doubled over, Shilong spun around to smash his heavy staff onto his back but it was obstructed by the black cleaver. The impact from the block was bone-jarring. Zuo Shilong's staff reverberated with the force but he ignored it to continue the momentum of his attacks, striking at the priest from various angles. It was not long until the priest caved-in from the pressure when Shilong broke through the handle of the cleaver and landed a crushing blow to his head.

The skull had caved in and spewed flesh and brain matter in every which way. The priests collapsed to the ground in a pool of black blood with both hands and arms twitching. Zuo Shilong did not make time for any celebration. The cleaver faded into smoke as Zuo Shilong leaped back into battle to aid the struggling Ming troops.

Not far from where the second priest fell, two warriors dueled for the life of the final Terukk priest. This time however, Sun Xin had turned the tide on his enemy. Sun Xin evaded and redirected Kurr's blows with an amazing calmness. He had peace. Xin foresaw every movement of his opponent's body and was able to predict where the blade would strike next. He had clarity. Xin also knew where to step and how to flow with his body's movements. He was effortless. These profound skills that had suddenly enlightened Xin caused Kurr to become increasingly frustrated and enraged. Just like Master Lo had said, darkness would not comprehend the light and so it was with Kurr who now could not comprehend his opponent. One final priest remained to hold back the Ming forces. If he could fall, the mutants could be quickly overrun and be cast into the sea.

"Time to finish this," Xin said in his cold, intimidating voice. He spun around Kurr's sword thrust and slammed a reverse elbow strike into Kurr's temple then in one continuous motion stabbed a dagger into his exposed inner thigh. Kurr roared with the pain. Just as soon as Xin proceeded to dispatch him once and for all, Kurr slashed his blade into the air, knocking away Xin with a powerful gust of wind. Kurr then fled into the heat of the battle in the background and disappeared amidst the chaos.

The final Terukk priest continued to recite incantations into the mutant army until his head fell clean off his shoulders and the body collapsed in a heap. Just as the final Terukk priest fell, Famin Jie played struck the final chord upon his zither. As the string' vibrations faded away, Famin Jie rolled onto his back in exhaustion and gave praise to Heaven. It was in that moment that the brunt of the Ming Imperial Army pushed against the Terukk with great force. Their shouts could be heard for many li and the ground shook with their thundering footfalls. General He Jin rounded up the rest of his commando and cavalry units and charged through the exposed flanks of the enemy. It was not long until the mutant army, severely lacking cavalry and artillery, and the dark magic of the Terukk priests, became completely overwhelmed by the Ming's unstoppable onslaught of swords, spears, and projectiles. Imperial Commander Feishen, though a veteran of many great battles, could not help but be in awe of this battle's immensity. When the priests had fallen, the infantry fought with a fiery inspiration as they cut down the mutant monstrosities who all of a sudden found themselves on the defensive. The cannons had ceased to fire after the two opposing armies had thoroughly defused in the battlefield. Coordinated battalions and their commanding officers systematically pressed forward against the receding Terukk mutants who still continued to resist. Cavalry units reformed their lines and swung around to cut them down as archer and gunner units concentrated their fire. No longer fueled by the mantras of the priests, the mutants had become just as mortal as any man despite maintaining the brute strength and ferocity of their mutations.

Little by little the mutant hordes, once so mighty and unrelenting, were pushed into the sea. Thousands plummeted off steep cliffs while hundreds of others were thrown off abandoned harbors and pulled down by the weight of their armor. Many of the remaining stragglers used what was left of their strength to run into the endless steppes, perhaps to die in the wilderness if they would not be hunted down by predators or powerful tribes.

Some tried to swim or row away in barges but were immediately destroyed by naval cannons or shot down by smaller Ming gunboats. Morale for the Ming reached a new high as they pushed forward onto the mutants and utterly destroyed them. The battle was won for the Ming Imperial Army. All mutants who had attempted to flee were either cut down by cavalry, or shot down by mounted archers. Those in the rear began to cheer as the last few thousand mutants who continued to resist were destroyed, no longer under the enchantment of the priests' incantations.

After the soldiers on the ground gained the upper hand in the battle, the Ming Navy proceeded west towards the light Terukk naval blockade where the Shandong and Liaodong Peninsulas met most closely. The Terukk transport ships were caught completely off guard and barely managed to get into formation by the time the Ming ships reached firing range. In unison, the Ming formation veered to starboard as the crews brought the cannons at the ready. The Terukk were outnumbered three to one though their light armaments were more than enough for a difficult fight. The hull of their vessels absorbed the brunt of the Ming's opening cannon salvo. Though buckled and splintered, a second volley of shells was needed to puncture the Terukk hull. As the broadside cannons of the Ming ships reloaded, they swung around to bring port cannons to fire. The Terukk ships answered the Ming attack with signature blue fires as piercing flames of intense heat slammed into several Ming ships puncturing hulls, spreading fires, and splintering decks. Many sailors fell overboard as others scrambled to douse fires and keep the cannons loaded.

Admiral Han Bin and two of the crew quickly spun the tiller around to avoid the enemy's return fire as the ship groaned and moaned with the strain. The Phoenix Spirit moved to the front of the formation and fired a salvo of winged rockets into the Terukk formation. The Scholars' warship targeted the lower hulls of the Terukk ships while simultaneously firing volleys of cannon grapeshot and mortar shells to decimate the enemy armor.

Commanding shouts, screams, and chatter filled the air between cannon and rocket volleys. The Terukk ships, still unable to get into their proper formation, were beginning to buckle from the harassing synchronized fire of the Ming ships. The Phoenix Spirit then used its signature speed and maneuverability to quickly evade the Terukks' line of fire as the rest of the circling Ming ships fired another salvo of bombs and shells. The Terukk, though outnumbered, managed to destroy a handful of the Ming battleships. Lu Guanying was on the stern of the Phoenix Spirit as he witnessed the decimated vessels sink beneath the waves.

Despite its size, the Phoenix Spirit swiftly evaded incoming bombs as it moved in to rescue any of the survivors clinging to chunks of driftwood and debris. The smaller Ming warships split into two formations in order to attack Terukk from two sides. Their signature battened sails swiveled to the left as it hauled wind from yet another angle. The enemy ships turned southwest in full sail to stay ahead of their pursuers. The two sides continued to exchange fire but the accuracy of the Terukk weapons were unmatched. Their concentrated fire tore holes through the rest of the Ming ships with their fiery projectiles to attempt to discourage their pursuit. It was an impressive feat given they were mere lightly armed transport vessels. Some of the Ming ships were even forced to break formation.

The Phoenix Spirit still managed to launch a trio of Fire Dragon missiles into the fleeing enemy ships. Two of the missiles slammed into the rear of one and the third veered off-course as the ordnance tore through the cabin of another. Admiral Han Bin swiveled the Phoenix Spirit to a hard port to prepare to launch another salvo of cannon fire as Tian Qiu, Lu Guanying, and Shang Jian were swept off their feet. Eight heavy cannons fired away in quick succession, their thunderous booms shook the entire ship. The rounds slammed into the nearest vessel, completely shredding apart its stern leaving a heap of twisted metals and wood. The crew cheered and jeered as the enemy ship began to list and sink beneath the waves.

Out from the ocean-blue horizon appeared a whole contingent of red sails soaring skyward. They approached the fleets with great speed in an attempt to cut off the Terukk retreat. The sails soon revealed to be the ships of the Ming Navy of Nanjing. They had finally arrived to participate in the battle of the gulf. The squadron's flagship opened fire and accompanying warships followed suit.

The pursuit lasted for another several dozen li until the Terukk finally revealed their oars and sailed out of range. At the battle's culmination, six of their ships had been destroyed while the remaining four managed to limp away severely damaged with smoke seeping from their hulls.

Admiral Han Bin desired to make chase but did not desire the risk of losing more ships or running into an ambush. The Ming had lost a total of seven ships and several others were in critical condition. There was only so much their superior numbers and the element of surprise could bring. This was a testament to the Ming military that the Terukk were indeed a force to be reckoned. The Phoenix Spirit did not survive the battle unscathed and had suffered a handful of breaches to the hull. Sturdy bulkhead compartments within its belly however have kept it afloat so far. After the survivors had been salvaged from the cold waters, the ships recalled to Liaodong and anchored at the shore near the battlefield.

The first great battle against the Terukk's forces had been won. Han Bin watched as the Terukk ships descended beneath the horizon trailing smoke and debris. A new squadron of box-shaped ships joined the Terukk from the west. It was a squadron loyal to the pirate lord Mizushima.

"Now, we can confirm that pirates from Riben have allied themselves with the Foreigner scum," commented Admiral Han.

"This is the beginning of our woes at sea. We barely managed to defeat a small squadron of their ships despite our numeric superiority. What we have experienced today is but a small taste of their naval capabilities. If we are to stand a chance against them, our own navy might require an overhaul," commented Shang Jian. Near the shores of Liaodong Peninsula, the Ming nursed its wounds. The Ming troops overall suffered low casualties relative to their enemy's numbers though it brought Imperial Commander Feishen great pain to count the fallen. It was something he would never be accustomed to. He loved his men sincerely and it wrenched his heart greatly when those very same men whom he had trained for years and marched with for thousands of li would make their sacrifices on the battlefield. Just over seven thousand were counted among the dead and thousands more were counted among the injured and the disabled.

Imperial Commander Feishen and his officers spent several minutes in silence as the dead were tallied and buried in a mass grave upon the plain. There were some among the dead whom he had known personally. He felt great regret for their loss though deep in his heart Feishen knew these were the inevitable daily realities of war that all officers had to reconcile. He must accept it gracefully so that it would not compromise his ability to lead.

Preparedness, naval support, and superior weaponry indeed have played their part in the victory but it was the company of Famin Jie who had truly won the battle for the Ming that day. Had the Terukk priests been allowed to continue their sorcery, the mutants' strength would have overwhelmed the Ming army even with the use of superior artillery. These truths did not pass by Commander Feishen and General Jin who along with their officers personally commended and honored the Scholars, their Academicians, and Famin Jie's company.

"Were it not for the efforts of the Scholars and these heroes from the provinces the battle would have continued to no end and many among us would have perished under the sorcery of the Terukk!" they said. Big Bang laughed maniacally as he usually did.

Jirgal however was only relieved to have survived the ordeal and urgently searched for some wine calm his nerves. Buff Baby celebrated with the rest of the troops in food and drink as he boasted about his 'mighty' feats during the battle. Zuo Shilong stood at the shore and silently stared into the sea which he was seeing for the very first time. Sun Xin, in his preoccupations with attending to his injured master, did not take the time to appreciate the commendations or the victory. Famin Jie however could not help but praise Heaven alone for the victory for he knew that it was Heaven who in supreme sovereignty had orchestrated the events that allowed these warriors to have assembled.

He later rejoined Imperial Commander Feishen and General Jin to set up camp not far from the edge of the battlefield as the dead were buried and the wounded were attended. The company regrouped and reported to the commander though Master Lo continued to be in severe pain after suffering the vicious blow of Kurr's kick. General Jin provided a bed for him to rest inside his own tent. His breath was labored and he coughed continuously.

"So you are the great Master Lo. I have had the rare privilege of personally bearing witness to the incredible feats of Sun Xin, but to have finally met his master is a rare and great honor," said General He Jin with a deep bow of respect.

"For many years I had been angry and resentful of him. He had chosen a path which I was sure there would be no return, but to see the alliances he has made, to witness where his path has brought him, gladness and peace have replaced my anger. He is destined for something monumental, General. Heaven has great plans for him, though I think my part in this tale is finally coming to a close," said Master Lo in a labored breath. He coughed profusely and blood poured from the corner of his mouth. General Jin then hurriedly searched for Sun Xin in the camp. His master did not have much time. Famin Jie approached Master Lo's bedside with tears welling up in his eyes. "Oh Lord Di, should this battle bear such a terrible cost?" he cried as his lips quivered.

"Do not lament for me, brother, for I long to be in the presence of the Most High. The spirits have posted here to anticipate my departure. Such a glorious sight it is!" Master Lo exclaimed.

"Look, the souls of my righteous ancestors descend and ascend from the right and left of Shang Di. I am overwhelmed."

"If your name is called, brother, do not neglect to answer it. I will find peace in your departure," said Famin Jie, his lips quivering and tears rolling from his cheeks. Sun Xin rushed to his master's side and fell on his knees. For the first time in ten years, Sun Xin began to cry.

"Master, forgive me for what I had done," he cried. "Do not leave my side, Master. You are the only father I have ever known."

"My son, the day I found you was the day I was made complete. You and Meiling have filled the aching abyss in my heart. Truly Heaven is gracious to have blessed me with the grand responsibility of raising you. The day you fled our home was the day I thought I had failed you, but little did I know of the grand master plan Heaven had already orchestrated for your life and now I am blessed have finally seen it unfold. Do not depart from the paths of righteousness. Walk in the Way, honor Heaven alone. The road ahead of you is dark and very treacherous; your faith will be tested. Always walk before the Light where the cracks upon the path you tread can be made visible," said Master Lo. He struggled to breathe but mustered the strength to speak his last words. "Xin, never forget my words. Hide them in your heart. I've told you how you can overcome the curse. Your hardships are only beginning. Only in the Way can you let peace, clarity, and effortless action embody your life and guide your hand in battle. Then, only then will you find victory. Take my sword; keep it with you always so it will remind you of my words."

The company, Tian Qiu, He Feishen, and He Jin stood around him with their hats and helmets in hand and with heads bowed. "Do not waste your breaths in lamentation for my loss, dear friends. Rejoice instead knowing that I have finished my mission in obedience to the will of Heaven. Xin, my son, do not pursue a campaign without acknowledging Heaven before all things. Only then will success follow in your wake. Do not forget about dear Meiling. After your task is complete return home, Xin. You are now the only loved one that remains for her." He turned his gaze to his beloved friend Famin Jie. "My dear brother in spirit, you have been tasked with a tremendous calling. Keep fighting the fight. Your battle is far from over. The next time we meet will be in victory." Famin Jie bowed his head and wept at his side.

Finally, in the tent of General He Jin, surrounded by friends and allies, Master Lo breathed his last breath. The departure of his spirit was felt by Xin and Famin Jie; like a veil that had been lifted, so too did they feel Master Lo depart from their midst. His body was wrapped in many cloths and readied to return to his home where proper funeral rites and ceremonies would be observed. Famin Jie wandered into the woods to briefly mourn in solitude and there he meditated and played his zither.

Though he greatly lamented the loss of his only master and adoptive father, Xin did not have the luxury to properly mourn. He swallowed his tears as he fastened Master Lo's sword right beside his own. There was a tremendous task at hand and Master Lo would have instructed him to remain focused on the mission. He meditated upon the highest hill on the field overlooking the battlefield to clear his mind. It was strange, however. He had expected anguish to dictate his emotions at this point but instead he was finding a small measure of peace. Now, he felt more ready than he ever had in the face of a mountainous trial and this time, a victorious outcome was more visible and more assured. He was going to claim it.

# 十五

# THE START OF A NEW CAMPAIGN

NIGHT HAD FALLEN OVER THE camp. Imperial Commander Feishen and the troops directly under his command were making preparations to return to the capital in the next day. Xin, Tian Qiu, Admiral Han and other Scholars surveyed the battlefield to record the activities taking place when the mutants and their Terukk overlords had occupied it.

"The Terukk appeared to have had some great plans in their campaigns against us. Much of what we see here were preparations for large-scale industries. This is but a first step in their plans for a militaristic colonization," said Tian Qiu.

"They have greatly underestimated our resolve and did not anticipate the ferocity of our forces," said Captain Liu Quan as he approached them. His armor was again spotted with blood and sported battle damage.

"Did they seriously think they could get away with settling on our land? They were fools."

"Our battle here today was nothing," emphasized Sun Xin. "The strength of the mutants, these projects they undertook, and the struggle we faced on this day were but a very small taste of what is to come. The mutant beasts were mere pawns, a means to test our forces, for the Terukk seek to know their enemy. This battle was just a ruse to discover our strengths, our weaknesses, and the true extent of the capabilities of our military. Our tactics and strategies are now being studied. The Terukk themselves will be arriving on our shores by the hundreds of thousands for what has transpired today is but the first step in their grander plan. Our woes have yet to begin and I'm afeared that the true power of the real Terukk army will be far more terrifying than what we have faced today." He then looked east to the open sea. "Their ships were not even constructed for war. Mere transport vessels with light armaments were all they were and yet they nearly devastated our own fleet. Everything we faced on this day barely qualified as an appetizer."

"I also need not mention that there are yet armies of the Underworld in the forests so that they may strike against us. Perhaps it is a grand strategy to destabilize the nation. I wouldn't be surprised if the Terukk are the primary organizers, supplying and arming them as well," added Tian Qiu.

"Sun Xin is correct. We cannot afford to relax for one moment.

Even celebration for our victory this day is a luxury. As we speak, many nations in the South have already been subjugated by the Terukk. There may be pockets of resistance scattered in the wilderness but of that we cannot be so sure. As far as we know, the Ming Empire is the only stronghold where resistance still thrives," said Lu Guanying.

"We cannot lie on our strength alone," Famin Jie interjected. "It must be in the Menggu horsemen and the Ashikaga warriors where we must find our aid." The rest of the group looked at him in disbelief.

"If we honestly think we can win this war on our own, we are already defeated," he added.

"The teacher certainly has a point. We now share a common enemy with the Menggu and the Ashikaga. An alliance is in order, for the Menggu still hold tremendous influence over the territories of their former empire in the western regions, though they have been in decline in recent times. I'm certain the Terukk have yet to influence the armies of Dayan Khan. The warrior class of the Ashikaga is extreme but has proven to be highly skilled in the art of war and knowledgeable in the profound teachings of our great philosopher Kongzi," said General Jin. "Our sister nation of Joseon lies just beyond the peninsulas. If we are to obtain their aid as well they must first be liberated, but with the coming invasions, our resources would be spread thin."

"It certainly seems to be the logical course of action, though the alliance should be forged with meekness and humility on our part.

Though it may seem unthinkable in the moment, the Ming must be willing to cooperate in unison with the Menggu and the Ashikaga," said Tian Qiu.

The counsel of Famin Jie was taken into deep consideration by the group and they decided that the plan be presented before the emperor and the rest of the Scholars. If the plan was to succeed, Famin Jie would personally make the journey to speak with the chieftains of the Menggu and the reigning military ruler of the Ashikaga regime. Little by little it seemed that their war against the Terukk would not have to be fought alone.

After the group had finished discussing the broad strategies for the war, Tian Qiu and Xin approached the large mechanisms Big Bang had destroyed a week before. It stood at the northern edge of the clearing where the battle took place and had remained untouched during the fighting. Tian Qiu surveyed the workings of the processing plant after Xin described how he had observed its use. The plant had many gears, chambers, and pipes leading in different directions in order to process and brew the liquid drug. It eventually led to overhead exhaust openings from which the liquid was converted to gas. Despite being severely damaged, the machine as a whole was still fairly recognizable and the mutants had apparently attempted to make repairs to it in the past several days. Tian Qiu walked to the rear and unlocked a large canister directly attached to the body of the device. In it contained a purplish-blue powdery substance. He analyzed its texture and sniffed it. It was foul.

"This substance is very similar to the drugs used to bribe many of the palace's officials and eunuchs when the Foreigners were in the process of puppeteering our government. This device processes this substance to create the gas you saw. Prolonged exposure to it creates the mutants we battled today, obviously, although this particular machine seems to be a mere unrefined prototype. It's an inefficient method of administering," concluded Tian Qiu. "It is very devilish, indeed. Imagine what a perfected mechanism or formula could do to enemy forces."

"I have seen very large devices very similar to this one in the forests where the rebel sects were gathering. I too saw the gasses spread over their armies. At the foot of Wudang Mountain, the sect I combated had it in liquid form to be readily ingested. It seems that there is more than one way of administering it," said Xin.

In a tent inside the army's camp, Tian Qiu examined the body of one of the mutants. He observed that the creature retained the fundamental form of a man though had greater muscle and bone density than the average soldier. The skin was rough, leathery, and a pale blue and its facial features had been distorted to more closely resemble the features of the Terukk. It was just as Xin had observed beneath the slopes of Wudang Mountain. It was undoubtedly clear that the devices were used to create an army incapable of independent thought and was yet stronger and faster than the average man. Such a soldier was dangerous. One that is incapable of experiencing fear or suffering in pain. It reminded Tian Qiu that their victory was due largely to effective tactics and planning. It was also terrifying for Tian Qiu to imagine all the terrorist groups and sects receiving this unnatural potion with all of its advantages. He did not yet even know what the fullest extent of exposure to the potion would result. At what point would exposure to the potion achieve the Terukk's "optimal" results for the mutants? At dawn, Tian Qiu summoned the Ming commanders, Famin Jie, Sun Xin, and the company to a meeting to discuss with them the matters concerning the assembly of the dark armies in the provinces, how to defend the people, and to locate and destroy the machines. What was most important was finding the enemy leadership and destroying it. Sun Xin volunteered to head the task.

"It is absolutely imperative that these machines be destroyed for every time our enemy makes use of it, they are gaining a significant physical edge over our troops no matter how well trained and disciplined they may be," insisted Tian Qiu.

"I will locate the machines and destroy them so the bulk of the Imperial Army can focus on the defense of the Empire from an invasion from the sea," said Xin. "We must anticipate the arrival of a Terukk Armada. I have many contacts and allies scattered across the provinces. The company and I will lead the Academicians for the campaign. If General He Jin be willing to provide us with a detachment of his elite commandos, my part in the campaign to defend the empire will succeed." General Jin agreed to help Xin in a heartbeat and already had in mind to dedicate some of the best of his personal commando units for future objectives.

"We must report to the capital immediately to present before the emperor our plans," said Feishen. "I must coordinate with the rest of army scattered throughout the provinces. I fear that Guangzhou may be the one of the first targets for the Terukk should their 'armada' arrive. I will immediately summon a considerable defense force for the protection of the city for it is of great strategic significance," he said.

"I agree," said Tian Qiu. "If the invasion comes from the south, Guangzhou would be caught right in the middle." The Ming Imperial Army under Feishen proceeded to return to the capital and the navy including the Phoenix Spirit, set sail for the harbor near Tianjin. Captain Liu Quan and several thousand troops, in coordination with the Great Wall's border garrison, stayed behind to fortify their recaptured territory on the Liaodong Peninsula installing a large garrison there. They had also built a makeshift shipyard for the loading, unloading, and repair of ships. Famin Jie and company sat in the bowels of the Phoenix Spirit with General He Jin and some Academicians.

Xin stood in the corner looking out of the window lost in deep thought and still mourning the loss of his master. Famin Jie as well could not fully accept the loss of his close friend. It would be a very long time before the wounds would begin to heal.

"I did not get the chance to personally express my gratitude for what you did on the battlefield. I saw what you did; I sincerely believe it was crucial for our hard-won victory," said General He Jin to Famin Jie.

"Ah, yes. I really did not do much of anything. All I did was cry out to Heaven. Any of you would have done the same. All glory belongs to Heaven," he said. "Indeed. Nevertheless, I am very pleased to have you on board and on our side, comrade," said General Jin. "The Scholars in the court may not understand nor accept it, but having personally experienced the supernatural unfold in the battlefield, your , er… Heaven's intervention is more important than ever. Even my brother knows this well."

Famin Jie and company sat quietly in the belly of the Phoenix Spirit unsure of the coming future. The fleet slowly sailed through the shimmering waters as Commander Feishen marched his troops back through the plains to return to the capital. Sun Xin grasped his master's sword in his hand feeling tremendous regret that he could not save him. He did not realize it until now – that he had all along, felt secure knowing that his master was still alive and that he could still seek his counsel. Now that he was gone, Sun Xin felt as a warrior who had been stripped of his armor. He promised in his heart that Master Lo's death would not be in vain and that through him, his memory would live to continue the mighty legacy of his ancestors. The best way he could honor his master's memory was to take into heart his teachings and apply them fully. Yet he felt conflicted.

His thoughts immediately returned to his second duel with Kurr. No matter how many times he recalled the battle, Sun Xin could not fully decipher the chain of events that allowed him to cause the Terukk warrior to flee. Was that what his Master Lo been trying to tell him? Was that the Wu Wei or effortless action of the swordsman? Was that the state of peace and clarity that could only be the reverse of the Swordsman's Curse? It was completely alien to him but he still well remembered the brief experience. He had to overcome the curse and apply the Wu Wei of the swordsman.

Zuo Shilong stood alone at the stern of the ship overlooking the blue horizon pondering whether he would be able to find an opportunity to valiantly fight alongside his temple brethren for the defense of their homeland.

As Buff Baby sharpened the broad, heavy blade of his weapon, he remembered his band of men as they were massacred by a dark horde. He had command of them for many years and forged a powerful bond with them as brothers. Since that fateful day he has not had the chance to grieve. He swore in that moment to honor their memories by exacting his revenge. For every one of his dead comrades, he would slay a thousand of the sect devils, he thought to himself.

Jirgal laid down onto a bunk and rested his head upon his arm. He was full of doubt and great worry wondering how he managed to get involved with the affairs of empire. He felt like he was just a "nobody" who was worthy of no one's attention. He was not even anything like his brave Menggu kin nor was he as wise as the sages of old. He gazed into the palms of his hands wondering if they would ever be capable of performing great deeds or if he himself would be any use to his newfound friends.

In a private quarter of the vessel, Big Bang worked furiously on new designs and improvements to the military's weapons. He wanted more than anything to defeat the enemy with the ingenuity of science and engineering. He laughed to himself as he fiddled with instruments of geometry and measurement while regularly consulting a copy of the Book of Changes… though he could never really grasp the logic behind the mysticism of divination or the ironies of metaphysics. Behind the seeming insanity and incoherence of Big Bang, whose real name has yet to have been revealed to the company, is the heart of a true patriot and a man who honors his word. It is in these six unlikely men chosen by Heaven who, through obedience and righteousness, would be able to bring light to extinguish a raging darkness consuming the nations.

# EPILOGUE

AT THE HEART OF THE bottom of the world, a winged messenger soared over frigid, desolate mountain ranges to reach the capital of the united Terukk nations. With great speed, he navigated the treacherous winds and jagged mountain slopes until the gargantuan castle fortress of the Terukk Overlord came into view in the valley below. Out of the darkness its lights flickered and radiated through the fog and snow. An army of 500,000 amassed upon the frozen plain under the shadow of the castle fortress. Many more were on their way. The winged Terukk messenger dove down to its very gates and ordered the towering guards to immediately allow him passage. The howling winds suddenly became silent as the massive castle doors slammed shut behind him so the only thing that could be heard were the echoes of his light-booted footsteps resounding across the marble halls of dark stones. Through the endless hallways and corridors, the winged messenger navigated his way to the highest level of the castle fortress where a large council of Terukk leaders had assembled before their Overlord.

"Come, Hadrukk, my reliable messenger. What news do you deliver from the world of men?" the Overlord asked with the large and reverberating voice of a giant.

"My lord," said Hadrukk. "I bring word from your warrior stationed upon the great Eastern civilization its people call The Middle Kingdom which is currently governed by a native empire called 'Ming'." The members of the council remained silent in anticipation of the news he bore. "Our experimentation with the mutant armies has… performed far below our expectations," Hadrukk gulped as a lump formed in his throat.

"However do you mean? Speak!" commanded the Overlord with a thunderous voice.

"Great battles have been fought against them and the mages in command over the field however have been assassinated," Hadrukk answered. "Our mutant armies have been overrun and defeated. Our prey's forces have also assembled far faster than we have anticipated. A powerful force works in their favor."

"Impossible! The mage priests wield the powers of the ancients! How were they defeated?" he questioned as he stood from his throne. His towering bulk cast a long shadow along the floor.

"It appears that they have a swordsman named Xin fighting for the cause of the Ming Empire. Kurr had also mentioned a prophet in their midst who vouched for the souls of the Ming warriors upon the battlefield. He managed to equalize the sorcery of our mages to buy time for their very own deaths. Kurr had fought valiantly but was unfortunately outmaneuvered and was forced to flee. Nonetheless, we have learned plenty from the battle. We know their weapons, their tactics, and – "

The Overlord slammed his giant fist onto the armrest of his throne and a gust of wind flew away from the impact as it shook the floor. "We cannot let this happen to the rest of the mages. Summon the Four Demon Generals of the Terukk nations. Send them posthaste into the Middle Kingdom to protect our sorcerers from this petty swordsman and this meaningless prophet. The Dark Hordes rising from within their own borders will grant us enough time to amass the rest of our forces for an invasion upon the world of men. Regardless of their military response, they will fall to the might of the Terukk. What is important is that we were able to understand their military tactics and methods, correct?

"Yes, my lord. A great deal has been learned from the first great battle."

"Hmm… and tell Kurr, if he ever fails me because of his pride and selfish pursuits again, I will personally cast him into the chasm where the other failures descend into the void."

Just like that, Hadrukk bowed low and made his way out of the castle fortress and took to the skies to summon the Four Demon Generals so they may be shipped immediately across the sea.

# BEIJING
## Ming Capital

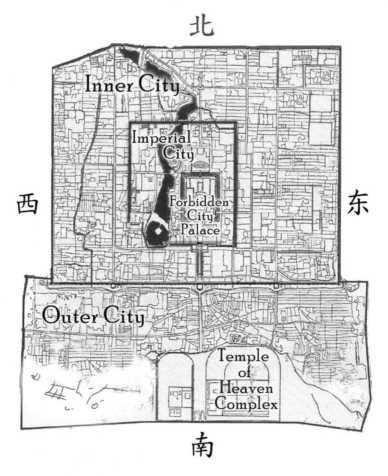

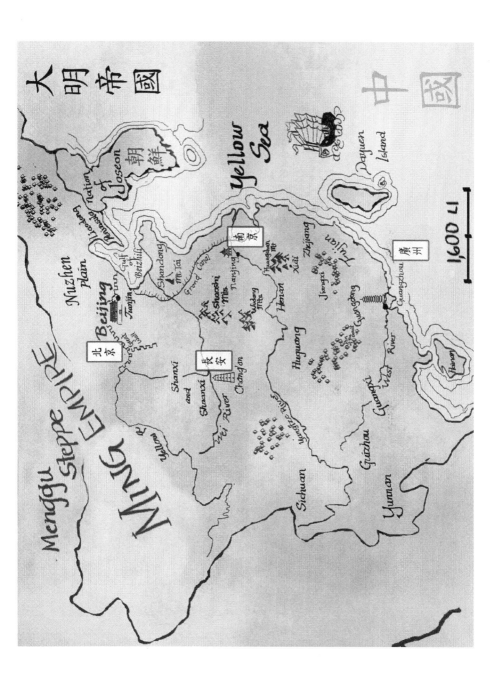

# ACKNOWLEDGMENTS

Though writing this book has been a great joy, it many times became overwhelming. It would have been impossible for me to complete it without the vital support from family and friends. I thank my mom for her prayers, timeless advice, and tremendous support. She cooks amazing food. I acknowledge my father as well for his support and understanding, especially for one as eccentric and peculiar as I am. I would also like to extend my gratitude to Prof. Drew for his encouragement and belief in me.

All glory, honor, and praise belong to Jesus Christ, my Redeemer and King. Without His grace and enabling, I am nothing.

## ABOUT THE AUTHOR

Pierre Dimaculangan is a digital artist, designer, and author of Trials of the Middle Kingdom series. He was born in Manila and grew up in Queens, New York. He's a lover of world history and is a self-proclaimed Sinophile. He loves to read, play story-driven video games, play drums, and practice Muay Thai and Parkour.

**Website**: www.pierredim.net
**Facebook**: TrialsoftheMiddleKingdom
**Artwork in Instagram**: @pierre_tomk

Made in the USA
Columbia, SC
03 May 2019